I0615117

William Walter Merry

The Clouds

William Walter Merry

The Clouds

ISBN/EAN: 9783337342838

Printed in Europe, USA, Canada, Australia, Japan

Cover: Foto ©Andreas Hilbeck / pixelio.de

More available books at **www.hansebooks.com**

Clarendon Press Series

ARISTOPHANES.

THE CLOUDS

WITH INTRODUCTION AND NOTES

BY

W. W. MERRY, D.D.

RECTOR OF LINCOLN COLLEGE AND PUBLIC ORATOR
IN THE UNIVERSITY OF OXFORD

New Edition

Oxford

AT THE CLARENDON PRESS

M DCCC LXXXIX

London

HENRY FROWDE

Oxford University Press Warehouse

Amen Corner, E.C.

PREFACE.

In preparing this edition of the 'Clouds' of Aristophanes I have endeavoured to give such full explanatory notes as to make it a helpful school-book for the use of the higher forms; while I have tried not to neglect the wants of somewhat more advanced scholars. The liveliness of the subject, the insight given into the political and social life of Athens, and the singular simplicity of the syntax, combine to recommend the study of Aristophanes in every way. The excisions that have been made are few; but they will be found, I hope, sufficient.

I gratefully acknowledge the help that I have derived from Teuffel's two editions (Teubner, Leips. 1863, 1867); and from the excellent introduction to the edition of Theo. Kock (Weidmann, Berlin, 1862).

W. W. M.

Oxford,
May, 1879.

CONTENTS.

INTRODUCTION.

It has been well said that the three great tragic poets of Athens are true representatives of three eras in her history. Aeschylus seems to breathe the spirit of Athens at the time of the Persian war, in which he himself had borne a part. Sophocles mirrors in absolute perfection the harmonious grace and artistic beauty of the age of Pericles. Euripides, though removed so little in point of time from his predecessors, seems to express a different tone of society. Some would go so far as to call him the poet of the decadence.

Aeschylus exhibits to us a mind deeply religious, and severely earnest—awed by the judicial power of the gods and reverently submissive to their binding laws. Sophocles, with a more genial spirit, can better appreciate the harmony of human freedom and divine ordinance. The triumph of moral order over self-will is with him rather a happy result than a crushing defeat.

Euripides, unlike the other two, cannot adopt unquestioningly the traditional code of morals, and claims of national faith. His attitude is critical: he is an inquirer more than a believer. The government of the world; the actions of the gods; the myths and legends of Hellenic religion; the common-places of morality —all are freely examined and freely judged. He is not irreligious and he is not immoral; but he is (if we choose to apply modern terms) a rationalist and a sceptic. His is the questioning spirit (*τοῦτο τοὐπιχώριον . . . τὸ τί λέγεις σύ*; Nub. 1173) applied to everything impartially, regarding nothing too sacred, or too time-honoured for its scrutiny. In short, he represents the tone of Athenian society that grew up in the period of the Peloponnesian war. We are rightly warned not to speak of it as a time of moral deterioration; but it no doubt marked a great crisis; as must always be the case when independent thought begins to protest against what has hitherto been universally accepted; especially when such protest takes the form of free criticism of those forms of government which have till then been taken for granted.

It is against this growing tone that Aristophanes, as an uncompromising conservative, fights with desperate energy. It seemed to him at once impious and immoral; and, above all, it represented a deep disloyalty to that glorious Athenian past, in the foreground of which he seemed to see the 'men who had fought at Marathon' as the only true type of national virtue. This free discussion, this unscrupulous independence of view, this setting up of individual judgment against immemorial tradition, was summed up under the general name *σοφιστική*, and the teachers who professed and disseminated such opinions were called *σοφισταί*, the very word gaining a tone of reproach by its application to them.

These professors, or Sophists, were not for the most part Athenian citizens. The most famous among them were Protagoras of Abdera, Prodicus of Ceos, Hippias of Elis, and Gorgias of Leontini. But they lectured to Athenian audiences, and their pupils were the wealthy Athenian youths. It was their business to meet the wants of the age; to introduce something like a systematic education; to furnish their pupils with a practical philosophy that should fit them for the various duties of life. And this seemed to be best attained by teaching them the art of speaking and arguing, and (as a necessary preparation) of speculation. But the celebrated dictum of Protagoras that 'man is the measure of all things' serves to show (however we may interpret it) that they did not profess to believe in an absolute standard of morality, or in any positive truth. Their aim was utilitarian. And so their antagonists had some ground for saying that their lessons in rhetoric and dialectic were intended to exhibit what was plausible rather than what was true; and they regarded with a not unreasonable suspicion the high fees charged for imparting wisdom—a practice which seemed to them not only sordid but positively sacrilegious.

The whole intention of this play of the 'Clouds' is to make

a vehement protest against the modern education introduced by these professors. Its radical fault consists in taking Socrates as their representative. Some such central figure is, of course, required, and there must always be an amount of unfairness, when the crimes or mistakes of a whole class are visited on the person of one man.

It is this necessity—as well as personal spite—which has over-drawn the caricature of Cleon in the 'Knights;' and which has done palpable injustice to Lamachus in the 'Acharnians,' as the type of the war-party. And in the 'Clouds' the relation of Socrates to the Sophists is wilfully or ignorantly misunderstood; so that the picture of him as their 'fugleman' is, consequently, notoriously unfair.

It must have been a great temptation to the Comic poet, and his mask-maker, to bring upon the stage that well-known, grotesque figure—that face with prominent eyes and flattened nose, which everyone was familiar with in the streets and in the market-place. No one could mistake him. But the temptation to present so familiar a character upon the stage, or even the conscientious desire to oppose the teaching of the Sophists, does not make the representation any more truthful. Nothing could be more unfair than to describe Socrates as taking exorbitant fees from his pupils, as being the type of the pale and squalid student, instead of the picture of rude health; or as being devoted to astronomy, and natural philosophy—studies which he had distinctly abjured long ago. Nor is it a truthful picture which represents Socrates shut up in a close and stuffy school, instead of enjoying that vagabond life which sent him to roam about the streets, and to haunt the shops and other places of public resort. Had Aristophanes really grasped the spirit of the Socratic teaching, he would have seen that it was rather a life-long protest against the shallowness of the Sophists. No one was further than he from accepting the evidence of the senses as the criterion of truth and falsehood; or the tendency of human desires as the criterion of what is truly desirable. Instead of this, he was profoundly convinced of the importance of a virtuous life as the source of all happiness.

But a superficial observer might, perhaps, be excused for not appreciating these radical differences. He would only see that Socrates did not raise his voice in protesting loudly against the spirit of the age in which he lived, nor cried in vain for the restoration of a past, which could never again be reproduced. For Socrates had set himself the difficult task of attempting to reform the faults of this modern spirit from within, instead of merely decrying it. And such a task was particularly open to misrepresentation, and was not likely to attract to itself the sympathy of ordinary men. There were, too, not a few points of actual resemblance between the Socratic method and that of the Sophists. They both employed the instrument of Dialectic, subjecting to the test of cross-examination the current views and common beliefs of the time—and, thus, they had alike a negative or destructive side to their philosophy. If the Sophists delighted to criticise, to question, to suggest doubts, and to raise objections; so Socrates had an unwelcome mission to perform, namely, to expose shams, to test severely, to weigh in the balances and find many things wanting, to disenchant, to disabuse. But his teaching had a constructive side as well; to rear what was true on the ruins of what was false; to make men think for themselves; to elicit the thought in their minds, and to force them to put it into shape.

Aristophanes was not alone in reckoning Socrates among the Sophists. Long after his sentence and death, when his character had been better studied and appreciated, Aeschines calls him 'Socrates the Sophist;' and, in still later times, Cato speaks of him as the corrupter of youth. Therefore we can hardly be surprised—we ought not even to be indignant—at a judgment passed upon him by his contemporaries in all the excitement of a party-struggle. When we remember, in the case of Cleon, the furious invectives which Aristophanes employed, we shall hardly be inclined to think his attack upon Socrates as personally malevolent. He conscientiously regarded him as the head and front of that modern spirit which was developing in Athens; and which threatened, as he thought, to sweep away all the old landmarks and hallowed memories of the past. His fault lay in his effort to stop the course of a torrent which could only gather strength by being held back; but which might, in the view of the more far-sighted Socrates, be directed into proper channels, and be adapted to the service of the generations to come.

Aristophanes may then be considered as conscientious, though mistaken, in his attack upon Socrates. Indeed, had he been asked to distinguish between the gratuitous teacher of the streets, and the paid and more regular professor, he would have said that the former was the more dangerous. For the fees which the professors charged had the effect of limiting the number of their pupils; but the gratuitous teaching of Socrates was accessible to every stratum of Athenian society.

How formidable Socrates felt this attack to be, let him tell in his own words in the Apologia (18 b.), ἐμοῦ γὰρ πολλοὶ κατήγοροι γεγόνασι πρὸς ὑμᾶς καὶ πάλαι πολλὰ ἤδη ἔτη καὶ οὐδὲν ἀληθὲς λέγοντες· οὓς ἐγὼ μᾶλλον φοβοῦμαι ἢ τοὺς ἀμφὶ Ἄνυτον, καίπερ ὄντας καὶ τούτους δεινούς. ἀλλ' ἐκεῖνοι δεινότεροι, ὦ ἄνδρες, οἳ ὑμῶν τοὺς πολλοὺς ἐκ παίδων παραλαμβάνοντες ἔπειθόν τε καὶ κατηγόρουν ἐμοῦ οὐδὲν ἀληθές, ὡς ἔστι τις Σωκράτης, σοφὸς ἀνήρ, τά τε μετέωρα φροντιστής, καὶ τὰ ὑπὸ γῆς ἅπαντα ἀνεζητηκώς, καὶ τὸν ἥττω λόγον κρείττω ποιῶν. οὗτοι, ὦ ἄνδρες Ἀθηναῖοι, ταύτην τὴν φήμην διασκεδάσαντες, οἱ δεινοί εἰσί μου κατήγοροι· οἱ γὰρ ἀκούοντες ἡγοῦνται τοὺς ταῦτα ζητοῦντας οὐδὲ θεοὺς νομίζειν. . . (ib. 19 c.), ταῦτα γὰρ ἑωρᾶτε καὶ αὐτοὶ ἐν τῇ Ἀριστοφάνους κωμῳδίᾳ, Σωκράτη τινὰ ἐκεῖ περιφερόμενον, φάσκοντά τε ἀεροβατεῖν, καὶ ἄλλην πολλὴν φλυαρίαν φλυαροῦντα, ὧν ἐγὼ οὐδὲν οὔτε μέγα οὔτε σμικρὸν πέρι ἐπαΐω.

The play of the 'Clouds' was acted in the year 423 B.C, at the Great Dionysia. But the author only gained the third prize, Cratinus winning the first with his Πυτίνη, and Ameipsias the second with his Κόννος. This failure disappointed Aristophanes, who thought it the very best play he had written: so he determined to make such alterations as were required, and to put it on the stage again. It is this altered form, or Second Edition, which we now possess; as we might indeed have inferred from the Parabasis (524 foll.), even had there been no external evidence to the same effect.

The exact relation between the two editions is best given in words from one of the Greek 'Arguments' prefixed to the play, probably the work of an Alexandrian grammarian: τοῦτο ταὐτόν ἐστι τῷ προτέρῳ. διασκεύασται δὲ ἐπὶ μέρους, ὡς ἂν δὴ ἀναδιδάξαι μὲν αὐτὸ τοῦ ποιητοῦ προθυμηθέντος, οὐκέτι δὲ τοῦτο δι' ἣν ποτε αἰτίαν ποιήσαντος. καθόλου μὲν οὖν σχεδὸν παρὰ πᾶν μέρος γεγενημένη [? γεγένηται ἡ] διόρθωσις. τὰ μὲν γὰρ περιῄρηται, τὰ δὲ παραπέπλεκται, καὶ ἐν τῇ τάξει καὶ ἐν τῇ τῶν προσώπων διαλλαγῇ μετεσχημάτισται. ἃ δὲ ὁλοσχερῆ τῆς διασκευῆς τοιαῦτα ὄντα τετύχηκεν, αὐτίκα ἡ παράβασις τοῦ χοροῦ ἤμειπται, καὶ ὅπου ὁ δίκαιος λόγος πρὸς τὸν ἄδικον λαλεῖ, καὶ τελευταῖον ὅπου καίεται ἡ διατριβὴ Σωκράτους.

'This edition is identical with the former one. But it has been to some extent recast, as though the poet had intended to reproduce it on the stage, but for some reason or other had never done so. A general revision too of nearly every part has been effected; some portions having been withdrawn; while others have been woven into the play, and alterations made in arrangement and interchange of characters.

'The main changes in the play, as recast, are the altered parabasis, the scene between the Just and Unjust Argument, and the burning of the house of Socrates.'

Here we must carefully distinguish between the διόρθωσις of details, and the διασκευή of the general plot.

What, we may ask, was the actual intention of these changes? Had the enmity to Socrates and his teaching deepened? Had Aristophanes learned, in the interim between the acting of the first edition and the preparation of the second for the stage, to regard Socrates as a dangerous citizen rather than as a silly pedant? It seems that these questions may be answered in the affirmative.

(In the passage quoted above from the Apologia (19 c.) the word ἑωρᾶτε limits the reference made by Socrates to the *acted*, or earlier, edition of the play.) [There he was represented only as engaged in idle speculations; but that a far more serious view was afterwards taken of his teaching we can gather from the nature of the charge made against him by Anytus and Meletus, Σωκράτη φησὶν ἀδικεῖν τούς τε νέους διαφθείροντα, καὶ θεοὺς οὓς ἡ πόλις νομίζει οὐ νομίζοντα, ἕτερα δὲ δαιμόνια καινά Apol. 24 b. If we take these words in connection with the views enunciated by the Unjust Argument, we shall see that Socrates distinctly appears as the champion of the new and pestilent form of education, to the utter ruin, as the Just Argument says, of that ill-fated city ἥτις σε τρέφει λυμαινόμενον τοῖς μειρακίοις (Nub. 1027). No wonder that the later edition ended with the firing of Socrates' house.

One of the Greek 'Arguments' to the 'Clouds' asserts that the play was produced in 422 B.C. in the Archonship of Ameinias, and that it failed more signally than before. But this was the year in which Aristophanes brought out his 'Wasps' and 'Proagon;' and the Parabasis of the 'Clouds' makes mention of the 'Maricas' of Eupolis, which was not represented till 421 B.C.; so that the second edition of the 'Clouds' must, under any circumstances, have been subsequent to that date. The most probable view is that this second edition was not only never reproduced, but that the recasting and revision were never quite completed. This is the only theory to account for such phenomena as the lacuna at l. 888 (see notes on text); the incongruity of ll. 1105–1112 with the foregoing scene, which was to decide whether Pheidippides should take his instruction from the Just or the Unjust Argument; the want of harmony between the strophe 700–706, and the antistrophe 804–813; the contradiction between ll. 550 and 581; the former of which speaks of Cleon as dead, the latter as living. All these marks of incompleteness would, we may suppose, have been obliterated, had the final revision ever been made. It is not unlikely that after the death of Aristophanes his sons published the imperfect recast of the 'Clouds,' without any further alterations; and that its evident superiority to the former edition soon caused that version to fall into disuse. A few lines are quoted in Athenaeus, Diogenes Laertius, and Photius as having occurred ἐν ταῖς προτέραις Νεφέλαις, which are not found in the extant form of the play. But, more than that, they seem to point to scenes so totally different from anything in the later edition, that we cannot help thinking that the διασκευή must have been very sweeping in its changes.

We might well ask at what point in our play we could insert this couplet, preserved by Diog. Laert. 2. 5, 18:

Εὐριπίδης δ' ὁ τὰς τραγῳδίας ποιῶν
τὰς περιλαλούσας οὗτός ἐστι, τὰς σοφάς?

or what offence offered to the Cloud-goddesses made them go off in a huff—(Phot. 398. 11):

ἐς τὴν Πάρνηθ' ὀργισθεῖσαι φροῦδαι κατὰ τὸν Λυκαβηττόν?

Indeed, the whole tendency of such evidence as we possess corroborates the general view expressed in the Greek Argument quoted above. But it forces us to give a very wide interpretation of the opening sentence *τοῦτο ταὐτόν ἐστι τῷ προτέρῳ.*

ΝΕΦΕΛΑΙ.

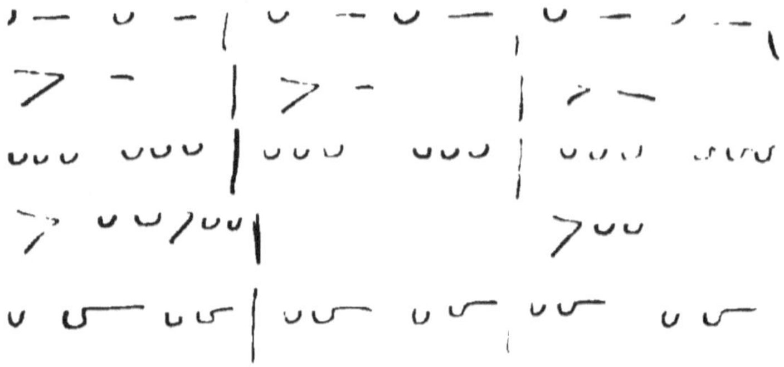

ΤΑ ΤΟΥ ΔΡΑΜΑΤΟΣ ΠΡΟΣΩΠΑ.

ΣΤΡΕΨΙΑΔΗΣ.
ΦΕΙΔΙΠΠΙΔΗΣ.
ΘΕΡΑΠΩΝ ΣΤΡΕΨΙΑΔΟΥ.
ΜΑΘΗΤΑΙ ΣΩΚΡΑΤΟΥΣ.
ΣΩΚΡΑΤΗΣ.

ΧΟΡΟΣ ΝΕΦΕΛΩΝ.
ΔΙΚΑΙΟΣ ΛΟΓΟΣ.
ΑΔΙΚΟΣ ΛΟΓΟΣ.
ΠΑΣΙΑΣ, *δανειστής.*
ΑΜΥΝΙΑΣ, *δανειστής.*

ΜΑΡΤΥΣ.

ΝΕΦΕΛΑΙ.

ΣΤΡΕΨΙΑΔΗΣ. ΦΕΙΔΙΠΠΙΔΗΣ. ΘΕΡΑΠΩΝ.

ΣΤΡ. Ἰοὺ ἰού·
ὦ Ζεῦ βασιλεῦ, τὸ χρῆμα τῶν νυκτῶν ὅσον·
ἀπέραντον· οὐδέποθ' ἡμέρα γενήσεται;
καὶ μὴν πάλαι γ' ἀλεκτρυόνος ἤκουσ' ἐγώ·
οἱ δ' οἰκέται ῥέγκουσιν· ἀλλ' οὐκ ἂν πρὸ τοῦ.
ἀπόλοιο δῆτ', ὦ πόλεμε, πολλῶν οὕνεκα,
ὅτ' οὐδὲ κολάσ' ἔξεστί μοι τοὺς οἰκέτας.
ἀλλ' οὐδ' ὁ χρηστὸς οὑτοσὶ νεανίας
ἐγείρεται τῆς νυκτός, ἀλλὰ πέρδεται
ἐν πέντε σισύραις ἐγκεκορδυλημένος.
ἀλλ' εἰ δοκεῖ, ῥέγκωμεν ἐγκεκαλυμμένοι.—
ἀλλ' οὐ δύναμαι δείλαιος εὕδειν δακνόμενος
ὑπὸ τῆς δαπάνης καὶ τῆς φάτνης καὶ τῶν χρεῶν,
διὰ τουτονὶ τὸν υἱόν. ὁ δὲ κόμην ἔχων
ἱππάζεταί τε καὶ ξυνωρικεύεται
ὀνειροπολεῖ θ' ἵππους· ἐγὼ δ' ἀπόλλυμαι,
ὁρῶν ἄγουσαν τὴν σελήνην εἰκάδας·
οἱ γὰρ τόκοι χωροῦσιν. ἅπτε, παῖ, λύχνον,
κἄκφερε τὸ γραμματεῖον, ἵν' ἀναγνῶ λαβὼν
ὁπόσοις ὀφείλω καὶ λογίσωμαι τοὺς τόκους.
φέρ' ἴδω, τί ὀφείλω; δώδεκα μνᾶς Πασίᾳ.
τοῦ δώδεκα μνᾶς Πασίᾳ; τί ἐχρησάμην;
ὅτ' ἐπριάμην τὸν κοππατίαν. οἴμοι τάλας,
εἴθ' ἐξεκόπην πρότερον τὸν ὀφθαλμὸν λίθῳ.
ΦΕΙ. Φίλων, ἀδικεῖς· ἔλαυνε τὸν σαυτοῦ δρόμον.

ΣΤΡ. τοῦτ' ἔστι τουτὶ τὸ κακὸν ὅ μ' ἀπολώλεκεν·
ὀνειροπολεῖ γὰρ καὶ καθεύδων ἱππικήν.
ΦΕΙ. πόσους δρόμους ἐλᾷ τὰ πολεμιστήρια;
ΣΤΡ. ἐμὲ μὲν σὺ πολλοὺς τὸν πατέρ' ἐλαύνεις δρόμους.
ἀτὰρ τί χρέος ἔβα με μετὰ τὸν Πασίαν;
τρεῖς μναῖ διφρίσκου καὶ τροχοῖν Ἀμυνίᾳ.
ΦΕΙ. ἄπαγε τὸν ἵππον ἐξαλίσας οἴκαδε.
ΣΤΡ. ἀλλ', ὦ μέλ', ἐξήλικας ἐμέ γ' ἐκ τῶν ἐμῶν,
ὅτε καὶ δίκας ὦφληκα χἄτεροι τόκου
ἐνεχυράσασθαί φασιν. ΦΕΙ. ἐτεόν, ὦ πάτερ,
τί δυσκολαίνεις καὶ στρέφει τὴν νύχθ' ὅλην;
ΣΤΡ. δάκνει με δήμαρχός τις ἐκ τῶν στρωμάτων.
ΦΕΙ. ἔασον, ὦ δαιμόνιε, καταδαρθεῖν τί με.
ΣΤΡ. σὺ δ' οὖν κάθευδε· τὰ δὲ χρέα ταῦτ' ἴσθ' ὅτι
εἰς τὴν κεφαλὴν ἅπαντα τὴν σὴν τρέψεται.
φεῦ.
εἴθ' ὤφελ' ἡ προμνήστρι' ἀπολέσθαι κακῶς,
ἥτις με γῆμ' ἐπῆρε τὴν σὴν μητέρα·
ἐμοὶ γὰρ ἦν ἄγροικος ἥδιστος βίος,
εὐρωτιῶν, ἀκόρητος, εἰκῆ κείμενος,
βρύων μελίτταις καὶ προβάτοις καὶ στεμφύλοις.
ἔπειτ' ἔγημα Μεγακλέους τοῦ Μεγακλέους
ἀδελφιδῆν ἄγροικος ὢν ἐξ ἄστεως,
σεμνήν, τρυφῶσαν, ἐγκεκοισυρωμένην.
ταύτην ὅτ' ἐγάμουν, συγκατεκλινόμην ἐγὼ
ὄζων τρυγός, τρασιᾶς, ἐρίων περιουσίας,
ἡ δ' αὖ μύρου, κρόκου, καταγλωττισμάτων,
δαπάνης, λαφυγμοῦ, Κωλιάδος, Γενετυλλίδος.
οὐ μὴν ἐρῶ γ' ὡς ἀργὸς ἦν, ἀλλ' ἐσπάθα.
ἐγὼ δ' ἂν αὐτῇ θοἰμάτιον δεικνὺς τοδὶ
πρόφασιν ἔφασκον, ὦ γύναι, λίαν σπαθᾷς.
ΘΕΡ. ἔλαιον ἡμῖν οὐκ ἔνεστ' ἐν τῷ λύχνῳ.

ΣΤΡ. οἴμοι· τί γάρ μοι τὸν πότην ἧπτες λύχνον;
δεῦρ' ἔλθ', ἵνα κλάῃς. ΘΕΡ. διὰ τί δῆτα κλαύσομαι;
ΣΤΡ. ὅτι τῶν παχειῶν ἐνετίθεις θρυαλλίδων.
μετὰ ταῦθ', ὅπως νῷν ἐγένεθ' υἱὸς οὑτοσί,
ἐμοί τε δὴ καὶ τῇ γυναικὶ τἀγαθῇ,
περὶ τοὐνόματος δὴ 'ντεῦθεν ἐλοιδορούμεθα·
ἡ μὲν γὰρ ἵππον προσετίθει πρὸς τοὔνομα,
Ξάνθιππον ἢ Χαίριππον ἢ Καλλιππίδην,
ἐγὼ δὲ τοῦ πάππου 'τιθέμην Φειδωνίδην.
τέως μὲν οὖν ἐκρινόμεθ'· εἶτα τῷ χρόνῳ
κοινῇ ξυνέβημεν κἀθέμεθα Φειδιππίδην.
τοῦτον τὸν υἱὸν λαμβάνουσ' ἐκορίζετο,
ὅταν σὺ μέγας ὢν ἅρμ' ἐλαύνῃς πρὸς πόλιν,
ὥσπερ Μεγακλέης, ξυστίδ' ἔχων. ἐγὼ δ' ἔφην,
ὅταν μὲν οὖν τὰς αἶγας ἐκ τοῦ φελλέως,
ὥσπερ ὁ πατήρ σου, διφθέραν ἐνημμένος.
ἀλλ' οὐκ ἐπίθετο τοῖς ἐμοῖς οὐδὲν λόγοις,
ἀλλ' ἵππερόν μου κατέχεεν τῶν χρημάτων.
νῦν οὖν ὅλην τὴν νύκτα φροντίζων ὁδοῦ
μίαν εὗρον ἀτραπὸν δαιμονίως ὑπερφυᾶ,
ἣν ἢν ἀναπείσω τουτονί, σωθήσομαι.
ἀλλ' ἐξεγεῖραι πρῶτον αὐτὸν βούλομαι.
πῶς δῆτ' ἂν ἥδιστ' αὐτὸν ἐπεγείραιμι; πῶς;
Φειδιππίδη, Φειδιππίδιον. ΦΕΙ. τί, ὦ πάτερ;
ΣΤΡ. κύσον με καὶ τὴν χεῖρα δὸς τὴν δεξιάν.
ΦΕΙ. ἰδού. τί ἔστιν; ΣΤΡ. εἰπέ μοι, φιλεῖς ἐμέ;
ΦΕΙ. νὴ τὸν Ποσειδῶ τουτονὶ τὸν ἵππιον.
ΣΤΡ. μή μοί γε τοῦτον μηδαμῶς τὸν ἵππιον·
οὗτος γὰρ ὁ θεὸς αἴτιός μοι τῶν κακῶν.
ἀλλ' εἴπερ ἐκ τῆς καρδίας μ' ὄντως φιλεῖς,
ὦ παῖ, πιθοῦ μοι. ΦΕΙ. τί δὲ πίθωμαι δῆτά σοι;
ΣΤΡ. ἔκστρεψον ὡς τάχιστα τοὺς σαυτοῦ τρόπους,

καὶ μάνθαν' ἐλθὼν ἂν ἐγὼ παραινέσω.
ΦΕΙ. λέγε δή, τί κελεύεις; ΣΤΡ. καί τι πείσει; ΦΕΙ. πείσομαι,
νὴ τὸν Διόνυσον. ΣΤΡ. δεῦρό νυν ἀπόβλεπε.
ὁρᾷς τὸ θύριον τοῦτο καὶ τῳκίδιον;
ΦΕΙ. ὁρῶ. τί οὖν τοῦτ' ἐστὶν ἐτεόν, ὦ πάτερ;
ΣΤΡ. ψυχῶν σοφῶν τοῦτ' ἐστὶ φροντιστήριον.
ἐνταῦθ' ἐνοικοῦσ' ἄνδρες οἳ τὸν οὐρανὸν
λέγοντες ἀναπείθουσιν ὡς ἔστιν πνιγεύς,
κἄστιν περὶ ἡμᾶς οὗτος, ἡμεῖς δ' ἄνθρακες.
οὗτοι διδάσκουσ', ἀργύριον ἤν τις διδῷ,
λέγοντα νικᾶν καὶ δίκαια κἄδικα.
ΦΕΙ. εἰσὶν δὲ τίνες; ΣΤΡ. οὐκ οἶδ' ἀκριβῶς τοὔνομα·
μεριμνοφροντισταὶ καλοί τε κἀγαθοί.
ΦΕΙ. αἰβοῖ, πονηροί γ', οἶδα. τοὺς ἀλαζόνας,
τοὺς ὠχριῶντας, τοὺς ἀνυποδήτους λέγεις·
ὧν ὁ κακοδαίμων Σωκράτης καὶ Χαιρεφῶν.
ΣΤΡ. ἢ ἤ, σιώπα· μηδὲν εἴπῃς νήπιον.
ἀλλ' εἴ τι κήδει τῶν πατρῴων ἀλφίτων,
τούτων γενοῦ μοι, σχασάμενος τὴν ἱππικήν.
ΦΕΙ. οὐκ ἂν μὰ τὸν Διόνυσον, εἰ δοίης γέ μοι
τοὺς φασιανοὺς οὓς τρέφει Λεωγόρας.
ΣΤΡ. ἴθ', ἀντιβολῶ σ', ὦ φίλτατ' ἀνθρώπων ἐμοί,
ἐλθὼν διδάσκου. ΦΕΙ. καὶ τί σοι μαθήσομαι;
ΣΤΡ. εἶναι παρ' αὐτοῖς φασὶν ἄμφω τὼ λόγω,
τὸν κρείττον', ὅστις ἐστί, καὶ τὸν ἥττονα.
τούτοιν τὸν ἕτερον τοῖν λόγοιν, τὸν ἥττονα,
νικᾶν λέγοντά φασι τἀδικώτερα.
ἢν οὖν μάθῃς μοι τὸν ἄδικον τοῦτον λόγον,
ἃ νῦν ὀφείλω διὰ σέ, τούτων τῶν χρεῶν
οὐκ ἂν ἀποδοίην οὐδ' ἂν ὀβολὸν οὐδενί.
ΦΕΙ. οὐκ ἂν πιθοίμην· οὐ γὰρ ἂν τλαίην ἰδεῖν

τοὺς ἱππέας τὸ χρῶμα διακεκναισμένος.
ΣΤΡ. οὐκ ἄρα μὰ τὴν Δήμητρα τῶν γ' ἐμῶν ἔδει,
οὔτ' αὐτὸς οὔθ' ὁ ζύγιος οὔθ' ὁ σαμφόρας·
ἀλλ' ἐξελῶ σ' ἐς κόρακας ἐκ τῆς οἰκίας.
ΦΕΙ. ἀλλ' οὐ περιόψεταί μ' ὁ θεῖος Μεγακλέης
ἄνιππον. ἀλλ' εἴσειμι, σοῦ δ' οὐ φροντιῶ.
ΣΤΡ. ἀλλ' οὐδ' ἐγὼ μέντοι πεσών γε κείσομαι·
ἀλλ' εὐξάμενος τοῖσιν θεοῖς διδάξομαι
αὐτὸς βαδίζων εἰς τὸ φροντιστήριον.
πῶς οὖν γέρων ὢν κἀπιλήσμων καὶ βραδὺς
λόγων ἀκριβῶν σκινδαλάμους μαθήσομαι;
ἰτητέον. τί ταῦτ' ἔχων στραγγεύομαι,
ἀλλ' οὐχὶ κόπτω τὴν θύραν; παῖ, παιδίον.

ΜΑΘΗΤΗΣ.

βάλλ' ἐς κόρακας· τίς ἐσθ' ὁ κόψας τὴν θύραν;
ΣΤΡ. Φείδωνος υἱὸς Στρεψιάδης Κικυννόθεν.
ΜΑΘ. ἀμαθής γε νὴ Δί', ὅστις οὑτωσὶ σφόδρα
ἀπεριμερίμνως τὴν θύραν λελάκτικας
καὶ φροντίδ' ἐξήμβλωκας ἐξευρημένην.
ΣΤΡ. σύγγνωθί μοι· τηλοῦ γὰρ οἰκῶ τῶν ἀγρῶν.
ἀλλ' εἰπέ μοι τὸ πρᾶγμα τοὐξημβλωμένον.
ΜΑΘ. ἀλλ' οὐ θέμις πλὴν τοῖς μαθηταῖσιν λέγειν.
ΣΤΡ. λέγε νυν ἐμοὶ θαρρῶν· ἐγὼ γὰρ οὑτοσὶ
ἥκω μαθητὴς εἰς τὸ φροντιστήριον.
ΜΑΘ. λέξω. νομίσαι δὲ ταῦτα χρὴ μυστήρια.
ἀνήρετ' ἄρτι Χαιρεφῶντα Σωκράτης
ψύλλαν ὁπόσους ἅλλοιτο τοὺς αὑτῆς πόδας·
δακοῦσα γὰρ τοῦ Χαιρεφῶντος τὴν ὀφρῦν
ἐπὶ τὴν κεφαλὴν τὴν Σωκράτους ἀφήλατο.
ΣΤΡ. πῶς τοῦτο διεμέτρησε; ΜΑΘ. δεξιώτατα.
κηρὸν διατήξας, εἶτα τὴν ψύλλαν λαβὼν

ἐνέβαψεν εἰς τὸν κηρὸν αὐτῆς τὼ πόδε,
κᾆτα ψυγείσῃ περιέφυσαν Περσικαί.
ταύτας ὑπολύσας ἀνεμέτρει τὸ χωρίον.
ΣΤΡ. ὦ Ζεῦ βασιλεῦ τῆς λεπτότητος τῶν φρενῶν.
ΜΑΘ. τί δῆτ' ἄν, ἕτερον εἰ πύθοιο Σωκράτους
φρόντισμα; ΣΤΡ. ποῖον; ἀντιβολῶ, κάτειπέ μοι.
ΜΑΘ. ἀνήρετ' αὐτὸν Χαιρεφῶν ὁ Σφήττιος
ὁπότερα τὴν γνώμην ἔχοι, τὰς ἐμπίδας
κατὰ τὸ στόμ' ᾄδειν, ἢ κατὰ τοὐρροπύγιον.
ΣΤΡ. τί δῆτ' ἐκεῖνος εἶπε περὶ τῆς ἐμπίδος;
ΜΑΘ. ἔφασκεν εἶναι τοὔντερον τῆς ἐμπίδος
στενόν· διὰ λεπτοῦ δ' ὄντος αὐτοῦ τὴν πνοὴν
βίᾳ βαδίζειν εὐθὺ τοὐρροπυγίου·
ἔπειτα κοῖλον πρὸς στενῷ προσκείμενον
τὸν πρωκτὸν ἠχεῖν ὑπὸ βίας τοῦ πνεύματος.
ΣΤΡ. σάλπιγξ ὁ πρωκτός ἐστιν ἄρα τῶν ἐμπίδων.
ὢ τρισμακάριος τοῦ διεντερεύματος.
ἦ ῥᾳδίως φεύγων ἂν ἀποφύγοι δίκην
ὅστις δίοιδε τοὔντερον τῆς ἐμπίδος.
ΜΑΘ. πρώην δέ γε γνώμην μεγάλην ἀφῃρέθη
ὑπ' ἀσκαλαβώτου. ΣΤΡ. τίνα τρόπον; κάτειπέ μοι.
ΜΑΘ. ζητοῦντος αὐτοῦ τῆς σελήνης τὰς ὁδοὺς
καὶ τὰς περιφοράς, εἶτ' ἄνω κεχηνότος
ἀπὸ τῆς ὀροφῆς νύκτωρ γαλεώτης κατέχεσεν.
ΣΤΡ. ἥσθην γαλεώτῃ καταχέσαντι Σωκράτους.
ΜΑΘ. ἐχθὲς δέ γ' ἡμῖν δεῖπνον οὐκ ἦν ἑσπέρας.
ΣΤΡ. εἶεν· τί οὖν πρὸς τἄλφιτ' ἐπαλαμήσατο;
ΜΑΘ. κατὰ τῆς τραπέζης καταπάσας λεπτὴν τέφραν,
κάμψας ὀβελίσκον, εἶτα διαβήτην λαβών,
ἐκ τῆς παλαίστρας θυμάτιον ὑφείλετο.
ΣΤΡ. τί δῆτ' ἐκεῖνον τὸν Θαλῆν θαυμάζομεν;
ἄνοιγ' ἄνοιγ' ἀνύσας τὸ φροντιστήριον,

καὶ δεῖξον ὡς τάχιστά μοι τὸν Σωκράτην.
μαθητιῶ γάρ· ἀλλ' ἄνοιγε τὴν θύραν.
ὦ Ἡράκλεις, ταυτὶ ποδαπὰ τὰ θηρία;
ΜΑΘ. τί ἐθαύμασας; τῷ σοι δοκοῦσιν εἰκέναι;
ΣΤΡ. τοῖς ἐκ Πύλου ληφθεῖσι, τοῖς Λακωνικοῖς.
ἀτὰρ τί ποτ' ἐς τὴν γῆν βλέπουσιν οὑτοιί;
ΜΑΘ. ζητοῦσιν οὗτοι τὰ κατὰ γῆς. ΣΤΡ. βολβοὺς ἄρα
ζητοῦσι. μή νυν τοῦτό γ' ἔτι φροντίζετε·
ἐγὼ γὰρ οἶδ' ἵν' εἰσὶ μεγάλοι καὶ καλοί.
τί γὰρ οἵδε δρῶσιν οἱ σφόδρ' ἐγκεκυφότες;
ΜΑΘ. οὗτοι δ' ἐρεβοδιφῶσιν ὑπὸ τὸν Τάρταρον.
ΣΤΡ. τί δῆθ' ὁ πρωκτὸς ἐς τὸν οὐρανὸν βλέπει;
ΜΑΘ. αὐτὸς καθ' αὑτὸν ἀστρονομεῖν διδάσκεται.
ἀλλ' εἴσιθ', ἵνα μὴ 'κεῖνος ὑμῖν ἐπιτύχῃ.
ΣΤΡ. μήπω γε, μήπω γ'· ἀλλ' ἐπιμεινάντων, ἵνα
αὐτοῖσι κοινώσω τι πραγμάτιον ἐμόν.
ΜΑΘ. ἀλλ' οὐχ οἷόν τ' αὐτοῖσι πρὸς τὸν ἀέρα
ἔξω διατρίβειν πολὺν ἄγαν ἐστὶν χρόνον.
ΣΤΡ. πρὸς τῶν θεῶν, τί γὰρ τάδ' ἐστίν; εἰπέ μοι.
ΜΑΘ. ἀστρονομία μὲν αὑτηί. ΣΤΡ. τουτὶ δὲ τί;
ΜΑΘ. γεωμετρία. ΣΤΡ. τοῦτ' οὖν τί ἐστι χρήσιμον;
ΜΑΘ. γῆν ἀναμετρεῖσθαι. ΣΤΡ. πότερα τὴν κληρουχικήν;
ΜΑΘ. οὔκ, ἀλλὰ τὴν σύμπασαν. ΣΤΡ. ἀστεῖον λέγεις.
τὸ γὰρ σόφισμα δημοτικὸν καὶ χρήσιμον.
ΜΑΘ. αὕτη δέ σοι γῆς περίοδος πάσης. ὁρᾷς;
αἵδε μὲν Ἀθῆναι. ΣΤΡ. τί σὺ λέγεις; οὐ πείθομαι,
ἐπεὶ δικαστὰς οὐχ ὁρῶ καθημένους.
ΜΑΘ. ὡς τοῦτ' ἀληθῶς Ἀττικὸν τὸ χωρίον.
ΣΤΡ. καὶ ποῦ Κικυννῆς εἰσὶν οὑμοὶ δημόται;
ΜΑΘ. ἐνταῦθ' ἔνεισιν. ἡ δέ γ' Εὔβοι', ὡς ὁρᾷς,
ἡδὶ παρατέταται μακρὰ πόρρω πάνυ.
ΣΤΡ. οἶδ'· ὑπὸ γὰρ ἡμῶν παρετάθη καὶ Περικλέους.

ἀλλ' ἡ Λακεδαίμων ποῦ 'στιν; ΜΑΘ. ὅπου 'στιν; αὐτηί.
ΣΤΡ. ὡς ἐγγὺς ἡμῶν. τοῦτο πάνυ φροντίζετε,
ταύτην ἀφ' ἡμῶν ἀπαγαγεῖν πόρρω πάνυ.
ΜΑΘ. ἀλλ' οὐχ οἷόν τε. ΣΤΡ. νὴ Δί', οἰμώξεσθ' ἄρα.
φέρε τίς γὰρ οὗτος οὑπὶ τῆς κρεμάθρας ἀνήρ;
ΜΑΘ. αὐτός. ΣΤΡ. τίς αὐτός; ΜΑΘ. Σωκράτης. ΣΤΡ. ὦ Σώκρατες.
ἴθ' οὗτος, ἀναβόησον αὐτόν μοι μέγα.
ΜΑΘ. αὐτὸς μὲν οὖν σὺ κάλεσον· οὐ γάρ μοι σχολή.
ΣΤΡ. ὦ Σώκρατες,
ὦ Σωκρατίδιον.

ΣΩΚΡΑΤΗΣ.

τί με καλεῖς, ὦ 'φήμερε;
ΣΤΡ. πρῶτον μὲν ὅ τι δρᾷς, ἀντιβολῶ, κάτειπέ μοι.
ΣΩ. ἀεροβατῶ καὶ περιφρονῶ τὸν ἥλιον.
ΣΤΡ. ἔπειτ' ἀπὸ ταρροῦ τοὺς θεοὺς ὑπερφρονεῖς,
ἀλλ' οὐκ ἀπὸ τῆς γῆς, εἴπερ; ΣΩ. οὐ γὰρ ἄν ποτε
ἐξεῦρον ὀρθῶς τὰ μετέωρα πράγματα,
εἰ μὴ κρεμάσας τὸ νόημα καὶ τὴν φροντίδα
λεπτὴν καταμίξας εἰς τὸν ὅμοιον ἀέρα.
εἰ δ' ὢν χαμαὶ τἄνω κάτωθεν ἐσκόπουν,
οὐκ ἄν ποθ' εὗρον· οὐ γὰρ ἀλλ' ἡ γῆ βίᾳ
ἕλκει πρὸς αὑτὴν τὴν ἰκμάδα τῆς φροντίδος.
πάσχει δὲ ταὐτὸ τοῦτο καὶ τὰ κάρδαμα.
ΣΤΡ. τί φῄς;
ἡ φροντὶς ἕλκει τὴν ἰκμάδ' εἰς τὰ κάρδαμα;
ἴθι νυν, κατάβηθ', ὦ Σωκρατίδιον, ὡς ἐμέ,
ἵνα με διδάξῃς ὧνπερ οὕνεκ' ἐλήλυθα.
ΣΩ. ἦλθες δὲ κατὰ τί; ΣΤΡ. βουλόμενος μαθεῖν λέγειν.

ὑπὸ γὰρ τόκων χρήστων τε δυσκολωτάτων
ἄγομαι, φέρομαι, τὰ χρήματ' ἐνεχυράζομαι.

ΣΩ. πόθεν δ' ὑπόχρεως σαυτὸν ἔλαθες γενόμενος;

ΣΤΡ. νόσος μ' ἐπέτριψεν ἱππική, δεινὴ φαγεῖν.
ἀλλά με δίδαξον τὸν ἕτερον τοῖν σοῖν λόγοιν,
τὸν μηδὲν ἀποδιδόντα. μισθὸν δ' ὅντιν' ἂν
πράττῃ μ' ὀμοῦμαί σοι καταθήσειν τοὺς θεούς.

ΣΩ. ποίους θεοὺς ὀμεῖ σύ; πρῶτον γὰρ θεοὶ
ἡμῖν νόμισμ' οὐκ ἔστι. ΣΤΡ. τῷ γὰρ ὄμνυτ'; ἢ
σιδαρέοισιν, ὥσπερ ἐν Βυζαντίῳ;

ΣΩ. βούλει τὰ θεῖα πράγματ' εἰδέναι σαφῶς
ἅττ' ἐστὶν ὀρθῶς; ΣΤΡ. νὴ Δί', εἴπερ ἔστι γε.

ΣΩ. καὶ ξυγγενέσθαι ταῖς Νεφέλαισιν ἐς λόγους,
ταῖς ἡμετέραισι δαίμοσιν; ΣΤΡ. μάλιστά γε.

ΣΩ. κάθιζε τοίνυν ἐπὶ τὸν ἱερὸν σκίμποδα.

ΣΤΡ. ἰδοὺ κάθημαι. ΣΩ. τουτονὶ τοίνυν λαβὲ
τὸν στέφανον. ΣΤΡ. ἐπὶ τί στέφανον; οἴμοι, Σώκρατες,
ὥσπερ με τὸν Ἀθάμανθ' ὅπως μὴ θύσετε.

ΣΩ. οὔκ, ἀλλὰ ταῦτα πάντα τοὺς τελουμένους
ἡμεῖς ποιοῦμεν. ΣΤΡ. εἶτα δὴ τί κερδανῶ;

ΣΩ. λέγειν γενήσει τρίμμα, κρόταλον, παιπάλη.
ἀλλ' ἔχ' ἀτρεμεί. ΣΤΡ. μὰ τὸν Δί' οὐ ψεύσει γέ με·
καταπαττόμενος γὰρ παιπάλη γενήσομαι.

ΣΩ. εὐφημεῖν χρὴ τὸν πρεσβύτην καὶ τῆς εὐχῆς ὑπακούειν.
ὦ δέσποτ' ἄναξ, ἀμέτρητ' Ἀήρ, ὃς ἔχεις τὴν γῆν μετέωρον,
λαμπρός τ' Αἰθήρ, σεμναί τε θεαὶ Νεφέλαι βροντησικέραυνοι,
ἄρθητε, φάνητ', ὦ δέσποιναι, τῷ φροντιστῇ μετέωροι.

ΣΤΡ. μήπω μήπω γε, πρὶν ἂν τουτὶ πτύξωμαι, μὴ καταβρεχθῶ.
τὸ δὲ μηδὲ κυνῆν οἴκοθεν ἐλθεῖν ἐμὲ τὸν κακοδαίμον᾽ ἔχοντα.
ΣΩ. ἔλθετε δῆτ᾽, ὦ πολυτίμητοι Νεφέλαι, τῷδ᾽ εἰς ἐπίδειξιν·
εἴτ᾽ ἐπ᾽ Ὀλύμπου κορυφαῖς ἱεραῖς χιονοβλήτοισι κάθησθε,
εἴτ᾽ Ὠκεανοῦ πατρὸς ἐν κήποις ἱερὸν χορὸν ἵστατε Νύμφαις,
εἴτ᾽ ἄρα Νείλου προχοαῖς ὑδάτων χρυσέαις ἀρύεσθε προχοῖσιν,
ἢ Μαιῶτιν λίμνην ἔχετ᾽ ἢ σκόπελον νιφόεντα Μίμαντος·
ἐπακούσατε δεξάμεναι θυσίαν καὶ τοῖς ἱεροῖσι χαρεῖσαι.

ΧΟΡΟΣ.

ἀέναοι Νεφέλαι,
ἀρθῶμεν φανεραὶ δροσερὰν φύσιν εὐάγητον,
πατρὸς ἀπ᾽ Ὠκεανοῦ βαρυαχέος
ὑψηλῶν ὀρέων κορυφὰς ἔπι
δενδροκόμους, ἵνα
τηλεφανεῖς σκοπιὰς ἀφορώμεθα,
καρπούς τ᾽ ἀρδομέναν ἱερὰν χθόνα,
καὶ ποταμῶν ζαθέων κελαδήματα,
καὶ πόντον κελάδοντα βαρύβρομον·
ὄμμα γὰρ αἰθέρος ἀκάματον σελαγεῖται
μαρμαρέαις ἐν αὐγαῖς.
ἀλλ᾽ ἀποσεισάμεναι νέφος ὄμβριον
ἀθανάτας ἰδέας ἐπιδώμεθα
τηλεσκόπῳ ὄμματι γαῖαν.

ΣΩ. ὦ μέγα σεμναὶ Νεφέλαι, φανερῶς ἠκούσατέ μου καλέσαντος.
ᾔσθου φωνῆς ἅμα καὶ βροντῆς μυκησαμένης θεοσέπτου;
οὐ μὴ σκώψεις, μηδὲ ποιήσεις ἅπερ οἱ τρυγοδαίμονες οὗτοι.
ἀλλ' εὐφήμει· μέγα γάρ τι θεῶν κινεῖται σμῆνος ἀοιδαῖς.
ΧΟΡ. παρθένοι ὀμβροφόροι,
ἔλθωμεν λιπαρὰν χθόνα Παλλάδος, εὔανδρον γᾶν
Κέκροπος ὀψόμεναι πολυήρατον·
οὗ σέβας ἀρρήτων ἱερῶν, ἵνα
μυστοδόκος δόμος
ἐν τελεταῖς ἁγίαις ἀναδείκνυται,
οὐρανίοις τε θεοῖς δωρήματα,
ναοί θ' ὑψερεφεῖς καὶ ἀγάλματα,
καὶ πρόσοδοι μακάρων ἱερώταται,
εὐστέφανοί τε θεῶν θυσίαι θαλίαι τε,
παντοδαπαῖς ἐν ὥραις,
ἦρί τ' ἐπερχομένῳ Βρομία χάρις,
εὐκελάδων τε χορῶν ἐρεθίσματα,
καὶ Μοῦσα βαρύβρομος αὐλῶν.
ΣΤΡ. πρὸς τοῦ Διὸς ἀντιβολῶ σε, φράσον, τίνες εἴσ', ὦ Σώκρατες, αὗται
αἱ φθεγξάμεναι τοῦτο τὸ σεμνόν; μῶν ἡρῷναί τινές εἰσιν;
ΣΩ. ἥκιστ', ἀλλ' οὐράνιαι Νεφέλαι, μεγάλαι θεαὶ ἀνδράσιν ἀργοῖς·
αἵπερ γνώμην καὶ διάλεξιν καὶ νοῦν ἡμῖν παρέχουσι,
καὶ τερατείαν καὶ περίλεξιν καὶ κροῦσιν καὶ κατάληψιν.
ΣΤΡ. ταῦτ' ἄρ' ἀκούσασ' αὐτῶν τὸ φθέγμ' ἡ ψυχή μου πεπότηται,
καὶ λεπτολογεῖν ἤδη ζητεῖ καὶ περὶ καπνοῦ στενολεσχεῖν,

καὶ γνωμιδίῳ γνώμην νύξασ' ἑτέρῳ λόγῳ ἀντιλογῆσαι·
ὥστ', εἴ πως ἔστιν, ἰδεῖν αὐτὰς ἤδη φανερῶς ἐπιθυμῶ.
ΣΩ. βλέπε νυν δευρὶ πρὸς τὴν Πάρνηθ'· ἤδη γὰρ ὁρῶ κατιούσας
ἡσυχῇ αὐτάς. ΣΤΡ. φέρε, ποῦ; δεῖξον. ΣΩ. χωροῦσ' αὗται πάνυ πολλαί,
διὰ τῶν κοίλων καὶ τῶν δασέων, αὗται πλάγιαι. ΣΤΡ. τί τὸ χρῆμα;
ὡς οὐ καθορῶ. ΣΩ. παρὰ τὴν εἴσοδον. ΣΤΡ. ἤδη νυνὶ μόλις οὕτως.
ΣΩ. νῦν γέ τοι ἤδη καθορᾷς αὐτάς, εἰ μὴ λημᾷς κολοκύνταις.
ΣΤΡ. νὴ Δί' ἔγωγ', ὦ πολυτίμητοι, πάντα γὰρ ἤδη κατέχουσι.
ΣΩ. ταύτας μέντοι σὺ θεὰς οὔσας οὐκ ᾔδεις οὐδ' ἐνόμιζες;
ΣΤΡ. μὰ Δί', ἀλλ' ὁμίχλην καὶ δρόσον αὐτὰς ἡγούμην καὶ καπνὸν εἶναι.
ΣΩ. οὐ γὰρ μὰ Δί' οἶσθ' ὁτιὴ πλείστους αὗται βόσκουσι σοφιστάς,
θουριομάντεις, ἰατροτέχνας, σφραγιδονυχαργοκομήτας,
κυκλίων τε χορῶν ᾀσματοκάμπτας, ἄνδρας μετεωροφένακας,
οὐδὲν δρῶντας βόσκουσ' ἀργούς, ὅτι ταύτας μουσοποιοῦσιν.
ΣΤΡ. ταῦτ' ἄρ' ἐποίουν ὑγρᾶν Νεφελᾶν στρεπταιγλᾶν δάϊον ὁρμάν,
πλοκάμους θ' ἑκατογκεφάλα Τυφῶ, πρημαινούσας τε θυέλλας,
εἶτ' ἀερίας, διεράς, γαμψοὺς οἰωνοὺς ἀερονηχεῖς,

ὄμβρους θ' ὑδάτων δροσερᾶν Νεφελᾶν· εἶτ' ἀντ' αὐτῶν κατέπινον
κεστρᾶν τεμάχη μεγαλᾶν ἀγαθᾶν, κρέα τ' ὀρνίθεια κιχηλᾶν.
ΣΩ. διὰ μέντοι τάσδ' οὐχὶ δικαίως; ΣΤΡ. λέξον δή μοι, τί παθοῦσαι,
εἴπερ Νεφέλαι γ' εἰσὶν ἀληθῶς, θνηταῖς εἴξασι γυναιξίν;
οὐ γὰρ ἐκεῖναί γ' εἰσὶ τοιαῦται. ΣΩ. φέρε, ποῖαι γάρ τινές εἰσιν;
ΣΤΡ. οὐκ οἶδα σαφῶς· εἴξασιν δ' οὖν ἐρίοισιν πεπταμένοισι,
κοὐχὶ γυναιξίν, μὰ Δί', οὐδ' ὁτιοῦν· αὗται δὲ ῥῖνας ἔχουσιν.
ΣΩ. ἀπόκριναί νυν ἅττ' ἂν ἔρωμαι. ΣΤΡ. λέγε νυν ταχέως ὅ τι βούλει.
ΣΩ. ἤδη ποτ' ἀναβλέψας εἶδες νεφέλην Κενταύρῳ ὁμοίαν
ἢ παρδάλει ἢ λύκῳ ἢ ταύρῳ; ΣΤΡ. νὴ Δί' ἔγωγ'. εἶτα τί τοῦτο;
ΣΩ. γίγνονται πάνθ' ὅ τι βούλονται· κᾆτ' ἢν μὲν ἴδωσι κομήτην,
ἄγριόν τινα τῶν λασίων τούτων, οἷόνπερ τὸν Ξενοφάντου,
σκώπτουσαι τὴν μανίαν αὐτοῦ Κενταύροις ᾔκασαν αὐτάς.
ΣΤΡ. τί γάρ, ἢν ἅρπαγα τῶν δημοσίων κατίδωσι Σίμωνα, τί δρῶσιν;
ΣΩ. ἀποφαίνουσαι τὴν φύσιν αὐτοῦ λύκοι ἐξαίφνης ἐγένοντο.
ΣΤΡ. ταῦτ' ἄρα, ταῦτα Κλεώνυμον αὗται τὸν ῥίψασπιν χθὲς ἰδοῦσαι,

ὅτι δειλότατον τοῦτον ἑώρων, ἔλαφοι διὰ τοῦτ' ἐγένοντο.

ΣΩ. καὶ νῦν γ' ὅτι Κλεισθένη εἶδον, ὁρᾷς, διὰ τοῦτ' ἐγένοντο γυναῖκες.

ΣΤΡ. χαίρετε τοίνυν, ὦ δέσποιναι· καὶ νῦν, εἴπερ τινὶ κἄλλῳ,
οὐρανομήκη ῥήξατε κἀμοὶ φωνήν, ὦ παμβασίλειαι.

ΧΟΡ. χαῖρ', ὦ πρεσβῦτα παλαιογενές, θηρατὰ λόγων φιλομούσων·
σύ τε, λεπτοτάτων λήρων ἱερεῦ, φράζε πρὸς ἡμᾶς ὅ τι χρῄζεις·
οὐ γὰρ ἂν ἄλλῳ γ' ὑπακούσαιμεν τῶν νῦν μετεωροσοφιστῶν
πλὴν ἢ Προδίκῳ, τῷ μὲν σοφίας καὶ γνώμης οὕνεκα, σοὶ δέ,
ὅτι βρενθύει τ' ἐν ταῖσιν ὁδοῖς καὶ τὠφθαλμὼ παραβάλλεις,
κἀνυπόδητος κακὰ πόλλ' ἀνέχει κἀφ' ἡμῖν σεμνοπροσωπεῖς.

ΣΤΡ. ὦ Γῆ τοῦ φθέγματος, ὡς ἱερὸν καὶ σεμνὸν καὶ τερατῶδες.

ΣΩ. αὗται γάρ τοι μόναι εἰσὶ θεαί· τἄλλα δὲ πάντ' ἐστὶ φλύαρος.

ΣΤΡ. ὁ Ζεὺς δ' ἡμῖν, φέρε, πρὸς τῆς Γῆς, οὑλύμπιος οὐ θεός ἐστιν;

ΣΩ. ποῖος Ζεύς; οὐ μὴ ληρήσεις· οὐδ' ἔστι Ζεύς. ΣΤΡ. τί λέγεις σύ;
ἀλλὰ τίς ὕει; τουτὶ γὰρ ἔμοιγ' ἀπόφηναι πρῶτον ἁπάντων.

ΣΩ. αὗται δή που· μεγάλοις δέ σ' ἐγὼ σημείοις αὐτὸ διδάξω.

φέρε, ποῦ γὰρ πώποτ' ἄνευ Νεφελῶν ὕοντ' ἤδη τεθέασαι;
καίτοι χρῆν αἰθρίας ὕειν αὐτόν, ταύτας δ' ἀποδημεῖν.
ΣΤΡ. νὴ τὸν Ἀπόλλω, τοῦτό γέ τοι τῷ νυνὶ λόγῳ εὖ προσέφυσας·
ἀλλ' ὅστις ὁ βροντῶν ἐστὶ φράσον, τοῦθ' ὅ με ποιεῖ τετρεμαίνειν.
ΣΩ. αὗται βροντῶσι κυλινδόμεναι. ΣΤΡ. τῷ τρόπῳ, ὦ πάντα σὺ τολμῶν;
ΣΩ. ὅταν ἐμπλησθῶσ' ὕδατος πολλοῦ κἀναγκασθῶσι φέρεσθαι,
κατακρημνάμεναι πλήρεις ὄμβρου δι' ἀνάγκην, εἶτα βαρεῖαι
εἰς ἀλλήλας ἐμπίπτουσαι ῥήγνυνται καὶ παταγοῦσιν.
ΣΤΡ. ὁ δ' ἀναγκάζων ἐστὶ τίς αὐτάς, οὐχ ὁ Ζεύς, ὥστε φέρεσθαι;
ΣΩ. ἥκιστ', ἀλλ' αἰθέριος δῖνος. ΣΤΡ. Δῖνος; τουτί μ' ἐλελήθει,
ὁ Ζεὺς οὐκ ὤν, ἀλλ' ἀντ' αὐτοῦ Δῖνος νυνὶ βασιλεύων.
ἀτὰρ οὐδέν πω περὶ τοῦ πατάγου καὶ τῆς βροντῆς μ' ἐδίδαξας.
ΣΩ. οὐκ ἤκουσάς μου τὰς Νεφέλας ὕδατος μεστὰς ὅτι φημὶ
ἐμπιπτούσας εἰς ἀλλήλας παταγεῖν διὰ τὴν πυκνότητα;
ΣΤΡ. φέρε τουτὶ τῷ χρὴ πιστεύειν; ΣΩ. ἀπὸ σαυτοῦ 'γώ σε διδάξω.
ἤδη ζωμοῦ Παναθηναίοις ἐμπλησθεὶς εἶτ' ἐταράχθης

τὴν γαστέρα, καὶ κλόνος ἐξαίφνης αὐτὴν διεκορκορύγησεν;
ΣΤΡ. νὴ τὸν Ἀπόλλω, καὶ δεινὰ ποιεῖ γ' εὐθύς μοι, καὶ τετάρακται.
χὤσπερ βροντὴ τὸ ζωμίδιον παταγεῖ, καὶ δεινὰ κέκραγεν,
ἀτρέμας πρῶτον παππὰξ παππάξ, κἄπειτ' ἐπάγει παπαπαππάξ.
ΣΩ. σκέψαι τοίνυν ἀπὸ γαστριδίου τυννουτουὶ οἷα κέκραγας·
τὸν δ' ἀέρα τόνδ' ὄντ' ἀπέραντον, πῶς οὐκ εἰκὸς μέγα βροντᾶν;
ΣΤΡ. ἀλλ' ὁ κεραυνὸς πόθεν αὖ φέρεται λάμπων πυρί, τοῦτο δίδαξον,
καὶ καταφρύγει βάλλων ἡμᾶς, τοὺς δὲ ζῶντας περιφλύει.
τοῦτον γὰρ δὴ φανερῶς ὁ Ζεὺς ἵησ' ἐπὶ τοὺς ἐπιόρκους.
ΣΩ. καὶ πῶς, ὦ μῶρε σὺ καὶ Κρονίων ὄζων καὶ βεκκεσέληνε,
εἴπερ βάλλει τοὺς ἐπιόρκους, πῶς οὐχὶ Σίμων' ἐνέπρησεν
οὐδὲ Κλεώνυμον οὐδὲ Θέωρον; καίτοι σφόδρα γ' εἴσ' ἐπίορκοι·
ἀλλὰ τὸν αὑτοῦ γε νεὼν βάλλει καὶ Σούνιον ἄκρον Ἀθηνέων,
καὶ τὰς δρῦς τὰς μεγάλας· τί μαθών; οὐ γὰρ δὴ δρῦς γ' ἐπιορκεῖ.
ΣΤΡ. οὐκ οἶδ'· ἀτὰρ εὖ σὺ λέγειν φαίνει. τί γάρ ἐστιν δῆθ' ὁ κεραυνός;
ΣΩ. ὅταν εἰς ταύτας ἄνεμος ξηρὸς μετεωρισθεὶς κατακλεισθῇ,

ἔνδοθεν αὐτὰς ὥσπερ κύστιν φυσᾷ, κἄπειθ' ὑπ' ἀνάγκης
ῥήξας αὐτὰς ἔξω φέρεται σοβαρὸς διὰ τὴν πυκνότητα,
ὑπὸ τοῦ ῥοίβδου καὶ τῆς ῥύμης αὐτὸς ἑαυτὸν κατακαίων.

ΣΤΡ. νὴ Δί', ἐγὼ γοῦν ἀτεχνῶς ἔπαθον τουτί ποτε Διασίοισιν·
ὤπτων γαστέρα τοῖς συγγενέσιν, κᾆτ' οὐκ ἔσχων ἀμελήσας·
ἡ δ' ἄρ' ἐφυσᾶτ', εἶτ' ἐξαίφνης διαλακήσασα πρὸς αὐτὼ
τὠφθαλμώ μου προσετίλησεν καὶ κατέκαυσεν τὸ πρόσωπον.

ΧΟΡ. ὦ τῆς μεγάλης ἐπιθυμήσας σοφίας ἄνθρωπε παρ' ἡμῶν,
ὡς εὐδαίμων ἐν Ἀθηναίοις καὶ τοῖς Ἕλλησι γενήσει,
εἰ μνήμων εἶ καὶ φροντιστὴς καὶ τὸ ταλαίπωρον ἔνεστιν
ἐν τῇ ψυχῇ, καὶ μὴ κάμνεις μήθ' ἑστὼς μήτε βαδίζων,
μήτε ῥιγῶν ἄχθει λίαν, μήτ' ἀριστᾶν ἐπιθυμεῖς,
οἴνου τ' ἀπέχει καὶ γυμνασίων καὶ τῶν ἄλλων ἀνοήτων,
καὶ βέλτιστον τοῦτο νομίζεις, ὅπερ εἰκὸς δεξιὸν ἄνδρα,
νικᾶν πράττων καὶ βουλεύων καὶ τῇ γλώττῃ πολεμίζων.

ΣΤΡ. ἀλλ' ἕνεκέν γε ψυχῆς στερρᾶς δυσκολοκοίτου τε μερίμνης,
καὶ φειδωλοῦ καὶ τρυσιβίου γαστρὸς καὶ θυμβρεπιδείπνου

ἀμέλει, θαρρῶν εἵνεκα τούτων ἐπιχαλκεύειν παρέχοιμ' ἄν.
ΣΩ. ἄλλο τι δῆτ' οὐ νομιεῖς ἤδη θεὸν οὐδένα πλὴν ἅπερ ἡμεῖς,
τὸ Χάος τουτὶ καὶ τὰς Νεφέλας καὶ τὴν γλῶτταν, τρία ταυτί;
ΣΤΡ. οὐδ' ἂν διαλεχθείην γ' ἀτεχνῶς τοῖς ἄλλοις, οὐδ' ἂν ἀπαντῶν·
οὐδ' ἂν θύσαιμ', οὐδ' ἂν σπείσαιμ', οὐδ' ἐπιθείην λιβανωτόν.
ΧΟΡ. λέγε νυν ἡμῖν ὅ τι σοι δρῶμεν θαρρῶν, ὡς οὐκ ἀτυχήσεις,
ἡμᾶς τιμῶν καὶ θαυμάζων καὶ ζητῶν δεξιὸς εἶναι.
ΣΤΡ. ὦ δέσποιναι, δέομαι τοίνυν ὑμῶν τουτὶ πάνυ μικρόν,
τῶν Ἑλλήνων εἶναί με λέγειν ἑκατὸν σταδίοισιν ἄριστον.
ΧΟΡ. ἀλλ' ἔσται σοι τοῦτο παρ' ἡμῶν· ὥστε τὸ λοιπόν γ' ἀπὸ τουδὶ
ἐν τῷ δήμῳ γνώμας οὐδεὶς νικήσει πλείονας ἢ σύ.
ΣΤΡ. μή μοί γε λέγειν γνώμας μεγάλας· οὐ γὰρ τούτων ἐπιθυμῶ,
ἀλλ' ὅσ' ἐμαυτῷ στρεψοδικῆσαι καὶ τοὺς χρήστας διολισθεῖν.
ΧΟΡ. τεύξει τοίνυν ὧν ἱμείρεις· οὐ γὰρ μεγάλων ἐπιθυμεῖς.
ἀλλὰ σεαυτὸν θαρρῶν παράδος τοῖς ἡμετέροις προπόλοισι.
ΣΤΡ. δράσω ταῦθ' ὑμῖν πιστεύσας· ἡ γὰρ ἀνάγκη με πιέζει
διὰ τοὺς ἵππους τοὺς κοππατίας καὶ τὸν γάμον, ὅς μ' ἐπέτριψεν.

νῦν οὖν τούτῳ χρήσθων ἀτεχνῶς
ὅ τι βούλονται.
τουτὶ τό γ' ἐμὸν σῶμ' αὐτοῖσιν
παρέχω τύπτειν, πεινῆν, διψῆν,
αὐχμεῖν, ῥιγῶν, ἀσκὸν δείρειν,
εἴπερ τὰ χρέα διαφευξοῦμαι,
τοῖς τ' ἀνθρώποις εἶναι δόξω
θρασύς, εὔγλωττος, τολμηρός, ἴτης,
βδελυρός, ψευδῶν συγκολλητής,
εὑρησιεπής, περίτριμμα δικῶν,
κύρβις, κρόταλον, κίναδος, τρύμη,
μάσθλης, εἴρων, γλοιός, ἀλαζών,
κέντρων, μιαρός, στρόφις, ἀργαλέος,
ματιολοιχός.
ταῦτ' εἴ με καλοῦσ' ἁπαντῶντες,
δρώντων ἀτεχνῶς ὅ τι χρῄζουσιν·
κεἰ βούλονται,
νὴ τὴν Δήμητρ' ἔκ μου χορδὴν
τοῖς φροντισταῖς παραθέντων. √

ΧΟΡ. λῆμα μὲν πάρεστι τῷδέ γ'
οὐκ ἄτολμον, ἀλλ' ἕτοιμον. ἴσθι δ' ὡς
ταῦτα μαθὼν παρ' ἐμοῦ κλέος οὐρανόμηκες
ἐν βροτοῖσιν ἕξεις.

ΣΤΡ. τί πείσομαι; ΧΟΡ. τὸν πάντα χρόνον μετ' ἐμοῦ
ζηλωτότατον βίον ἀνθρώπων διάξεις.

ΣΤΡ. ἆρά γε τοῦτ' ἄρ' ἐγώ ποτ'
ὄψομαι; ΧΟΡ. ὥστε γε σοῦ πολλοὺς ἐπὶ ταῖσι
θύραις ἀεὶ καθῆσθαι,
βουλομένους ἀνακοινοῦσθαί τε καὶ ἐς λόγον ἐλθεῖν,
πράγματα κἀντιγραφὰς πολλῶν ταλάντων,
ἄξια σῇ φρενί, συμβουλευσομένους μετὰ σοῦ.

ἀλλ' ἐγχείρει τὸν πρεσβύτην ὅ τι περ μέλλεις προδιδάσκειν,
καὶ διακίνει τὸν νοῦν αὐτοῦ, καὶ τῆς γνώμης ἀποπειρῶ.
ΣΩ. ἄγε δή, κάτειπέ μοι σὺ τὸν σαυτοῦ τρόπον,
ἵν' αὐτὸν εἰδὼς ὅστις ἐστὶ μηχανὰς
ἤδη 'πὶ τούτοις πρὸς σὲ καινὰς προσφέρω.
ΣΤΡ. τί δέ; τειχομαχεῖν μοι διανοεῖ, πρὸς τῶν θεῶν;
ΣΩ. οὔκ, ἀλλὰ βραχέα σου πυθέσθαι βούλομαι.
ἦ μνημονικὸς εἶ; ΣΤΡ. δύο τρόπω νὴ τὸν Δία·
ἢν μὲν γὰρ ὀφείληταί τί μοι, μνήμων πάνυ·
ἐὰν δ' ὀφείλω σχέτλιος, ἐπιλήσμων πάνυ.
ΣΩ. ἔνεστι δῆτά σοι λέγειν ἐν τῇ φύσει;
ΣΤΡ. λέγειν μὲν οὐκ ἔνεστ', ἀποστερεῖν δ' ἔνι.
ΣΩ. πῶς οὖν δυνήσει μανθάνειν; ΣΤΡ. ἀμέλει, καλῶς.
ΣΩ. ἄγε νυν ὅπως, ὅταν τι προβάλωμαι σοφὸν
περὶ τῶν μετεώρων, εὐθέως ὑφαρπάσει.
ΣΤΡ. τί δαί; κυνηδὸν τὴν σοφίαν σιτήσομαι;
ΣΩ. ἄνθρωπος ἀμαθὴς οὑτοσὶ καὶ βάρβαρος,
δέδοικά σ', ὦ πρεσβῦτα, μὴ πληγῶν δέει.
φέρ' ἴδω, τί δρᾷς, ἤν τίς σε τύπτῃ; ΣΤΡ. τύπτομαι,
ἔπειτ' ἐπισχὼν ὀλίγον ἐπιμαρτύρομαι,
εἶτ' αὖθις ἀκαρῆ διαλιπὼν δικάζομαι.
ΣΩ. ἴθι νυν, κατάθου θοἰμάτιον. ΣΤΡ. ἠδίκηκά τι;
ΣΩ. οὔκ, ἀλλὰ γυμνοὺς εἰσιέναι νομίζεται.
ΣΤΡ. ἀλλ' οὐχὶ φωράσων ἔγωγ' εἰσέρχομαι.
ΣΩ. κατάθου. τί ληρεῖς; ΣΤΡ. εἰπὲ δή νύν μοι τοδί.
ἢν ἐπιμελὴς ὦ καὶ προθύμως μανθάνω,
τῷ τῶν μαθητῶν ἐμφερὴς γενήσομαι;
ΣΩ. οὐδὲν διοίσεις Χαιρεφῶντος τὴν φύσιν.
ΣΤΡ. οἴμοι κακοδαίμων, ἡμιθνὴς γενήσομαι.
ΣΩ. οὐ μὴ λαλήσεις, ἀλλ' ἀκολουθήσεις ἐμοὶ

ἀνύσας τι δευρὶ θᾶττον. ΣΤΡ. ἐς τὼ χεῖρέ νυν
δός μοι μελιτοῦτταν πρότερον· ὡς δέδοικ᾽ ἐγὼ
εἴσω καταβαίνων ὥσπερ εἰς Τροφωνίου.
ΣΩ. χώρει· τί κυπτάζεις ἔχων περὶ τὴν θύραν;
ΧΟΡ. ἀλλ᾽ ἴθι χαίρων τῆς ἀνδρείας
εἵνεκα ταύτης.
εὐτυχία γένοιτο τἀν-
θρώπῳ, ὅτι προήκων
ἐς βαθὺ τῆς ἡλικίας,
νεωτέροις τὴν φύσιν αὑ-
τοῦ πράγμασιν χρωτίζεται
καὶ σοφίαν ἐπασκεῖ.
ὦ θεώμενοι, κατερῶ πρὸς ὑμᾶς ἐλευθέρως
τἀληθῆ, νὴ τὸν Διόνυσον τὸν ἐκθρέψαντά με.
οὕτω νικήσαιμί τ᾽ ἐγὼ καὶ νομιζοίμην σοφός,
ὡς ὑμᾶς ἡγούμενος εἶναι θεατὰς δεξιοὺς
καὶ ταύτην σοφώτατ᾽ ἔχειν τῶν ἐμῶν κωμῳδιῶν,
πρώτους ἠξίωσ᾽ ἀναγεῦσ᾽ ὑμᾶς, ἣ παρέσχε μοι
ἔργον πλεῖστον· εἶτ᾽ ἀνεχώρουν ὑπ᾽ ἀνδρῶν φορτικῶν
ἡττηθείς, οὐκ ἄξιος ὤν· ταῦτ᾽ οὖν ὑμῖν μέμφομαι
τοῖς σοφοῖς, ὧν εἵνεκ᾽ ἐγὼ ταῦτ᾽ ἐπραγματευόμην.
ἀλλ᾽ οὐδ᾽ ὣς ὑμῶν ποθ᾽ ἑκὼν προδώσω τοὺς δεξιούς.
ἐξ ὅτου γὰρ ἐνθάδ᾽ ὑπ᾽ ἀνδρῶν, οἷς ἡδὺ καὶ λέγειν,
ὁ σώφρων τε χὠ καταπύγων ἄριστ᾽ ἠκουσάτην,
κἀγώ, παρθένος γὰρ ἔτ᾽ ἦν, κοὐκ ἐξῆν πώ μοι τεκεῖν,
ἐξέθηκα, παῖς δ᾽ ἑτέρα τις λαβοῦσ᾽ ἀνείλετο,
ὑμεῖς δ᾽ ἐξεθρέψατε γενναίως κἀπαιδεύσατε·
ἐκ τούτου μοι πιστὰ παρ᾽ ὑμῶν γνώμης ἔσθ᾽ ὅρκια.
νῦν οὖν Ἠλέκτραν κατ᾽ ἐκείνην ἥδ᾽ ἡ κωμῳδία
ζητοῦσ᾽ ἦλθ᾽, ἤν που ᾽πιτύχῃ θεαταῖς οὕτω σοφοῖς·
γνώσεται γάρ, ἤνπερ ἴδῃ, τἀδελφοῦ τὸν βόστρυχον.
ὡς δὲ σώφρων ἐστὶ φύσει σκέψασθ᾽· ἥτις πρῶτα μὲν

οὐδ' ἔσκωψε τοὺς φαλακρούς, οὐδὲ κόρδαχ' εἵλκυσεν,
οὐδὲ πρεσβύτης ὁ λέγων τἄπη τῇ βακτηρίᾳ
τύπτει τὸν παρόντ', ἀφανίζων πονηρὰ σκώμματα,
οὐδ' εἰσῆξε δᾷδας ἔχουσ', οὐδ' ἰοὺ ἰοὺ βοᾷ,
ἀλλ' αὐτῇ καὶ τοῖς ἔπεσιν πιστεύουσ' ἐλήλυθεν.
κἀγὼ μὲν τοιοῦτος ἀνὴρ ὢν ποιητὴς οὐ κομῶ,
οὐδ' ὑμᾶς ζητῶ 'ξαπατᾶν δὶς καὶ τρὶς ταὔτ' εἰσάγων,
ἀλλ' ἀεὶ καινὰς ἰδέας εἰσφέρων σοφίζομαι,
οὐδὲν ἀλλήλαισιν ὁμοίας καὶ πάσας δεξιάς·
ὃς μέγιστον ὄντα Κλέων' ἔπαισ' εἰς τὴν γαστέρα,
κοὐκ ἐτόλμησ' αὖθις ἐπεμπηδῆσ' αὐτῷ κειμένῳ.
οὗτοι δ', ὡς ἅπαξ παρέδωκεν λαβὴν Ὑπέρβολος,
τοῦτον δείλαιον κολετρῶσ' ἀεὶ καὶ τὴν μητέρα.
Εὔπολις μὲν τὸν Μαρικᾶν πρώτιστον παρείλκυσεν
ἐκστρέψας τοὺς ἡμετέρους Ἱππέας κακὸς κακῶς,
προσθεὶς αὐτῷ γραῦν μεθύσην τοῦ κόρδακος εἵνεχ', ἣν
Φρύνιχος πάλαι πεποίηχ', ἣν τὸ κῆτος ἤσθιεν.
εἶθ' Ἕρμιππος αὖθις ἐποίησεν εἰς Ὑπέρβολον,
ἄλλοι τ' ἤδη πάντες ἐρείδουσιν εἰς Ὑπέρβολον,
τὰς εἰκοὺς τῶν ἐγχέλεων τὰς ἐμὰς μιμούμενοι.
ὅστις οὖν τούτοισι γελᾷ, τοῖς ἐμοῖς μὴ χαιρέτω·
ἢν δ' ἐμοὶ καὶ τοῖσιν ἐμοῖς εὐφραίνησθ' εὑρήμασιν,
ἐς τὰς ὥρας τὰς ἑτέρας εὖ φρονεῖν δοκήσετε.
ὑψιμέδοντα μὲν θεῶν
Ζῆνα τύραννον ἐς χορὸν
πρῶτα μέγαν κικλήσκω·
τόν τε μεγασθενῆ τριαίνης ταμίαν,
γῆς τε καὶ ἁλμυρᾶς θαλάσσης ἄγριον μοχλευτήν·
καὶ μεγαλώνυμον ἡμέτερον πατέρ',
Αἰθέρα σεμνότατον, βιοθρέμμονα πάντων·
τόν θ' ἱππονώμαν, ὃς ὑπερ-

λάμπροις ἀκτῖσιν κατέχει
γῆς πέδον, μέγας ἐν θεοῖς
ἐν θνητοῖσί τε δαίμων.
ὦ σοφώτατοι θεαταί, δεῦρο τὸν νοῦν προσέχετε.
ἠδικημέναι γὰρ ὑμῖν μεμφόμεσθ' ἐναντίον·
πλεῖστα γὰρ θεῶν ἁπάντων ὠφελούσαις τὴν πόλιν,
δαιμόνων ἡμῖν μόναις οὐ θύετ' οὐδὲ σπένδετε,
αἵτινες τηροῦμεν ὑμᾶς. ἢν γὰρ ᾖ τις ἔξοδος
μηδενὶ ξὺν νῷ, τότ' ἢ βροντῶμεν ἢ ψακάζομεν.
εἶτα τὸν θεοῖσιν ἐχθρὸν βυρσοδέψην Παφλαγόνα
ἡνίχ' ᾑρεῖσθε στρατηγόν, τὰς ὀφρῦς συνήγομεν
κἀποιοῦμεν δεινά· βροντὴ δ' ἐρράγη δι' ἀστραπῆς·
ἡ σελήνη δ' ἐξέλειπε τὰς ὁδούς· ὁ δ' ἥλιος
τὴν θρυαλλίδ' εἰς ἑαυτὸν εὐθέως ξυνελκύσας
οὐ φανεῖν ἔφασκεν ὑμῖν, εἰ στρατηγήσει Κλέων.
ἀλλ' ὅμως εἵλεσθε τοῦτον. φασὶ γὰρ δυσβουλίαν
τῇδε τῇ πόλει προσεῖναι, ταῦτα μέντοι τοὺς θεοὺς
ἅττ' ἂν ὑμεῖς ἐξαμάρτητ', ἐπὶ τὸ βέλτιον τρέπειν.
ὡς δὲ καὶ τοῦτο ξυνοίσει ῥᾳδίως διδάξομεν.
ἢν Κλέωνα τὸν λάρον δώρων ἑλόντες καὶ κλοπῆς,
εἶτα φιμώσητε τούτου τῷ ξύλῳ τὸν αὐχένα,
αὖθις ἐς τἀρχαῖον ὑμῖν, εἴ τι κἀξημάρτετε,
ἐπὶ τὸ βέλτιον τὸ πρᾶγμα τῇ πόλει συνοίσεται.
ἀμφί μοι αὖτε, Φοῖβ' ἄναξ
Δήλιε, Κυνθίαν ἔχων
ὑψικέρατα πέτραν·
ἥ τ' Ἐφέσου μάκαιρα πάγχρυσον ἔχεις
οἶκον, ἐν ᾧ κόραι σε Λυδῶν μεγάλως σέβουσιν·
ἥ τ' ἐπιχώριος ἡμετέρα θεός,
αἰγίδος ἡνίοχος, πολιοῦχος Ἀθάνα·
Παρνασίαν θ' ὃς κατέχων
πέτραν σὺν πεύκαις σελαγεῖ

Βάκχαις Δελφίσιν ἐμπρέπων,
κωμαστὴς Διόνυσος.
ἡνίχ' ἡμεῖς δεῦρ' ἀφορμᾶσθαι παρεσκευάσμεθα,
ἡ Σελήνη συντυχοῦσ' ἡμῖν ἐπέστειλεν φράσαι,
πρῶτα μὲν χαίρειν Ἀθηναίοισι καὶ τοῖς ξυμμάχοις.
εἶτα θυμαίνειν ἔφασκε· δεινὰ γὰρ πεπονθέναι,
ὠφελοῦσ' ὑμᾶς ἅπαντας, οὐ λόγοις, ἀλλ' ἐμφανῶς.
πρῶτα μὲν τοῦ μηνὸς εἰς δᾳδ' οὐκ ἔλαττον ἢ δραχμήν,
ὥστε καὶ λέγειν ἅπαντας ἐξιόντας ἑσπέρας,
μὴ πρίῃ, παῖ, δᾳδ', ἐπειδὴ φῶς Σεληναίης καλόν.
ἄλλα τ' εὖ δρᾶν φησιν, ὑμᾶς δ' οὐκ ἄγειν τὰς ἡμέρας
οὐδὲν ὀρθῶς, ἀλλ' ἄνω τε καὶ κάτω κυδοιδοπᾶν·
ὥστ' ἀπειλεῖν φησιν αὐτῇ τοὺς θεοὺς ἑκάστοτε
ἡνίκ' ἂν ψευσθῶσι δείπνου, κἀπίωσιν οἴκαδε,
τῆς ἑορτῆς μὴ τυχόντες κατὰ λόγον τῶν ἡμερῶν.
κᾳθ' ὅταν θύειν δέῃ, στρεβλοῦτε καὶ δικάζετε·
πολλάκις δ' ἡμῶν ἀγόντων τῶν θεῶν ἀπαστίαν,
ἡνίκ' ἂν πενθῶμεν ἢ τὸν Μέμνον' ἢ Σαρπηδόνα,
σπένδεθ' ὑμεῖς καὶ γελᾶτ'· ἀνθ' ὧν λαχὼν Ὑπέρβολος
τῆτες ἱερομνημονεῖν, κἄπειθ' ὑφ' ἡμῶν τῶν θεῶν
τὸν στέφανον ἀφῃρέθη· μᾶλλον γὰρ οὕτως εἴσεται
κατὰ σελήνην ὡς ἄγειν χρὴ τοῦ βίου τὰς ἡμέρας.

ΣΩΚΡΑΤΗΣ. ΣΤΡΕΨΙΑΔΗΣ. ΧΟΡΟΣ.

ΣΩ. μὰ τὴν Ἀναπνοήν, μὰ τὸ Χάος, μὰ τὸν Ἀέρα,
οὐκ εἶδον οὕτως ἄνδρ' ἄγροικον οὐδένα
οὐδ' ἄπορον οὐδὲ σκαιὸν οὐδ' ἐπιλήσμονα·
ὅστις σκαλαθυρμάτι' ἄττα μικρὰ μανθάνων,
ταῦτ' ἐπιλέλησται πρὶν μαθεῖν· ὅμως γε μὴν
αὐτὸν καλῶ θύραζε δευρὶ πρὸς τὸ φῶς.

ποῦ Στρεψιάδης; ἔξει τὸν ἀσκάντην λαβών.
ΣΤΡ. ἀλλ' οὐκ ἐῶσί μ' ἐξενεγκεῖν οἱ κόρεις.
ΣΩ. ἀνύσας τι κατάθου, καὶ πρόσεχε τὸν νοῦν.
ΣΤΡ. ἰδού.
ΣΩ. ἄγε δή, τί βούλει πρῶτα νυνὶ μανθάνειν
ὧν οὐκ ἐδιδάχθης πώποτ' οὐδέν; εἰπέ μοι.
πότερον περὶ μέτρων ἢ ῥυθμῶν ἢ περὶ ἐπῶν;
ΣΤΡ. περὶ τῶν μέτρων ἔγωγ'· ἔναγχος γάρ ποτε
ὑπ' ἀλφιταμοιβοῦ παρεκόπην διχοινίκῳ.
ΣΩ. οὐ τοῦτ' ἐρωτῶ σ', ἀλλ' ὅ τι κάλλιστον μέτρον
ἡγεῖ· πότερον τὸ τρίμετρον ἢ τὸ τετράμετρον;
ΣΤΡ. ἐγὼ μὲν οὐδὲν πρότερον ἡμιεκτέου.
ΣΩ. οὐδὲν λέγεις, ὤνθρωπε. ΣΤΡ. περίδου νυν ἐμοί,
εἰ μὴ τετράμετρόν ἐστιν ἡμιεκτέον.
ΣΩ. ἐς κόρακας, ὡς ἄγροικος εἶ καὶ δυσμαθής.
ταχύ γ' ἂν δύναιο μανθάνειν περὶ ῥυθμῶν.
ΣΤΡ. τί δέ μ' ὠφελήσουσ' οἱ ῥυθμοὶ πρὸς τἄλφιτα;
ΣΩ. πρῶτον μὲν εἶναι κομψὸν ἐν συνουσίᾳ,
ἐπαΐονθ' ὁποῖός ἐστι τῶν ῥυθμῶν
κατ' ἐνόπλιον, χὠποῖος αὖ κατὰ δάκτυλον.
ΣΤΡ. κατὰ δάκτυλον; ΣΩ. νὴ τὸν Δί'. ΣΤΡ. ἀλλ' οἶδ'.
ΣΩ. εἰπὲ δή.
ΣΤΡ. τίς ἄλλος ἀντὶ τουτουὶ τοῦ δακτύλου;
πρὸ τοῦ μέν, ἐπ' ἐμοῦ παιδὸς ὄντος, οὑτοσί.
ΣΩ. ἀγρεῖος εἶ καὶ σκαιός. ΣΤΡ. οὐ γάρ, ᾠζυρέ,
τούτων ἐπιθυμῶ μανθάνειν οὐδέν. ΣΩ. τί δαί;
ΣΤΡ. ἐκεῖν' ἐκεῖνο, τὸν ἀδικώτατον λόγον.
ΣΩ. ἀλλ' ἕτερα δεῖ σε πρότερα τούτων μανθάνειν,
τῶν τετραπόδων ἅττ' ἐστὶν ὀρθῶς ἄρρενα.
ΣΤΡ. ἀλλ' οἶδ' ἔγωγε τἄρρεν', εἰ μὴ μαίνομαι·
κριός, τράγος, ταῦρος, κύων, ἀλεκτρυών.
ΣΩ. ὁρᾷς ὃ πάσχεις; τήν τε θήλειαν καλεῖς

ἀλεκτρυόνα κατὰ ταὐτὸ καὶ τὸν ἄρρενα.
ΣΤΡ. πῶς δή; φέρε. ΣΩ. πῶς; ἀλεκτρυὼν κἀλεκτρυών.
ΣΤΡ. νὴ τὸν Ποσειδῶ. νῦν δὲ πῶς με χρὴ καλεῖν;
ΣΩ. ἀλεκτρύαιναν, τὸν δ' ἕτερον ἀλέκτορα.
ΣΤΡ. ἀλεκτρύαιναν; εὖ γε νὴ τὸν Ἀέρα·
ὥστ' ἀντὶ τούτου τοῦ διδάγματος μόνου
διαλφιτώσω σου κύκλῳ τὴν κάρδοπον.
ΣΩ. ἰδοὺ μάλ' αὖθις τοῦθ' ἕτερον. τὴν κάρδοπον
ἄρρενα καλεῖς, θήλειαν οὖσαν. ΣΤΡ. τῷ τρόπῳ
ἄρρενα καλῶ 'γὼ κάρδοπον; ΣΩ. μάλιστά γε,
ὥσπερ γε καὶ Κλεώνυμον. ΣΤΡ. πῶς δή; φράσον.
ΣΩ. ταὐτὸν δύναταί σοι κάρδοπος Κλεωνύμῳ.
ΣΤΡ. ἀλλ', ὦγάθ', οὐδ' ἦν κάρδοπος Κλεωνύμῳ,
ἀλλ' ἐν θυείᾳ στρογγύλῃ γ' ἀνεμάττετο.
ἀτὰρ τὸ λοιπὸν πῶς με χρὴ καλεῖν; ΣΩ. ὅπως;
τὴν καρδόπην, ὥσπερ καλεῖς τὴν Σωστράτην.
ΣΤΡ. τὴν καρδόπην θήλειαν; ΣΩ. ὀρθῶς γὰρ λέγεις.
ΣΤΡ. ἐκεῖνο δ' ἦν ἄν, καρδόπη, Κλεωνύμη.
ΣΩ. ἔτι δή γε περὶ τῶν ὀνομάτων μαθεῖν σε δεῖ,
ἅττ' ἄρρεν' ἐστίν, ἅττα δ' αὐτῶν θήλεα.
ΣΤΡ. ἀλλ' οἶδ' ἔγωγ' ἃ θήλε' ἐστίν. ΣΩ. εἰπὲ δή.
ΣΤΡ. Λύσιλλα, Φίλιννα, Κλειταγόρα, Δημητρία.
ΣΩ. ἄρρενα δὲ ποῖα τῶν ὀνομάτων; ΣΤΡ. μυρία.
Φιλόξενος, Μελησίας, Ἀμυνίας.
ΣΩ. ἀλλ', ὦ πονηρέ, ταῦτά γ' ἔστ' οὐκ ἄρρενα.
ΣΤΡ. οὐκ ἄρρεν' ὑμῖν ἐστιν; ΣΩ. οὐδαμῶς γ', ἐπεὶ
πῶς ἂν καλέσειας ἐντυχὼν Ἀμυνίᾳ;
ΣΤΡ. ὅπως ἄν; ὡδί, δεῦρο δεῦρ', Ἀμυνία.
ΣΩ. ὁρᾷς; γυναῖκα τὴν Ἀμυνίαν καλεῖς.
ΣΤΡ. οὔκουν δικαίως ἥτις οὐ στρατεύεται;
ἀτὰρ τί ταῦθ' ἃ πάντες ἴσμεν μανθάνω;
ΣΩ. οὐδὲν μὰ Δί', ἀλλὰ κατακλινεὶς δευρὶ—ΣΤΡ. τί δρῶ;

ΣΩ. ἐκφρόντισόν τι τῶν σεαυτοῦ πραγμάτων.
ΣΤΡ. μὴ δῆθ', ἱκετεύω, 'νταῦθά γ'· ἀλλ' εἴπερ γε χρή,
χαμαί μ' ἔασον αὐτὰ ταῦτ' ἐκφροντίσαι.
ΣΩ. οὐκ ἔστι παρὰ ταῦτ' ἄλλα. ΣΤΡ. κακοδαίμων ἐγώ,
οἵαν δίκην τοῖς κόρεσι δώσω τήμερον.
ΧΟΡ. φρόντιζε δὴ καὶ διάθρει, πάντα τρόπον τε σαυτὸν
στρόβει πυκνώσας·
ταχὺς δ', ὅταν εἰς ἄπορον πέσῃς,
ἐπ' ἄλλο πήδα
νόημα φρενός· ὕπνος δ' ἀπέστω γλυκύθυμος ὀμ-
μάτων.
ΣΤΡ. ἀτταταῖ ἀτταταῖ.
ΧΟΡ. τί πάσχεις; τί κάμνεις;
ΣΤΡ. ἀπόλλυμαι δείλαιος· ἐκ τοῦ σκίμποδος
δάκνουσί μ' ἐξέρποντες οἱ Κορίνθιοι,
καὶ τὰς πλευρὰς δαρδάπτουσιν
καὶ τὴν ψυχὴν ἐκπίνουσιν,
καί μ' ἀπολοῦσιν.
ΧΟΡ. μή νυν βαρέως ἄλγει λίαν.
ΣΤΡ. καὶ πῶς; ὅτε μου
φροῦδα τὰ χρήματα, φρούδη χροιά,
φρούδη ψυχή, φρούδη δ' ἐμβάς·
καὶ πρὸς τούτοις ἔτι τοῖσι κακοῖς
φρουρᾶς ᾄδων
ὀλίγου φροῦδος γεγένημαι.
ΣΩ. οὗτος, τί ποιεῖς; οὐχὶ φροντίζεις; ΣΤΡ. ἐγώ;
νὴ τὸν Ποσειδῶ. ΣΩ. καὶ τί δῆτ' ἐφρόντισας;
ΣΤΡ. ὑπὸ τῶν κόρεων εἴ μού τι περιλειφθήσεται.
ΣΩ. ἀπολεῖ κάκιστ'. ΣΤΡ. ἀλλ', ὦγάθ', ἀπόλωλ' ἀρτίως.
ΣΩ. οὐ μαλθακιστέ', ἀλλὰ περικαλυπτέα.
ἐξευρετέος γὰρ νοῦς ἀποστερητικὸς
κἀπαιόλημ'. ΣΤΡ. οἴμοι, τίς ἂν δῆτ' ἐπιβάλοι

ἐξ ἀρνακίδων γνώμην ἀποστερητρίδα;
ΣΩ. φέρε νυν, ἀθρήσω πρῶτον, ὅ τι δρᾷ, τουτονί.
οὗτος, καθεύδεις; ΣΤΡ. μὰ τὸν Ἀπόλλω ᾿γὼ μὲν οὔ.
ΣΩ. ἔχεις τι; ΣΤΡ. μὰ Δί᾿ οὐ δῆτ᾿ ἔγωγ᾿. ΣΩ. οὐδὲν πάνυ;
οὐκ ἐγκαλυψάμενος ταχέως τι φροντιεῖς;
ΣΤΡ. περὶ τοῦ; σὺ γάρ μοι τοῦτο φράσον, ὦ Σώκρατες.
ΣΩ. αὐτὸς ὅ τι βούλει πρῶτος ἐξευρὼν λέγε.
ΣΤΡ. ἀκήκοας μυριάκις ἁγὼ βούλομαι,
περὶ τῶν τόκων, ὅπως ἂν ἀποδῶ μηδενί.
ΣΩ. ἴθι νυν, καλύπτου καὶ σχάσας τὴν φροντίδα
λεπτὴν κατὰ μικρὸν περιφρόνει τὰ πράγματα,
ὀρθῶς διαιρῶν καὶ σκοπῶν. ΣΤΡ. οἴμοι τάλας.
ΣΩ. ἔχ᾿ ἀτρέμα· κἂν ἀπορῇς τι τῶν νοημάτων,
ἀφεὶς ἄπελθε· κᾆτα τὴν γνώμην πάλιν
κίνησον αὖθις αὐτὸ καὶ ζυγώθρισον·
ΣΤΡ. ὦ Σωκρατίδιον φίλτατον. ΣΩ. τί, ὦ γέρον;
ΣΤΡ. ἔχω τόκου γνώμην ἀποστερητικήν.
ΣΩ. ἐπίδειξον αὐτήν. ΣΤΡ. εἰπὲ δή νύν μοι—ΣΩ. τὸ τί;
ΣΤΡ. γυναῖκα φαρμακίδ᾿ εἰ πριάμενος Θετταλήν,
καθέλοιμι νύκτωρ τὴν σελήνην, εἶτα δὴ
αὐτὴν καθείρξαιμ᾿ ἐς λοφεῖον στρογγύλον,
ὥσπερ κάτοπτρον, κᾆτα τηροίην ἔχων,
ΣΩ. τί δῆτα τοῦτ᾿ ἂν ὠφελήσειέν σ᾿; ΣΤΡ. ὅ τι;
εἰ μηκέτ᾿ ἀνατέλλοι σελήνη μηδαμοῦ,
οὐκ ἂν ἀποδοίην τοὺς τόκους. ΣΩ. ὁτιὴ τί δή;
ΣΤΡ. ὁτιὴ κατὰ μῆνα τἀργύριον δανείζεται.
ΣΩ. εὖ γ᾿· ἀλλ᾿ ἕτερον αὖ σοι προβαλῶ τι δεξιόν,
εἴ σοι γράφοιτο πεντετάλαντός τις δίκη,
ὅπως ἂν αὐτὴν ἀφανίσειας εἰπέ μοι.
ΣΤΡ. ὅπως; ὅπως; οὐκ οἶδ᾿· ἀτὰρ ζητητέον.
ΣΩ. μή νυν περὶ σαυτὸν εἶλλε τὴν γνώμην ἀεί,

ἀλλ᾽ ἀποχάλα τὴν φροντίδ᾽ εἰς τὸν ἀέρα,
λινόδετον ὥσπερ μηλολόνθην τοῦ ποδός·
ΣΤΡ. εὕρηκ᾽ ἀφάνισιν τῆς δίκης σοφωτάτην,
ὥστ᾽ αὐτὸν ὁμολογεῖν σ᾽ ἐμοί. ΣΩ. ποίαν τινά;
ΣΤΡ. ἤδη παρὰ τοῖσι φαρμακοπώλαις τὴν λίθον
ταύτην ἑόρακας, τὴν καλήν, τὴν διαφανῆ,
ἀφ᾽ ἧς τὸ πῦρ ἅπτουσι; ΣΩ. τὴν ὕαλον λέγεις;
ΣΤΡ. ἔγωγε. φέρε, τί δῆτ᾽ ἄν, εἰ ταύτην λαβών,
ὁπότε γράφοιτο τὴν δίκην ὁ γραμματεύς,
ἀπωτέρω στὰς ὧδε πρὸς τὸν ἥλιον
τὰ γράμματ᾽ ἐκτήξαιμι τῆς ἐμῆς δίκης;
ΣΩ. σοφῶς γε νὴ τὰς Χάριτας. ΣΤΡ. οἴμ᾽ ὡς ἥδομαι
ὅτι πεντετάλαντος διαγέγραπταί μοι δίκη. draw a line through.
ΣΩ. ἄγε δὴ ταχέως τουτὶ ξυνάρπασον. ΣΤΡ. τὸ τί;
ΣΩ. ὅπως ἀποστρέψαις ἂν ἀντιδικῶν δίκην,
μέλλων ὀφλήσειν, μὴ παρόντων μαρτύρων.
ΣΤΡ. φαυλότατα καὶ ῥᾷστ᾽. ΣΩ. εἰπὲ δή. ΣΤΡ. καὶ δὴ λέγω.
εἰ πρόσθεν ἔτι μιᾶς ἐνεστώσης δίκης,
πρὶν τὴν ἐμὴν καλεῖσθ᾽, ἀπαγξαίμην τρέχων.
ΣΩ. οὐδὲν λέγεις. ΣΤΡ. νὴ τοὺς θεοὺς ἔγωγ᾽, ἐπεὶ
οὐδεὶς κατ᾽ ἐμοῦ τεθνεῶτος εἰσάξει δίκην.
ΣΩ. ὑθλεῖς· ἄπερρ᾽, οὐκ ἂν διδαξαίμην σ᾽ ἔτι.
ΣΤΡ. ὁτιὴ τί; ναὶ πρὸς τῶν θεῶν, ὦ Σώκρατες.
ΣΩ. ἀλλ᾽ εὐθὺς ἐπιλήθει σύ γ᾽ ἅττ᾽ ἂν καὶ μάθῃς·
ἐπεὶ τί νῦν δὴ πρῶτον ἐδιδάχθης; λέγε.
ΣΤΡ. φέρ᾽ ἴδω, τί μέντοι πρῶτον ἦν; τί πρῶτον ἦν;
τίς ἦν ἐν ᾗ ματτόμεθα μέντοι τἄλφιτα;
οἴμοι, τίς ἦν; ΣΩ. οὐκ ἐς κόρακας ἀποφθερεῖ,
ἐπιλησμότατον καὶ σκαιότατον γερόντιον;
ΣΤΡ. οἴμοι, τί οὖν δῆθ᾽ ὁ κακοδαίμων πείσομαι;
ἀπὸ γὰρ ὀλοῦμαι μὴ μαθὼν γλωττοστροφεῖν.

ἀλλ', ὦ Νεφέλαι, χρηστόν τι συμβουλεύσατε.
ΧΟΡ. ἡμεῖς μέν, ὦ πρεσβῦτα, συμβουλεύομεν,
εἴ σοί τις υἱός ἐστιν ἐκτεθραμμένος,
πέμπειν ἐκεῖνον ἀντὶ σαυτοῦ μανθάνειν.
ΣΤΡ. ἀλλ' ἔστ' ἔμοιγ' υἱὸς καλός τε κἀγαθός·
ἀλλ' οὐκ ἐθέλει γὰρ μανθάνειν, τί ἐγὼ πάθω;
ΧΟΡ. σὺ δ' ἐπιτρέπεις; ΣΤΡ. εὐσωματεῖ γὰρ καὶ σφριγᾷ,
κἄστ' ἐκ γυναικῶν εὐπτέρων τῶν Κοισύρας.
ἀτὰρ μέτειμί γ' αὐτόν· ἢν δὲ μὴ θέλῃ,
οὐκ ἔσθ' ὅπως οὐκ ἐξελῶ 'κ τῆς οἰκίας.
ἀλλ' ἐπανάμεινόν μ' ὀλίγον εἰσελθὼν χρόνον.
ΧΟΡ. ἆρ' αἰσθάνει πλεῖστα δι' ἡμᾶς ἀγάθ' αὐτίχ' ἕξων
μόνας θεῶν; ὡς
ἕτοιμος ὅδ' ἐστὶν ἅπαντα δρᾶν
ὅσ' ἂν κελεύῃς.
σὺ δ' ἀνδρὸς ἐκπεπληγμένου καὶ φανερῶς ἐπηρμένου
γνοὺς ἀπολάψεις, ὅ τι πλεῖστον δύνασαι,
ταχέως· φιλεῖ γάρ πως τὰ τοιαῦθ' ἑτέρᾳ τρέπεσθαι.

ΣΤΡΕΨΙΑΔΗΣ. ΦΕΙΔΙΠΠΙΔΗΣ. ΣΩΚΡΑΤΗΣ.
ΧΟΡΟΣ.

ΣΤΡ. οὔτοι μὰ τὴν Ὁμίχλην ἔτ' ἐνταυθοῖ μενεῖς·
ἀλλ' ἔσθι' ἐλθὼν τοὺς Μεγακλέους κίονας.
ΦΕΙ. ὦ δαιμόνιε, τί χρῆμα πάσχεις, ὦ πάτερ;
οὐκ εὖ φρονεῖς μὰ τὸν Δία τὸν Ὀλύμπιον.
ΣΤΡ. ἰδού γ' ἰδοὺ Δί' Ὀλύμπιον· τῆς μωρίας·
τὸ Δία νομίζειν, ὄντα τηλικουτονί.
ΦΕΙ. τί δὲ τοῦτ' ἐγέλασας ἐτεόν; ΣΤΡ. ἐνθυμούμενος
ὅτι παιδάριον εἶ καὶ φρονεῖς ἀρχαϊκά.

ὅμως γε μὴν πρόσελθ', ἵν' εἰδῇς πλείονα,
καί σοι φράσω τι πρᾶγμ' ὃ μαθὼν ἀνὴρ ἔσει.
ὅπως δὲ τοῦτο μὴ διδάξεις μηδένα.
ΦΕΙ. ἰδού· τί ἔστιν; ΣΤΡ. ὤμοσας νῦν δὴ Δία.
ΦΕΙ. ἔγωγ'. ΣΤΡ. ὁρᾷς οὖν ὡς ἀγαθὸν τὸ μανθάνειν;
οὐκ ἔστιν, ὦ Φειδιππίδη, Ζεύς. ΦΕΙ. ἀλλὰ τίς;
ΣΤΡ. Δῖνος βασιλεύει, τὸν Δί' ἐξεληλακώς.
ΦΕΙ. αἰβοῖ, τί ληρεῖς; ΣΤΡ. ἴσθι τοῦθ' οὕτως ἔχον.
ΦΕΙ. τίς φησι ταῦτα; ΣΤΡ. Σωκράτης ὁ Μήλιος
καὶ Χαιρεφῶν, ὃς οἶδε τὰ ψυλλῶν ἴχνη.
ΦΕΙ. σὺ δ' εἰς τοσοῦτον τῶν μανιῶν ἐλήλυθας
ὥστ' ἀνδράσιν πείθει χολῶσιν; ΣΤΡ. εὐστόμει,
καὶ μηδὲν εἴπῃς φλαῦρον ἄνδρας δεξιοὺς
καὶ νοῦν ἔχοντας· ὧν ὑπὸ τῆς φειδωλίας
ἀπεκείρατ' οὐδεὶς πώποτ' οὐδ' ἠλείψατο
οὐδ' εἰς βαλανεῖον ἦλθε λουσόμενος· σὺ δὲ
ὥσπερ τεθνεῶτος καταλόει μου τὸν βίον.
ἀλλ' ὡς τάχιστ' ἐλθὼν ὑπὲρ ἐμοῦ μάνθανε.
ΦΕΙ. τί δ' ἂν παρ' ἐκείνων καὶ μάθοι χρηστόν τις ἄν;
ΣΤΡ. ἄληθες; ὅσαπερ ἔστ' ἐν ἀνθρώποις σοφά·
γνώσει δὲ σαυτὸν ὡς ἀμαθὴς εἶ καὶ παχύς.
ἀλλ' ἐπανάμεινόν μ' ὀλίγον ἐνταυθοῖ χρόνον.
ΦΕΙ. οἴμοι, τί δράσω παραφρονοῦντος τοῦ πατρός;
πότερον παρανοίας αὐτὸν εἰσαγαγὼν ἕλω,
ἢ τοῖς σοροπηγοῖς τὴν μανίαν αὐτοῦ φράσω;
ΣΤΡ. φέρ' ἴδω, σὺ τουτονὶ τί νομίζεις; εἰπέ μοι.
ΦΕΙ. ἀλεκτρυόνα. ΣΤΡ. καλῶς γε. ταυτηνὶ δὲ τί;
ΦΕΙ. ἀλεκτρυόν'. ΣΤΡ. ἄμφω ταὐτό; καταγέλαστος εἶ.
μή νυν τὸ λοιπόν, ἀλλὰ τήνδε μὲν καλεῖν
ἀλεκτρύαιναν, τουτονὶ δ' ἀλέκτορα.
ΦΕΙ. ἀλεκτρύαιναν; ταῦτ' ἔμαθες τὰ δεξιὰ
εἴσω παρελθὼν ἄρτι παρὰ τοὺς γηγενεῖς;

ΣΤΡ. χἄτερά γε πόλλ᾽· ἀλλ᾽ ὅ τι μάθοιμ᾽ ἑκάστοτε,
ἐπελανθανόμην ἂν εὐθὺς ὑπὸ πλήθους ἐτῶν.
ΦΕΙ. διὰ ταῦτα δὴ καὶ θοἰμάτιον ἀπώλεσας;
ΣΤΡ. ἀλλ᾽ οὐκ ἀπολώλεκ᾽, ἀλλὰ καταπεφρόντικα.
ΦΕΙ. τὰς δ᾽ ἐμβάδας ποῖ τέτροφας, ὦνόητε σύ;
ΣΤΡ. ὥσπερ Περικλέης εἰς τὸ δέον ἀπώλεσα.
ἀλλ᾽ ἴθι, βάδιζ᾽, ἴωμεν· εἶτα τῷ πατρὶ
πειθόμενος ἐξάμαρτε· κἀγώ τοί ποτε
οἶδ᾽ ἑξέτει σοι τραυλίσαντι πιθόμενος·
ὃν πρῶτον ὀβολὸν ἔλαβον Ἡλιαστικόν,
τούτου ᾽πριάμην σοι Διασίοις ἁμαξίδα.
ΦΕΙ. ἦ μὴν σὺ τούτοις τῷ χρόνῳ ποτ᾽ ἀχθέσει.
ΣΤΡ. εὖ γ᾽, ὅτι ἐπείσθης. δεῦρο δεῦρ᾽, ὦ Σώκρατες,
ἔξελθ᾽· ἄγω γάρ σοι τὸν υἱὸν τουτονί,
ἄκοντ᾽ ἀναπείσας. ΣΩ. νηπύτιος γάρ ἐστ᾽ ἔτι,
καὶ τῶν κρεμαθρῶν οὐ τρίβων τῶν ἐνθάδε.
ΦΕΙ. αὐτὸς τρίβων εἴης ἄν, εἰ κρέμαιό γε.
ΣΤΡ. οὐκ ἐς κόρακας; καταρᾷ σὺ τῷ διδασκάλῳ;
ΣΩ. ἰδοὺ κρέμαι᾽, ὡς ἠλίθιον ἐφθέγξατο
καὶ τοῖσι χείλεσιν διερρυηκόσιν.
πῶς ἂν μάθοι ποθ᾽ οὗτος ἀπόφευξιν δίκης
ἢ κλῆσιν ἢ χαύνωσιν ἀναπειστηρίαν;
καίτοι γε ταλάντου τοῦτ᾽ ἔμαθεν Ὑπέρβολος.
ΣΤΡ. ἀμέλει, δίδασκε· θυμόσοφός ἐστιν φύσει·
εὐθύς γέ τοι παιδάριον ὂν τυννουτονὶ
ἔπλαττεν ἔνδον οἰκίας ναῦς τ᾽ ἔγλυφεν,
ἁμαξίδας τε σκυτίνας εἰργάζετο,
κἀκ τῶν σιδίων βατράχους ἐποίει πῶς δοκεῖς.
ὅπως δ᾽ ἐκείνω τὼ λόγω μαθήσεται,
τὸν κρείττον᾽, ὅστις ἐστί, καὶ τὸν ἥττονα,
ὃς τἄδικα λέγων ἀνατρέπει τὸν κρείττονα·
ἐὰν δὲ μή, τὸν γοῦν ἄδικον πάσῃ τέχνῃ.

ΣΩ. αὐτὸς μαθήσεται παρ' αὐτοῖν τοῖν λόγοιν.
ἐγὼ δ' ἄπειμι. ΣΤΡ. τοῦτό νυν μέμνησ', ὅπως
πρὸς πάντα τὰ δίκαι' ἀντιλέγειν δυνήσεται.

ΧΟΡΟΣ.

* * * * * * * *

ΔΙΚΑΙΟΣ ΛΟΓΟΣ. ΑΔΙΚΟΣ ΛΟΓΟΣ. ΧΟΡΟΣ.

ΔΙΚ. χώρει δευρί, δεῖξον σαυτὸν
τοῖσι θεαταῖς, καίπερ θρασὺς ὤν.
ΑΔ. ἴθ' ὅποι χρῄζεις. πολὺ γὰρ μᾶλλόν σ'
ἐν τοῖς πολλοῖσι λέγων ἀπολῶ.
ΔΙΚ. ἀπολεῖς σύ; τίς ὤν; ΑΔ. λόγος. ΔΙΚ. ἥττων γ' ὤν.
ΑΔ. ἀλλά σε νικῶ, τὸν ἐμοῦ κρείττω
φάσκοντ' εἶναι. ΔΙΚ. τί σοφὸν ποιῶν;
ΑΔ. γνώμας καινὰς ἐξευρίσκων.
ΔΙΚ. ταῦτα γὰρ ἀνθεῖ διὰ τουτουσὶ
τοὺς ἀνοήτους.
ΑΔ. οὔκ, ἀλλὰ σοφούς. ΔΙΚ. ἀπολῶ σε κακῶς.
ΑΔ. εἰπέ, τί ποιῶν; ΔΙΚ. τὰ δίκαια λέγων.
ΑΔ. ἀλλ' ἀνατρέψω γ' αὔτ' ἀντιλέγων·
οὐδὲ γὰρ εἶναι πάνυ φημὶ δίκην.
ΔΙΚ. οὐκ εἶναι φής; ΑΔ. φέρε γάρ, ποῦ 'στιν;
ΔΙΚ. παρὰ τοῖσι θεοῖς.
ΑΔ. πῶς δῆτα δίκης οὔσης ὁ Ζεὺς
οὐκ ἀπόλωλεν τὸν πατέρ' αὑτοῦ
δήσας; ΔΙΚ. αἰβοῖ, τουτὶ καὶ δὴ
χωρεῖ τὸ κακόν· δότε μοι λεκάνην.
ΑΔ. τυφογέρων εἶ κἀνάρμοστος.
ΔΙΚ. καταπύγων εἶ κἀναίσχυντος.
ΑΔ. ῥόδα μ' εἴρηκας. ΔΙΚ. καὶ βωμολόχος.

ΑΔ. κρίνεσι στεφανοῖς. ΔΙΚ. καὶ πατραλοίας.
ΑΔ. χρυσῷ πάττων μ' οὐ γιγνώσκεις.
ΔΙΚ. οὐ δῆτα πρὸ τοῦ γ', ἀλλὰ μολύβδῳ.
ΑΔ. νῦν δέ γε κόσμος τοῦτ' ἐστὶν ἐμοί.
ΔΙΚ. θρασὺς εἶ πολλοῦ. ΑΔ. σὺ δέ γ' ἀρχαῖος.
ΔΙΚ. διὰ σὲ δὲ φοιτᾶν
οὐδεὶς ἐθέλει τῶν μειρακίων·
γνωσθήσει τοί ποτ' Ἀθηναίοις
οἷα διδάσκεις τοὺς ἀνοήτους.
ΑΔ. αὐχμεῖς αἰσχρῶς. ΔΙΚ. σὺ δέ γ' εὖ πράττεις.
καίτοι πρότερόν γ' ἐπτώχευες,
Τήλεφος εἶναι Μυσὸς φάσκων,
ἐκ πηριδίου
γνώμας τρώγων Πανδελετείους.
ΑΔ. ὤμοι σοφίας—ΔΙΚ. ὤμοι μανίας—
ΑΔ. ἧς ἐμνήσθης. ΔΙΚ. τῆς σῆς, πόλεώς θ'
ἥτις σε τρέφει
λυμαινόμενον τοῖς μειρακίοις.
ΑΔ. οὐχὶ διδάξεις τοῦτον Κρόνος ὤν.
ΔΙΚ. εἴπερ γ' αὐτὸν σωθῆναι χρὴ
καὶ μὴ λαλιὰν μόνον ἀσκῆσαι.
ΑΔ. δεῦρ' ἴθι, τοῦτον δ' ἔα μαίνεσθαι.
ΔΙΚ. κλαύσει, τὴν χεῖρ' ἢν ἐπιβάλλῃς.
ΧΟΡ. παύσασθε μάχης καὶ λοιδορίας.
ἀλλ' ἐπίδειξαι
σύ τε τοὺς προτέρους ἅττ' ἐδίδασκες,
σύ τε τὴν καινὴν
παίδευσιν, ὅπως ἂν ἀκούσας σφῷν
ἀντιλεγόντοιν κρίνας φοιτᾷ.
ΔΙΚ. δρᾶν ταῦτ' ἐθέλω. ΑΔ. κἄγωγ' ἐθέλω.
ΧΟΡ. φέρε δὴ πότερος λέξει πρότερος;
ΑΔ. τούτῳ δώσω·

κᾆτ' ἐκ τούτων ὧν ἂν λέξῃ
ῥηματίοισιν καινοῖς αὐτὸν
καὶ διανοίαις κατατοξεύσω.
τὸ τελευταῖον δ', ἢν ἀναγρύξῃ,
τὸ πρόσωπον ἅπαν καὶ τὠφθαλμὼ
κεντούμενος ὥσπερ ὑπ' ἀνθρηνῶν
ὑπὸ τῶν γνωμῶν ἀπολεῖται.

ΧΟΡ. νῦν δείξετον τὼ πισύνω τοῖς περιδεξίοισι
λόγοισι καὶ φροντίσι καὶ γνωμοτύποις μερίμναις,
ὁπότερος αὐτοῖν λέγων ἀμείνων φανήσεται.
νῦν γὰρ ἅπας ἐνθάδε κίνδυνος ἀνεῖται σοφίας,
ἧς πέρι τοῖς ἐμοῖς φίλοις ἔστιν ἀγὼν μέγιστος.
ἀλλ' ὦ πολλοῖς τοὺς πρεσβυτέρους ἤθεσι χρηστοῖς στεφανώσας,
ῥῆξον φωνὴν ᾗτινι χαίρεις, καὶ τὴν σαυτοῦ φύσιν εἰπέ.

ΔΙΚ. λέξω τοίνυν τὴν ἀρχαίαν παιδείαν, ὡς διέκειτο,
ὅτ' ἐγὼ τὰ δίκαια λέγων ἤνθουν καὶ σωφροσύνη 'νενόμιστο.
πρῶτον μὲν ἔδει παιδὸς φωνὴν γρύξαντος μηδέν' ἀκοῦσαι·
εἶτα βαδίζειν ἐν ταῖσιν ὁδοῖς εὐτάκτως εἰς κιθαριστοῦ
τοὺς κωμήτας γυμνοὺς ἁθρόους, κεἰ κριμνώδη κατανίφοι.
εἶτ' αὖ προμαθεῖν ᾆσμ' ἐδίδασκεν, τὼ μηρὼ μὴ ξυνέχοντας,
ἢ Παλλάδα περσέπολιν δεινάν, ἢ Τηλέπορόν τι βόαμα,
ἐντειναμένους τὴν ἁρμονίαν, ἣν οἱ πατέρες παρέδωκαν.

εἰ δέ τις αὐτῶν βωμολοχεύσαιτ' ἢ κάμψειέν τινα καμπήν,
οἵας οἱ νῦν τὰς κατὰ Φρῦνιν ταύτας τὰς δυσκολοκάμπτους,
ἐπετρίβετο τυπτόμενος πολλὰς ὡς τὰς Μούσας ἀφανίζων.
οὐδ' ἂν ἑλέσθαι δειπνοῦντ' ἐξῆν κεφάλαιον τῆς ῥαφανῖδος,
οὐδ' ἄννηθον τῶν πρεσβυτέρων ἁρπάζειν οὐδὲ σέλινον,
οὐδ' ὀψοφαγεῖν, οὐδὲ κιχλίζειν, οὐδ' ἴσχειν τὼ πόδ' ἐναλλάξ.
ΑΔ. ἀρχαῖά γε καὶ Διπολιώδη καὶ τεττίγων ἀνάμεστα
καὶ Κηκείδου καὶ Βουφονίων. ΔΙΚ. ἀλλ' οὖν ταῦτ' ἐστὶν ἐκεῖνα,
ἐξ ὧν ἄνδρας Μαραθωνομάχους ἡμὴ παίδευσις ἔθρεψεν.
σὺ δὲ τοὺς νῦν εὐθὺς ἐν ἱματίοισι διδάσκεις ἐντετυλίχθαι·
πρὸς ταῦτ', ὦ μειράκιον, θαρρῶν ἐμὲ τὸν κρείττω λόγον αἱροῦ·
κἀπιστήσει μισεῖν ἀγορὰν καὶ βαλανείων ἀπέχεσθαι,
καὶ τοῖς αἰσχροῖς αἰσχύνεσθαι, κἂν σκώπτῃ τίς σε, φλέγεσθαι·
καὶ τῶν θάκων τοῖς πρεσβυτέροις ὑπανίστασθαι προσιοῦσιν,
καὶ μὴ περὶ τοὺς σαυτοῦ γονέας σκαιουργεῖν, ἄλλο τε μηδὲν
αἰσχρὸν ποιεῖν, ὅτι τῆς Αἰδοῦς μέλλεις τἄγαλμ' ἀναπλάττειν·
μηδ' εἰς ὀρχηστρίδος εἰσάττειν, ἵνα μὴ πρὸς ταῦτα κεχηνώς,

μήλῳ βληθεὶς ὑπὸ πορνιδίου, τῆς εὐκλείας ἀποθραυσθῇς·
μηδ' ἀντειπεῖν τῷ πατρὶ μηδέν, μηδ' Ἰαπετὸν καλέσαντα
μνησικακῆσαι τὴν ἡλικίαν, ἐξ ἧς ἐνεοττοτροφήθης.
ΑΔ. εἰ ταῦτ', ὦ μειράκιον, πείσει τούτῳ, νὴ τὸν Διόνυσον
τοῖς Ἱπποκράτους υἱέσιν εἴξεις, καί σε καλοῦσι βλιτομάμμαν.
ΔΙΚ. ἀλλ' οὖν λιπαρός γε καὶ εὐανθὴς ἐν γυμνασίοις διατρίψεις,
οὐ στωμύλλων κατὰ τὴν ἀγορὰν τριβολεκτράπελ', οἷάπερ οἱ νῦν,
οὐδ' ἑλκόμενος περὶ πραγματίου γλισχραντιλογεξεπιτρίπτου·
ἀλλ' εἰς Ἀκαδήμειαν κατιὼν ὑπὸ ταῖς μορίαις ἀποθρέξει
στεφανωσάμενος καλάμῳ λευκῷ μετὰ σώφρονος ἡλικιώτου,
μίλακος ὄζων καὶ ἀπραγμοσύνης καὶ λεύκης φυλλοβολούσης,
ἦρος ἐν ὥρᾳ χαίρων, ὁπόταν πλάτανος πτελέᾳ ψιθυρίζῃ.
ἢν ταῦτα ποιῇς ἁγὼ φράζω,
καὶ πρὸς τούτοις προσέχῃς τὸν νοῦν,
ἕξεις ἀεὶ στῆθος λιπαρόν,
χροιὰν λευκήν, ὤμους μεγάλους
γλῶτταν βαιάν.
ἢν δ' ἅπερ οἱ νῦν ἐπιτηδεύῃς,
πρῶτα μὲν ἕξεις χροιὰν ὠχράν,
ὤμους μικρούς, στῆθος λεπτόν,
γλῶτταν μεγάλην, ψήφισμα μακρόν,

καί σ' ἀναπείσει
τὸ μὲν αἰσχρὸν ἅπαν καλὸν ἡγεῖσθαι,
τὸ καλὸν δ' αἰσχρόν·
καὶ πρὸς τούτοις τῆς Ἀντιμάχου
καταπυγοσύνης ἀναπλήσει.

ΧΟΡ. ὦ καλλίπυργον σοφίαν κλεινοτάτην ἐπασκῶν,
ὡς ἡδύ σου τοῖσι λόγοις σῶφρον ἔπεστιν ἄνθος.
εὐδαίμονες δ' ἦσαν ἄρ' οἱ ζῶντες τότ' ἐπὶ τῶν προτέρων.
πρὸς οὖν τάδ', ὦ κομψοπρεπῆ μοῦσαν ἔχων,
δεῖ σε λέγειν τι καινόν, ὡς εὐδοκίμηκεν ἀνήρ.
δεινῶν δέ σοι βουλευμάτων ἔοικε δεῖν πρὸς αὐτόν,
εἴπερ τὸν ἄνδρ' ὑπερβαλεῖ καὶ μὴ γέλωτ' ὀφλήσεις.

ΑΔ. καὶ μὴν πάλαι γ' ἐπνιγόμην τὰ σπλάγχνα, κἀπεθύμουν
ἅπαντα ταῦτ' ἐναντίαις γνώμαισι συνταράξαι.
ἐγὼ γὰρ ἥττων μὲν λόγος δι' αὐτὸ τοῦτ' ἐκλήθην
ἐν τοῖσι φροντισταῖσιν, ὅτι πρώτιστος ἐπενόησα
τοῖσιν νόμοις καὶ ταῖς δίκαις τἀναντί' ἀντιλέξαι.
καὶ τοῦτο πλεῖν ἢ μυρίων ἔστ' ἄξιον στατήρων,
αἱρούμενον τοὺς ἥττονας λόγους ἔπειτα νικᾶν.
σκέψαι δὲ τὴν παίδευσιν ᾗ πέποιθεν ὡς ἐλέγξω·
ὅστις σε θερμῷ φησι λοῦσθαι πρῶτον οὐκ ἐάσειν.
καίτοι τίνα γνώμην ἔχων ψέγεις τὰ θερμὰ λουτρά;

ΔΙΚ. ὁτιὴ κάκιστόν ἐστι καὶ δειλὸν ποιεῖ τὸν ἄνδρα.

ΑΔ. ἐπίσχες· εὐθὺς γάρ σ' ἔχω μέσον λαβὼν ἄφυκτον.
καί μοι φράσον, τῶν τοῦ Διὸς παίδων τίν' ἄνδρ' ἄριστον
ψυχὴν νομίζεις, εἰπέ, καὶ πλείστους πόνους πονῆσαι;

ΔΙΚ. ἐγὼ μὲν οὐδέν' Ἡρακλέους βελτίον' ἄνδρα κρίνω.
ΑΔ. ποῦ ψυχρὰ δῆτα πώποτ' εἶδες Ἡράκλεια λουτρά;
καίτοι τίς ἀνδρειότερος ἦν; ΔΙΚ. ταῦτ' ἐστί, ταῦτ' ἐκεῖνα,
ἃ τῶν νεανίσκων ἀεὶ δι' ἡμέρας λαλούντων
πλῆρες τὸ βαλανεῖον ποιεῖ, κενὰς δὲ τὰς παλαίστρας.
ΑΔ. εἶτ' ἐν ἀγορᾷ τὴν διατριβὴν ψέγεις· ἐγὼ δ' ἐπαινῶ.
εἰ γὰρ πονηρὸν ἦν, Ὅμηρος οὐδέποτ' ἂν ἐποίει
τὸν Νέστορ' ἀγορητὴν ἂν οὐδὲ τοὺς σοφοὺς ἅπαντας.
ἄνειμι δῆτ' ἐντεῦθεν εἰς τὴν γλῶτταν, ἣν ὁδὶ μὲν
οὔ φησι χρῆναι τοὺς νέους ἀσκεῖν, ἐγὼ δὲ φημί.
καὶ σωφρονεῖν αὖ φησι χρῆναι· δύο κακὼ μεγίστω.
ἐπεὶ σὺ διὰ τὸ σωφρονεῖν τῷ πώποτ' εἶδες ἤδη
ἀγαθόν τι γενόμενον, φράσον, καί μ' ἐξέλεγξον εἰπών.
ΔΙΚ. πολλοῖς. ὁ γοῦν Πηλεὺς ἔλαβε διὰ τοῦτο τὴν μάχαιραν.
ΑΔ. μάχαιραν; ἀστεῖον τὸ κέρδος ἔλαβεν ὁ κακοδαίμων.
Ὑπέρβολος δ' οὑκ τῶν λύχνων πλεῖν ἢ τάλαντα πολλὰ
εἴληφε διὰ πονηρίαν, ἀλλ' οὐ μὰ Δί' οὐ μάχαιραν.
ΔΙΚ. καὶ τὴν Θέτιν γ' ἔγημε διὰ τὸ σωφρονεῖν ὁ Πηλεύς.
ΑΔ. κᾆτ' ἀπολιποῦσά γ' αὐτὸν ᾤχετ'· ἴσθι δ' ὢν Κρόνιππος.
σκέψαι γάρ, ὦ μειράκιον, ἐν τῷ σωφρονεῖν ἅπαντα
ἅνεστιν, ἡδονῶν θ' ὅσων μέλλεις ἀποστερεῖσθαι.
καίτοι τί σοι ζῆν ἄξιον, τούτων ἐὰν στερηθῇς;
εἶεν. πάρειμ' ἐντεῦθεν ἐς τὰς τῆς φύσεως ἀνάγκας.
ἥμαρτες, ἠράσθης, ἐμοίχευσάς τι, κᾆτ' ἐλήφθης·
ἀπόλωλας· ἀδύνατος γὰρ εἶ λέγειν. ἐμοὶ δ' ὁμιλῶν,
χρῶ τῇ φύσει, σκίρτα, γέλα, νόμιζε μηδὲν αἰσχρόν.

μοιχὸς γὰρ ἢν τύχῃς ἁλούς, τάδ' ἀντερεῖς πρὸς αὐτόν,
ὡς οὐδὲν ἠδίκηκας· εἶτ' εἰς τὸν Δί' ἐπανενεγκεῖν,
κἀκεῖνος ὡς ἥττων ἔρωτός ἐστι καὶ γυναικῶν·
καίτοι σὺ θνητὸς ὢν θεοῦ πῶς μεῖζον ἂν δύναιο;
τί δῆτ' ἐρεῖς;
ΔΙΚ. ἡττήμεθα,
πρὸς τῶν θεῶν δέξασθέ μου
θοἰμάτιον, ὡς
ἐξαυτομολῶ πρὸς ὑμᾶς.

ΣΩΚΡΑΤΗΣ. ΣΤΡΕΨΙΑΔΗΣ. ΦΕΙΔΙΠΠΙΔΗΣ.

ΣΩ. τί δῆτα; πότερα τοῦτον ἀπάγεσθαι λαβὼν
βούλει τὸν υἱόν, ἢ διδάσκω σοι λέγειν;
ΣΤΡ. δίδασκε καὶ κόλαζε, καὶ μέμνησ' ὅπως
εὖ μοι στομώσεις αὐτόν, ἐπὶ μὲν θἄτερα
οἷαν δικιδίοις, τὴν δ' ἑτέραν αὐτοῦ γνάθον
στόμωσον οἷαν ἐς τὰ μείζω πράγματα.
ΣΩ. ἀμέλει, κομιεῖ τοῦτον σοφιστὴν δεξιόν.
ΦΕΙ. ὠχρὸν μὲν οὖν οἶμαί γε καὶ κακοδαίμονα.
ΧΟΡ. χωρεῖτέ νυν. οἶμαι δέ σοι ταῦτα μεταμελήσειν.—
τοὺς κριτὰς ἃ κερδανοῦσιν, ἤν τι τόνδε τὸν χορὸν
ὠφελῶσ' ἐκ τῶν δικαίων, βουλόμεσθ' ἡμεῖς φράσαι.
πρῶτα μὲν γάρ, ἢν νεᾶν βούλησθ' ἐν ὥρᾳ τοὺς ἀγρούς,
ὕσομεν πρώτοισιν ὑμῖν, τοῖσι δ' ἄλλοις ὕστερον.
εἶτα τὸν καρπόν τε καὶ τὰς ἀμπέλους φυλάξομεν,
ὥστε μήτ' αὐχμὸν πιέζειν μήτ' ἄγαν ἐπομβρίαν.
ἢν δ' ἀτιμάσῃ τις ἡμᾶς θνητὸς ὢν οὔσας θεάς,
προσεχέτω τὸν νοῦν, πρὸς ἡμῶν οἷα πείσεται κακά,
λαμβάνων οὔτ' οἶνον οὔτ' ἄλλ' οὐδὲν ἐκ τοῦ χωρίου.

ἡνίκ᾽ ἂν γὰρ αἵ τ᾽ ἐλᾶαι βλαστάνωσ᾽ αἵ τ᾽ ἄμπελοι,
ἀποκεκόψονται· τοιαύταις σφενδόναις παιήσομεν.
ἢν δὲ πλινθεύοντ᾽ ἴδωμεν, ὕσομεν καὶ τοῦ τέγους
τὸν κέραμον αὐτοῦ χαλάζαις στρογγύλαις συντρί-
ψομεν.
κἂν γαμῇ ποτ᾽ αὐτὸς ἢ τῶν ξυγγενῶν ἢ τῶν φίλων,
ὕσομεν τὴν νύκτα πᾶσαν· ὥστ᾽ ἴσως βουλήσεται
κἂν ἐν Αἰγύπτῳ τυχεῖν ὢν μᾶλλον ἢ κρῖναι κακῶς.

ΣΤΡ. πέμπτη, τετράς, τρίτη, μετὰ ταύτην δευτέρα,
εἶθ᾽ ἣν ἐγὼ μάλιστα πασῶν ἡμερῶν
δέδοικα καὶ πέφρικα καὶ βδελύττομαι,
εὐθὺς μετὰ ταύτην ἔσθ᾽ ἕνη τε καὶ νέα.
πᾶς γάρ τις ὀμνὺς οἷς ὀφείλων τυγχάνω
θείς μοι πρυτανεῖ᾽ ἀπολεῖν μέ φησι κἀξολεῖν·
κἀμοῦ μέτρι᾽ ἄττα καὶ δίκαι᾽ αἰτουμένου,
"ὦ δαιμόνιε, τὸ μέν τι νυνὶ μὴ λάβῃς,
τὸ δ᾽ ἀναβαλοῦ μοι, τὸ δ᾽ ἄφες", οὔ φασίν ποτε
οὕτως ἀπολήψεσθ᾽, ἀλλὰ λοιδοροῦσί με
ὡς ἄδικός εἰμι, καὶ δικάσασθαί φασί μοι.
νῦν οὖν δικαζέσθων· ὀλίγον γάρ μοι μέλει,
εἴπερ μεμάθηκεν εὖ λέγειν Φειδιππίδης.
τάχα δ᾽ εἴσομαι κόψας τὸ φροντιστήριον.
παῖ, ἠμί, παῖ παῖ. ΣΩ. Στρεψιάδην ἀσπάζομαι.

ΣΤΡ. κἄγωγέ σ᾽· ἀλλὰ τουτονὶ πρῶτον λαβέ·
χρὴ γὰρ ἐπιθαυμάζειν τι τὸν διδάσκαλον.
καί μοι τὸν υἱόν, εἰ μεμάθηκε τὸν λόγον
ἐκεῖνον, εἴφ᾽, ὃν ἀρτίως εἰσήγαγες.

ΣΩ. μεμάθηκεν. ΣΤΡ. εὖ γ᾽, ὦ παμβασίλει᾽ Ἀπαιόλη.

ΣΩ. ὥστ᾽ ἀποφύγοις ἂν ἥντιν᾽ ἂν βούλῃ δίκην.

ΣΤΡ. κεἰ μάρτυρες παρῆσαν, ὅτ᾽ ἐδανειζόμην;

ΣΩ. πολλῷ γε μᾶλλον, κἂν παρῶσι χίλιοι.

ΣΤΡ. βοάσομαί τἄρα τὰν ὑπέρτονον

βοάν. ἰώ, κλάετ' ὦβολοστάται,
αὐτοί τε καὶ τἀρχαῖα καὶ τόκοι τόκων·
οὐδὲν γὰρ ἄν με φλαῦρον ἐργάσαισθ' ἔτι·
οἷος ἐμοὶ τρέφεται
τοῖσδ' ἐνὶ δώμασι παῖς,
ἀμφήκει γλώττῃ λάμπων,
πρόβολος ἐμός, σωτὴρ δόμοις, ἐχθροῖς βλάβη,
λυσανίας πατρῴων μεγάλων κακῶν·
ὃν κάλεσον τρέχων ἔνδοθεν ὡς ἐμέ.

ΣΩ. ὦ τέκνον, ὦ παῖ,
ἔξελθ' οἴκων, ἄϊε σοῦ πατρός.
ὅδ' ἐκεῖνος ἀνήρ.

ΣΤΡ. ὦ φίλος, ὦ φίλος.

ΣΩ. ἄπιθι λαβὼν τὸν υἱόν.

ΣΤΡ. ἰὼ ἰὼ τέκνον.
ἰοῦ ἰοῦ.
ὡς ἥδομαί σου πρῶτα τὴν χροιὰν ἰδών.
νῦν μέν γ' ἰδεῖν εἶ πρῶτον ἐξαρνητικὸς
κἀντιλογικός, καὶ τοῦτο τοὐπιχώριον
ἀτεχνῶς ἐπανθεῖ, τὸ τί λέγεις σύ; καὶ δοκεῖν
ἀδικοῦντ' ἀδικεῖσθαι καὶ κακουργοῦντ', οἶδ' ὅτι.
ἐπὶ τοῦ προσώπου τ' ἐστὶν Ἀττικὸν βλέπος.
νῦν οὖν ὅπως σώσεις μ', ἐπεὶ κἀπώλεσας.

ΦΕΙ. φοβεῖ δὲ δὴ τί; ΣΤΡ. τὴν ἕνην τε καὶ νέαν.

ΦΕΙ. ἕνη γάρ ἐστι καὶ νέα τις; ΣΤΡ. ἡμέρα,
εἰς ἥν γε θήσειν τὰ πρυτανεῖά φασί μοι.

ΦΕΙ. ἀπολοῦσ' ἄρ' αὔθ' οἱ θέντες· οὐ γὰρ ἔσθ' ὅπως
μί' ἡμέρα γένοιτ' ἂν ἡμέραι δύο.

ΣΤΡ. οὐκ ἂν γένοιτο; ΦΕΙ. πῶς γάρ; εἰ μή πέρ γ' ἅμα
αὐτὴ γένοιτο γραῦς τε καὶ νέα γυνή.

ΣΤΡ. καὶ μὴν νενόμισταί γ'. ΦΕΙ. οὐ γάρ, οἶμαι, τὸν
νόμον

ἴσασιν ὀρθῶς ὅ τι νοεῖ. ΣΤΡ. νοεῖ δὲ τί;
ΦΕΙ. ὁ Σόλων ὁ παλαιὸς ἦν φιλόδημος τὴν φύσιν.
ΣΤΡ. τουτὶ μὲν οὐδέν πω πρὸς ἕνην τε καὶ νέαν.
ΦΕΙ. ἐκεῖνος οὖν τὴν κλῆσιν εἰς δύ' ἡμέρας
ἔθηκεν, εἴς γε τὴν ἕνην τε καὶ νέαν,
ἵν' αἱ θέσεις γίγνοιντο τῇ νουμηνίᾳ.
ΣΤΡ. ἵνα δὴ τί τὴν ἕνην προσέθηκεν; ΦΕΙ. ἵν', ὦ μέλε,
παρόντες οἱ φεύγοντες ἡμέρᾳ μιᾷ
πρότερον ἀπαλλάττοινθ' ἑκόντες, εἰ δὲ μή,
ἕωθεν ὑπανιῷντο τῇ νουμηνίᾳ.
ΣΤΡ. πῶς οὐ δέχονται δῆτα τῇ νουμηνίᾳ
ἀρχαὶ τὰ πρυτανεῖ', ἀλλ' ἕνῃ τε καὶ νέᾳ;
ΦΕΙ. ὅπερ οἱ προτένθαι γὰρ δοκοῦσί μοι παθεῖν·
ὅπως τάχιστα τὰ πρυτανεῖ' ὑφελοίατο,
διὰ τοῦτο προὐτένθευσαν ἡμέρᾳ μιᾷ.
ΣΤΡ. εὖ γ', ὦ κακοδαίμονες, τί κάθησθ' ἀβέλτεροι,
ἡμέτερα κέρδη τῶν σοφῶν ὄντες, λίθοι,
ἀριθμός, πρόβατ' ἄλλως, ἀμφορῆς νενησμένοι;
ὥστ' εἰς ἐμαυτὸν καὶ τὸν υἱὸν τουτονὶ
ἐπ' εὐτυχίαισιν ᾀστέον μοὐγκώμιον.
"μάκαρ ὦ Στρεψίαδες,
αὐτός τ' ἔφυς ὡς σοφός,
χοῖον τὸν υἱὸν τρέφεις,"
φήσουσι δή μ' οἱ φίλοι
χοἰ δημόται,
ζηλοῦντες ἡνίκ' ἂν σὺ νικᾷς λέγων τὰς δίκας.
ἀλλ' εἰσάγων σε βούλομαι πρῶτον ἑστιᾶσαι.

ΠΑΣΙΑΣ.

εἶτ' ἄνδρα τῶν αὑτοῦ τι χρὴ προϊέναι;
οὐδέποτέ γ', ἀλλὰ κρεῖττον εὐθὺς ἦν τότε
ἀπερυθριᾶσαι μᾶλλον ἢ σχεῖν πράγματα,

ὅτε τῶν ἐμαυτοῦ γ᾽ ἕνεκα νυνὶ χρημάτων
ἕλκω σε κλητεύσοντα, καὶ γενήσομαι
ἐχθρὸς ἔτι πρὸς τούτοισιν ἀνδρὶ δημότῃ.
ἀτὰρ οὐδέποτέ γε τὴν πατρίδα καταισχυνῶ
ζῶν, ἀλλὰ καλοῦμαι Στρεψιάδην ΣΤΡ. τίς οὑτοσί;
ΠΑ. ἐς τὴν ἕνην τε καὶ νέαν. ΣΤΡ. μαρτύρομαι,
ὅτι ἐς δύ᾽ εἶπεν ἡμέρας. τοῦ χρήματος;
ΠΑ. τῶν δώδεκα μνῶν, ἃς ἔλαβες ὠνούμενος
τὸν ψαρὸν ἵππον. ΣΤΡ. ἵππον; οὐκ ἀκούετε,
ὃν πάντες ὑμεῖς ἴστε μισοῦνθ᾽ ἱππικήν;
ΠΑ. καὶ νὴ Δί᾽ ἀποδώσειν γ᾽ ἐπώμνυς τοὺς θεούς.
ΣΤΡ. μὰ τὸν Δί᾽· οὐ γάρ πω τότ᾽ ἐξηπίστατο
Φειδιππίδης μοι τὸν ἀκατάβλητον λόγον.
ΠΑ. νῦν δὲ διὰ τοῦτ᾽ ἔξαρνος εἶναι διανοεῖ;
ΣΤΡ. τί γὰρ ἄλλ᾽ ἂν ἀπολαύσαιμι τοῦ μαθήματος;
ΠΑ. καὶ ταῦτ᾽ ἐθελήσεις ἀπομόσαι μοι τοὺς θεούς;
ΣΤΡ. ποίους θεούς;
ΠΑ. τὸν Δία, τὸν Ἑρμῆν, τὸν Ποσειδῶ. ΣΤΡ. νὴ Δία,
κἂν προσκαταθείην γ᾽, ὥστ᾽ ὀμόσαι, τριώβολον.
ΠΑ. ἀπόλοιο τοίνυν ἕνεκ᾽ ἀναιδείας ἔτι.
ΣΤΡ. ἁλσὶν διασμηχθεὶς ὄναιτ᾽ ἂν οὑτοσί.
ΠΑ. οἴμ᾽ ὡς καταγελᾷς. ΣΤΡ. ἓξ χόας χωρήσεται.
ΠΑ. οὔ τοι μὰ τὸν Δία τὸν μέγαν καὶ τοὺς θεοὺς
ἐμοῦ καταπροίξει. ΣΤΡ. θαυμασίως ἥσθην θεοῖς,
καὶ Ζεὺς γέλοιος ὀμνύμενος τοῖς εἰδόσιν.
ΠΑ. ἦ μὴν σὺ τούτων τῷ χρόνῳ δώσεις δίκην.
ἀλλ᾽ εἴτ᾽ ἀποδώσεις μοι τὰ χρήματ᾽ εἴτε μή,
ἀπόπεμψον ἀποκρινάμενος. ΣΤΡ. ἔχε νυν ἥσυχος.
ἐγὼ γὰρ αὐτίκ᾽ ἀποκρινοῦμαί σοι σαφῶς.
ΠΑ. τί σοι δοκεῖ δράσειν; ἀποδώσειν σοι δοκεῖ;
ΣΤΡ. ποῦ 'σθ᾽ οὗτος ἁπαιτῶν με τἀργύριον; λέγε,
τουτὶ τί ἔστι; ΠΑ. τοῦθ᾽ ὅ τι ἐστί; κάρδοπος.

ΣΤΡ. ἔπειτ' ἀπαιτεῖς τἀργύριον τοιοῦτος ὤν;
οὐκ ἂν ἀποδοίην οὐδ' ἂν ὀβολὸν οὐδενί,
ὅστις καλέσειε κάρδοπον τὴν καρδόπην.
ΠΑ. οὐκ ἄρ' ἀποδώσεις; ΣΤΡ. οὔχ, ὅσον γέ μ' εἰδέναι.
οὔκουν ἀνύσας τι θᾶττον ἀπολιταργιεῖς
ἀπὸ τῆς θύρας; ΠΑ. ἄπειμι, καὶ τοῦτ' ἴσθ', ὅτι
θήσω πρυτανεῖ', ἢ μηκέτι ζῴην ἐγώ.
ΣΤΡ. προσαποβαλεῖς ἄρ' αὐτὰ πρὸς ταῖς δώδεκα.
καίτοι σε τοῦτό γ' οὐχὶ βούλομαι παθεῖν,
ὀτιὴ 'κάλεσας εὐηθικῶς τὴν κάρδοπον.

ΑΜΥΝΙΑΣ.

ἰώ μοί μοι.
ΣΤΡ. ἔα· τίς οὑτοσί ποτ' ἔσθ' ὁ θρηνῶν; οὔ τί που
τῶν Καρκίνου τις δαιμόνων ἐφθέγξατο;
ΑΜ. τί δ' ὅστις εἰμί, τοῦτο βούλεσθ' εἰδέναι;
ἀνὴρ κακοδαίμων. ΣΤΡ. κατὰ σεαυτόν νυν τρέπου.
ΑΜ. ὦ σκληρὲ δαῖμον, ὦ τύχαι θραυσάντυγες
ἵππων ἐμῶν· ὦ Παλλάς, ὥς μ' ἀπώλεσας.
ΣΤΡ. τί δαί σε Τληπόλεμός ποτ' εἴργασται κακόν;
ΑΜ. μὴ σκῶπτέ μ', ὦ τάν, ἀλλά μοι τὰ χρήματα
τὸν υἱὸν ἀποδοῦναι κέλευσον ἅλαβεν,
ἄλλως τε μέντοι καὶ κακῶς πεπραγότι.
ΣΤΡ. τὰ ποῖα ταῦτα χρήμαθ'; ΑΜ. ἁδανείσατο.
ΣΤΡ. κακῶς ἄρ' ὄντως εἶχες, ὥς γ' ἐμοὶ δοκεῖς.
ΑΜ. ἵππους ἐλαύνων ἐξέπεσον νὴ τοὺς θεούς.
ΣΤΡ. τί δῆτα ληρεῖς ὥσπερ ἀπ' ὄνου καταπεσών;
ΑΜ. ληρῶ, τὰ χρήματ' ἀπολαβεῖν εἰ βούλομαι;
ΣΤΡ. οὐκ ἔσθ' ὅπως σύ γ' αὐτὸς ὑγιαίνεις. ΑΜ. τί δαί;
ΣΤΡ. τὸν ἐγκέφαλον ὥσπερ σεσεῖσθαί μοι δοκεῖς.
ΑΜ. σὺ δὲ νὴ τὸν Ἑρμῆν προσκεκλῆσθαί μοι δοκεῖς,

εἰ μἀποδώσεις τἀργύριον. ΣΤΡ. κάτειπέ νυν,
πότερα νομίζεις καινὸν ἀεὶ τὸν Δία
ὕειν ὕδωρ ἑκάστοτ', ἢ τὸν ἥλιον
ἕλκειν κάτωθεν ταὐτὸ τοῦθ' ὕδωρ πάλιν;
ΑΜ. οὐκ οἶδ' ἔγωγ' ὁπότερον, οὐδέ μοι μέλει.
ΣΤΡ. πῶς οὖν ἀπολαβεῖν τἀργύριον δίκαιος εἶ,
εἰ μηδὲν οἶσθα τῶν μετεώρων πραγμάτων;
ΑΜ. ἀλλ' εἰ σπανίζεις, τἀργυρίου μοι τὸν τόκον
ἀπόδοτε. ΣΤΡ. τοῦτο δ' ἔσθ' ὁ τόκος τί θηρίον;
ΑΜ. τί δ' ἄλλο γ' ἢ κατὰ μῆνα καὶ καθ' ἡμέραν
πλέον πλέον τἀργύριον ἀεὶ γίγνεται,
ὑπορρέοντος τοῦ χρόνου; ΣΤΡ. καλῶς λέγεις.
τί δῆτα; τὴν θάλατταν ἔσθ' ὅτι πλείονα
νυνὶ νομίζεις ἢ πρὸ τοῦ; ΑΜ. μὰ Δί', ἀλλ' ἴσην.
οὐ γὰρ δίκαιον πλείον' εἶναι. ΣΤΡ. κᾆτα πῶς
αὕτη μέν, ὦ κακόδαιμον, οὐδὲν γίγνεται
ἐπιρρεόντων τῶν ποταμῶν πλείων, σὺ δὲ
ζητεῖς ποιῆσαι τἀργύριον πλεῖον τὸ σόν;
οὐκ ἀποδιώξεις σαυτὸν ἀπὸ τῆς οἰκίας;
φέρε μοι τὸ κέντρον. ΑΜ. ταῦτ' ἐγὼ μαρτύρομαι.
ΣΤΡ. ὕπαγε, τί μέλλεις; οὐκ ἐλᾷς, ὦ σαμφόρα;
ΑΜ. ταῦτ' οὐχ ὕβρις δῆτ' ἐστίν; ΣΤΡ. ἄξεις; ἐπιαλῶ
κεντῶν ὑπὸ τὸν πρωκτόν σε τὸν σειραφόρον.
φεύγεις; ἔμελλόν σ' ἆρα κινήσειν ἐγὼ
αὐτοῖς τροχοῖς τοῖς σοῖσι καὶ ξυνωρίσιν.
ΧΟΡ. οἷον τὸ πραγμάτων ἐρᾶν φλαύρων· ὁ γὰρ
γέρων ὅδ' ἐρασθεὶς
ἀποστερῆσαι βούλεται
τὰ χρήμαθ' ἁδανείσατο·
κοὐκ ἔσθ' ὅπως οὐ τήμερόν τι λήψεται
πρᾶγμ', ὃ τοῦτον ποιήσει τὸν σοφιστήν,
ἀνθ' ὧν πανουργεῖν ἤρξατ', ἐξαίφνης κακὸν λαβεῖν τι.

οἶμαι γὰρ αὐτὸν αὐτίχ' εὑρήσειν ὅπερ
πάλαι ποτ' ἐπῄτει,
εἶναι τὸν υἱὸν δεινόν οἱ
γνώμας ἐναντίας λέγειν 1314
τοῖσιν δικαίοις, ὥστε νικᾶν οἷσπερ ἂν
ξυγγένηται, κἂν λέγῃ παμπόνηρα.
ἴσως δ', ἴσως βουλήσεται κἄφωνον αὐτὸν εἶναι.

ΣΤΡΕΨΙΑΔΗΣ. ΦΕΙΔΙΠΠΙΔΗΣ. ΧΟΡΟΣ.

ΣΤΡ. ἰοὺ ἰού. 1321
ὦ γείτονες καὶ ξυγγενεῖς καὶ δημόται,
ἀμυνάθετέ μοι τυπτομένῳ πάσῃ τέχνῃ.
οἴμοι κακοδαίμων τῆς κεφαλῆς καὶ τῆς γνάθου.
ὦ μιαρέ, τύπτεις τὸν πατέρα; ΦΕΙ. φήμ', ὦ πάτερ. 1325
ΣΤΡ. ὁρᾶθ' ὁμολογοῦνθ' ὅτι με τύπτει. ΦΕΙ. καὶ μάλα.
ΣΤΡ. ὦ μιαρὲ καὶ πατραλοῖα καὶ τοιχωρύχε.
ΦΕΙ. αὖθίς με ταὐτὰ ταῦτα καὶ πλείω λέγε.
ἆρ' οἶσθ' ὅτι χαίρω πόλλ' ἀκούων καὶ κακά; 1329
ΣΤΡ. ὦ λακκόπρωκτε. ΦΕΙ. πάττε πολλοῖς τοῖς ῥόδοις.
ΣΤΡ. τὸν πατέρα τύπτεις; ΦΕΙ. κἀποφανῶ γε νὴ Δία
ὡς ἐν δίκῃ σ' ἔτυπτον. ΣΤΡ. ὦ μιαρώτατε,
καὶ πῶς γένοιτ' ἂν πατέρα τύπτειν ἐν δίκῃ;
ΦΕΙ. ἔγωγ' ἀποδείξω, καί σε νικήσω λέγων.
ΣΤΡ. τουτὶ σὺ νικήσεις; ΦΕΙ. πολύ γε καὶ ῥᾳδίως. 1335
ἑλοῦ δ' ὁπότερον τοῖν λόγοιν βούλει λέγειν.
ΣΤΡ. ποίοιν λόγοιν; ΦΕΙ. τὸν κρείττον', ἢ τὸν ἥττονα;
ΣΤΡ. ἐδιδαξάμην μέντοι σε νὴ Δί', ὦ μέλε,
τοῖσιν δικαίοις ἀντιλέγειν, εἰ ταῦτά γε
μέλλεις ἀναπείσειν, ὡς δίκαιον καὶ καλὸν 1340

τὸν πατέρα τύπτεσθ' ἐστὶν ὑπὸ τῶν υἱέων.
ΦΕΙ. ἀλλ' οἴομαι μέντοι σ' ἀναπείσειν, ὥστε γε
οὐδ' αὐτὸς ἀκροασάμενος οὐδὲν ἀντερεῖς.
ΣΤΡ. καὶ μὴν ὅ τι καὶ λέξεις ἀκοῦσαι βούλομαι.
ΧΟΡ. σὸν ἔργον, ὦ πρεσβῦτα, φροντίζειν ὅπη
τὸν ἄνδρα κρατήσεις,
ὡς οὗτος, εἰ μή τῳ 'πεποίθειν, οὐκ ἂν ἦν
οὕτως ἀκόλαστος.
ἀλλ' ἔσθ' ὅτῳ θρασύνεται· δῆλόν γε τἀν-
θρώπου 'στὶ τὸ λῆμα.
ἀλλ' ἐξ ὅτου τὸ πρῶτον ἤρξαθ' ἡ μάχη γενέσθαι
ἤδη λέγειν χρὴ πρὸς χορόν· πάντως δὲ τοῦτο δράσεις.
ΣΤΡ. καὶ μὴν ὅθεν γε πρῶτον ἠρξάμεσθα λοιδορεῖσθαι
ἐγὼ φράσω· 'πειδὴ γὰρ εἱστιώμεθ', ὥσπερ ἴστε,
πρῶτον μὲν αὐτὸν τὴν λύραν λαβόντ' ἐγὼ 'κέλευσα
ᾆσαι Σιμωνίδου μέλος, τὸν Κριόν, ὡς ἐπέχθη.
ὁ δ' εὐθέως ἀρχαῖον εἶν' ἔφασκε τὸ κιθαρίζειν
ᾄδειν τε πίνονθ', ὡσπερεὶ κάχρυς γυναῖκ' ἀλοῦσαν.
ΦΕΙ. οὐ γὰρ τότ' εὐθὺς χρῆν σ' ἄρα τύπτεσθαί τε καὶ πατεῖσθαι,
ᾄδειν κελεύονθ', ὡσπερεὶ τέττιγας ἑστιῶντα;
ΣΤΡ. τοιαῦτα μέντοι καὶ τότ' ἔλεγεν ἔνδον, οἷάπερ νῦν,
καὶ τὸν Σιμωνίδην ἔφασκ' εἶναι κακὸν ποιητήν.
κἀγὼ μόλις μέν, ἀλλ' ὅμως ἠνεσχόμην τὸ πρῶτον·
ἔπειτα δ' ἐκέλευσ' αὐτὸν ἀλλὰ μυρρίνην λαβόντα
τῶν Αἰσχύλου λέξαι τί μοι· κᾆθ' οὗτος εὐθὺς εἶπεν,
ἐγὼ γὰρ Αἰσχύλον νομίζω πρῶτον ἐν ποιηταῖς,
ψόφου πλέων, ἀξύστατον, στόμφακα, κρημνοποιόν.
κἀνταῦθα πῶς οἴεσθέ μου τὴν καρδίαν ὀρεχθεῖν;
ὅμως δὲ τὸν θυμὸν δακὼν ἔφην, σὺ δ' ἀλλὰ τούτων
λέξον τι τῶν νεωτέρων, ἅττ' ἐστὶ τὰ σοφὰ ταῦτα.

ὁ δ' εὐθὺς ᾖσ' Εὐριπίδου ῥῆσίν τιν', ὡς ἐκίνει
ἀδελφός, ὦλεξίκακε, τὴν ὁμομητρίαν ἀδελφήν.
κἀγὼ οὐκέτ' ἐξηνεσχόμην, ἀλλ' εὐθὺς ἐξαράττω
πολλοῖς κακοῖς καἰσχροῖσι· κᾆτ' ἐντεῦθεν, οἷον εἰκός,
ἔπος πρὸς ἔπος ἠρειδόμεσθ'· εἶθ' οὗτος ἐπαναπηδᾷ,
κἄπειτ' ἔφλα με κἀσπόδει κἄπνιγε κἀπέτριβεν.
ΦΕΙ. οὔκουν δικαίως, ὅστις οὐκ Εὐριπίδην ἐπαινεῖς,
σοφώτατον; ΣΤΡ. σοφώτατόν γ' ἐκεῖνον, ὦ—τί σ' εἴπω;
ἀλλ' αὖθις αὖ τυπτήσομαι. ΦΕΙ. νὴ τὸν Δί', ἐν δίκῃ γ' ἄν.
ΣΤΡ. καὶ πῶς δικαίως; ὅστις ὦναίσχυντέ σ' ἐξέθρεψα,
αἰσθανόμενός σου πάντα τραυλίζοντος, ὅ τι νοοίης.
εἰ μέν γε βρῦν εἴποις, ἐγὼ γνοὺς ἂν πιεῖν ἐπέσχον·
μαμμᾶν δ' ἂν αἰτήσαντος ἧκόν σοι φέρων ἂν ἄρτον.
ΧΟΡ. οἶμαί γε τῶν νεωτέρων τὰς καρδίας
πηδᾶν, ὅ τι λέξει.
εἰ γὰρ τοιαῦτά γ' οὗτος ἐξειργασμένος
λαλῶν ἀναπείσει,
τὸ δέρμα τῶν γεραιτέρων λάβοιμεν ἂν
ἀλλ' οὐδ' ἐρεβίνθου.
σὸν ἔργον, ὦ καινῶν ἐπῶν κινητὰ καὶ μοχλευτά,
πειθώ τινα ζητεῖν, ὅπως δόξεις λέγειν δίκαια.
ΦΕΙ. ὡς ἡδὺ καινοῖς πράγμασιν καὶ δεξιοῖς ὁμιλεῖν,
καὶ τῶν καθεστώτων νόμων ὑπερφρονεῖν δύνασθαι.
ἐγὼ γὰρ ὅτε μὲν ἱππικῇ τὸν νοῦν μόνον προσεῖχον,
οὐδ' ἂν τρί' εἰπεῖν ῥήμαθ' οἷός τ' ἦν πρὶν ἐξαμαρτεῖν·
νυνὶ δ' ἐπειδή μ' οὑτοσὶ τούτων ἔπαυσεν αὐτός,
γνώμαις δὲ λεπταῖς καὶ λόγοις ξύνειμι καὶ μερίμναις,

οἶμαι διδάξειν ὡς δίκαιον τὸν πατέρα κολάζειν.
ΣΤΡ. ἵππευε τοίνυν νὴ Δί', ὡς ἔμοιγε κρεῖττόν ἐστιν
ἵππων τρέφειν τέθριππον ἢ τυπτόμενον ἐπιτριβῆναι.
ΦΕΙ. ἐκεῖσε δ' ὅθεν ἀπέσχισάς με τοῦ λόγου μέτειμι,
καὶ πρῶτ' ἐρήσομαί σε τουτί· παῖδά μ' ὄντ' ἔτυπτες;
ΣΤΡ. ἔγωγέ σ', εὐνοῶν γε καὶ κηδόμενος. ΦΕΙ. εἰπὲ δή μοι,
οὐ κἀμέ σοι δίκαιόν ἐστιν εὐνοεῖν ὁμοίως,
τύπτειν τ', ἐπειδήπερ γε τοῦτ' ἔστ' εὐνοεῖν, τὸ τύπτειν;
πῶς γὰρ τὸ μὲν σὸν σῶμα χρὴ πληγῶν ἀθῷον εἶναι,
τοὐμὸν δὲ μή; καὶ μὴν ἔφυν ἐλεύθερός γε κἀγώ.
"κλάουσι παῖδες, πατέρα δ' οὐ κλάειν δοκεῖς;"
φήσεις νομίζεσθαι σὺ παιδὸς τοῦτο τοὔργον εἶναι·
ἐγὼ δέ γ' ἀντείποιμ' ἂν ὡς δὶς παῖδες οἱ γέροντες.
εἰκὸς δὲ μᾶλλον τοὺς γέροντας ἢ νέους τι κλάειν,
ὅσῳπερ ἐξαμαρτάνειν ἧττον δίκαιον αὐτούς.
ΣΤΡ. ἀλλ' οὐδαμοῦ νομίζεται τὸν πατέρα τοῦτο πάσχειν.
ΦΕΙ. οὔκουν ἀνὴρ ὁ τὸν νόμον θεὶς τοῦτον ἦν τὸ πρῶτον,
ὥσπερ σὺ κἀγώ, καὶ λέγων ἔπειθε τοὺς παλαιούς;
ἧττόν τι δῆτ' ἔξεστι κἀμοὶ καινὸν αὖ τὸ λοιπὸν
θεῖναι νόμον τοῖς υἱέσιν, τοὺς πατέρας ἀντιτύπτειν;
ὅσας δὲ πληγὰς εἴχομεν πρὶν τὸν νόμον τεθῆναι,
ἀφίεμεν, καὶ δίδομεν αὐτοῖς προῖκα συγκεκόφθαι.
σκέψαι δὲ τοὺς ἀλεκτρυόνας καὶ τἄλλα τὰ βοτὰ ταυτί,
ὡς τοὺς πατέρας ἀμύνεται· καίτοι τί διαφέρουσιν
ἡμῶν ἐκεῖνοι, πλὴν ὅτι ψηφίσματ' οὐ γράφουσιν;
ΣΤΡ. τί δῆτ', ἐπειδὴ τοὺς ἀλεκτρυόνας ἅπαντα μιμεῖ,

οὐκ ἐσθίεις καὶ τὴν κόπρον κἀπὶ ξύλου καθεύδεις;
ΦΕΙ. οὐ ταὐτόν, ὦ τάν, ἐστίν, οὐδ' ἂν Σωκράτει δοκοίη.
ΣΤΡ. πρὸς ταῦτα μὴ τύπτ'· εἰ δὲ μή, σαυτόν ποτ' αἰτιάσει.
ΦΕΙ. καὶ πῶς; ΣΤΡ. ἐπεὶ σὲ μὲν δίκαιός εἰμ' ἐγὼ κολάζειν,
σὺ δ', ἢν γένηταί σοι, τὸν υἱόν. ΦΕΙ. ἢν δὲ μὴ γένηται,
μάτην ἐμοὶ κεκλαύσεται, σὺ δ' ἐγχανὼν τεθνήξεις.
ΣΤΡ. ἐμοὶ μέν, ὦνδρες ἥλικες, δοκεῖ λέγειν δίκαια·
κἄμοιγε συγχωρεῖν δοκεῖ τούτοισι τἀπιεικῆ.
κλάειν γὰρ ἡμᾶς εἰκός ἐστ', ἢν μὴ δίκαια δρῶμεν.
ΦΕΙ. σκέψαι δὲ χἀτέραν ἔτι γνώμην. ΣΤΡ. ἀπὸ γὰρ ὀλοῦμαι.
ΦΕΙ. καὶ μὴν ἴσως γ' οὐκ ἀχθέσει παθὼν ἃ νῦν πέπονθας.
ΣΤΡ. πῶς δή; δίδαξον γὰρ τί μ' ἐκ τούτων ἐπωφελήσεις·
ΦΕΙ. τὴν μητέρ' ὥσπερ καὶ σὲ τυπτήσω. ΣΤΡ. τί δῆτα φῂς σύ;
τοῦθ' ἕτερον αὖ μεῖζον κακόν. ΦΕΙ. τί δ', ἢν ἔχων τὸν ἥττω
λόγον σὲ νικήσω λέγων
τὴν μητέρ' ὡς τύπτειν χρεών;
ΣΤΡ. τί δ' ἄλλο γ' ἢ ταῦτ' ἢν ποιῇς
οὐδέν σε κωλύσει σεαυ-
τὸν ἐμβαλεῖν ἐς τὸ βάραθρον
μετὰ Σωκράτους
καὶ τὸν λόγον τὸν ἥττω.
ταυτὶ δι' ὑμᾶς, ὦ Νεφέλαι, πέπονθ' ἐγώ,
ὑμῖν ἀναθεὶς ἅπαντα τἀμὰ πράγματα.
ΧΟΡ. αὐτὸς μὲν οὖν σαυτῷ σὺ τούτων αἴτιος,
στρέψας σεαυτὸν ἐς πονηρὰ πράγματα.

ΣΤΡ. τί δῆτα ταῦτ' οὔ μοι τότ' ἠγορεύετε,
ἀλλ' ἄνδρ' ἄγροικον καὶ γέροντ' ἐπήρετε;
ΧΟΡ. ἡμεῖς ποιοῦμεν ταῦθ' ἑκάστοθ', ὅντιν' ἂν
γνῶμεν πονηρῶν ὄντ' ἐραστὴν πραγμάτων,
ἕως ἂν αὐτὸν ἐμβάλωμεν εἰς κακόν,
ὅπως ἂν εἰδῇ τοὺς θεοὺς δεδοικέναι.
ΣΤΡ. ὤμοι, πονηρά γ', ὦ Νεφέλαι, δίκαια δέ.
οὐ γάρ μ' ἐχρῆν τὰ χρήμαθ' ἁδανεισάμην
ἀποστερεῖν. νῦν οὖν ὅπως, ὦ φίλτατε,
τὸν Χαιρεφῶντα τὸν μιαρὸν καὶ Σωκράτην
ἀπολεῖς μετελθών, οἵ σὲ κἄμ' ἐξηπάτων.
ΦΕΙ. ἀλλ' οὐκ ἂν ἀδικήσαιμι τοὺς διδασκάλους.
ΣΤΡ. ναὶ ναί, καταιδέσθητι πατρῷον Δία.
ΦΕΙ. ἰδού γε Δία πατρῷον· ὡς ἀρχαῖος εἶ.
Ζεὺς γάρ τις ἔστιν; ΣΤΡ. ἔστιν. ΦΕΙ. οὐκ ἔστ', οὔκ, ἐπεὶ
Δῖνος βασιλεύει, τὸν Δί' ἐξεληλακώς.
ΣΤΡ. οὐκ ἐξελήλακ', ἀλλ' ἐγὼ τοῦτ' ᾠόμην,
διὰ τουτονὶ τὸν δῖνον. οἴμοι δείλαιος,
ὅτε καὶ σὲ χυτρεοῦν ὄντα θεὸν ἡγησάμην.
ΦΕΙ. ἐνταῦθα σαυτῷ παραφρόνει καὶ φληνάφα.
ΣΤΡ. οἴμοι παρανοίας· ὡς ἐμαινόμην ἄρα,
ὅτ' ἐξέβαλλον τοὺς θεοὺς διὰ Σωκράτην.
ἀλλ', ὦ φίλ' Ἑρμῆ, μηδαμῶς θύμαινέ μοι,
μηδέ μ' ἐπιτρίψῃς, ἀλλὰ συγγνώμην ἔχε
ἐμοῦ παρανοήσαντος ἀδολεσχίᾳ.
καί μοι γενοῦ ξύμβουλος, εἴτ' αὐτοὺς γραφὴν
διωκάθω γραψάμενος, εἴθ' ὅ τι σοι δοκεῖ.—
ὀρθῶς παραινεῖς οὐκ ἐῶν δικορραφεῖν,
ἀλλ' ὡς τάχιστ' ἐμπιμπράναι τὴν οἰκίαν
τῶν ἀδολεσχῶν. δεῦρο δεῦρ', ὦ Ξανθία,
κλίμακα λαβὼν ἔξελθε καὶ σμινύην φέρων,

κἄπειτ' ἐπαναβὰς ἐπὶ τὸ φροντιστήριον
τὸ τέγος κατάσκαπτ', εἰ φιλεῖς τὸν δεσπότην,
ἕως ἂν αὐτοῖς ἐμβάλῃς τὴν οἰκίαν·
ἐμοὶ δὲ δᾷδ' ἐνεγκάτω τις ἡμμένην,
κἀγώ τιν' αὐτῶν τήμερον δοῦναι δίκην
ἐμοὶ ποιήσω, κεἰ σφόδρ' εἴσ' ἀλαζόνες.

ΜΑΘΗΤΗΣ.

ἰοὺ ἰού.
ΣΤΡ. σὸν ἔργον, ὦ δᾴς, ἱέναι πολλὴν φλόγα.
ΜΑΘ. ἄνθρωπε, τί ποιεῖς; ΣΤΡ. ὅ τι ποιῶ; τί δ' ἄλλο γ' ἢ
διαλεπτολογοῦμαι ταῖς δοκοῖς τῆς οἰκίας.
ΜΑΘ. οἴμοι, τίς ἡμῶν πυρπολεῖ τὴν οἰκίαν;
ΣΤΡ. ἐκεῖνος οὗπερ θοἰμάτιον εἰλήφατε.
ΜΑΘ. ἀπολεῖς ἀπολεῖς. ΣΤΡ. τοῦτ' αὐτὸ γὰρ καὶ βούλομαι,
ἢν ἡ σμινύη μοι μὴ προδῷ τὰς ἐλπίδας,
ἢ 'γὼ πρότερόν πως ἐκτραχηλισθῶ πεσών.

ΣΩΚΡΑΤΗΣ.

οὗτος, τί ποιεῖς ἐτεόν, οὑπὶ τοῦ τέγους;
ΣΤΡ. ἀεροβατῶ, καὶ περιφρονῶ τὸν ἥλιον.
ΣΩ. οἴμοι τάλας, δείλαιος ἀποπνιγήσομαι.
ΜΑΘ. ἐγὼ δὲ κακοδαίμων γε κατακαυθήσομαι.
ΣΤΡ. τί γὰρ μαθόντες τοὺς θεοὺς ὑβρίζετε,
καὶ τῆς Σελήνης ἐσκοπεῖσθε τὴν ἕδραν;
δίωκε, βάλλε, παῖε, πολλῶν οὕνεκα,
μάλιστα δ' εἰδὼς τοὺς θεοὺς ὡς ἠδίκουν.
ΧΟΡ. ἡγεῖσθ' ἔξω· κεχόρευται γὰρ μετρίως τό γε τήμερον ἡμῖν.

NOTES.

The opening scene presents the interior of a room, shown by means of the *ἐκκύκλημα*, containing two beds. Strepsiades is tossing, wideawake, upon one, and his son Pheidippides is sleeping under a pile of blankets on the other. Several slaves are snoring on mats upon the floor.

l. 1. **ἰού.** Equivalent here to 'heigh-ho,' the sound made by a man stretching and yawning.

l. 2. **τὸ χρῆμα τῶν νυκτῶν,** 'the length of the night-watches, how tremendous it is—interminable!' So *τὸ χρῆμα τῶν κόπων ὅσον* Ran. 1278, and *συὸς μέγα χρῆμα* to describe a 'huge wild boar,' Hdt. 1. 36. For **νυκτῶν** in this sense cp. *μέσαι νύκτες* Plato, Rep. 621 b.

l. 5. **οὐκ ἂν πρὸ τοῦ,** 'they wouldn't have dared to do so in bygone times.' But, since the Peloponnesian war, masters cannot venture 'so much as to chastise their slaves' (v. 7), much less put them to the torture, for fear they should desert to the enemy. The opening scene of the 'Knights' introduces slaves preparing for desertion; cp. Thuc. 7. 27 *ἀνδραπόδων πλέον ἢ δύο μυριάδες ηὐτομολήκεσαν.*

l. 7. **ὅτ',** i. e. *ὅτε* (not *ὅτι*, the final syllable of which is never elided); the days of war,—'a time when.'

l. 8. **οὐδ'** 'not even,' though it is far less excusable in him. **χρηστός** is used ironically, 'nice.'

l. 11. **ἀλλ', εἰ δοκεῖ,** 'well, if you please!' Strepsiades tries to resign himself, and take a nap; but he soon breaks out with **ἀλλ' οὐ δύναμαι.**

l. 12. **δακνόμενος.** This suggests an immediate allusion to the vermin in the bed, sc *ὑπὸ τῶν κόρεων.* But Aristophanes delights in this sort of surprise (or 'sell'). The technical name for this form of joke is *σκῶμμα παρὰ προσδοκίαν*, 'a jest with an unexpected conclusion.'

l. 13. **φάτνης.** Young Pheidippides has involved his father in debt, by keeping a stud of horses. The character of Pheidippides was intended to remind the audience of Alcibiades, who sought *θαυμάζεσθαι ἀπὸ τῆς ἱπποτροφίας* Thuc. 6. 12. The phrase *οἰκίη τεθριπποτρόφος* (Hdt. 6. 35) meant a wealthy family that could afford to compete in the most expensive contest of the Olympian games. Pheidippides belonged, on his mother's side (inf. 46), to the family of the Alcmaeonidae, and Alcmaeon himself *τεθριπποτροφήσας* *'Ολυμπιάδα ἀναιρέεται* Hdt. 6. 125.

l. 14. **κόμην ἔχων**, 'wearing his hair long,' the distinguishing mark of a fop, cp. *κομᾶν* inf. 545.

l. 17. **εἰκάδας**, 'the twenties;' i.e. the 20th and following days up to the end of the month, on the last day of which (*ἕνη καὶ νέα* inf. 1134) demand was made for interest on money borrowed. Cp. *tristes Kalendae* (Hor. Sat. 1. 3. 87), to describe the pay-day in Rome.

l. 22. **τοῦ**, i.e. *τίνος*, 'for what [do I owe] twelve minae to Pasias?' **τί ἐχρησάμην** seems to mean, 'for what purpose did I employ them?' It might equally well be rendered, 'why did I borrow them?' but then the two clauses would both mean the same thing. Cp. inf. 439 **χρήσθων** . . **ὅ τι** *βούλονται*.

l. 23. **ὅτ' ἐπριάμην**, 'when I bought the hack with the Corinthian brand;' i.e. marked with the ancient letter Koppa ϙ, equivalent to the Latin Q, and the initial, in old spelling, of *Κόρινθος*, famous for its breed of horses. Another distinguishing brand was the old sigma, or **σάν**, the horse so marked being called **σαμφόρας**, inf. 122, 1298. 'I wish,' he says, 'that I had had my eye "hacked" out, before I had ever seen this "hack,"' for he plays upon **κοππατίας** and **ἐξεκόπην**.

l. 25. **ἀδικεῖς**. Pheidippides, talking in his sleep, accuses some competitor named Philon of 'cheating,' by trying to 'foul' him in the race, where the chariots ran abreast.

l. 27. **καὶ καθεύδων**. That is, not only does he devote himself all day to 'horseflesh' (**ἱππική**, sc. *τέχνη*), but 'even when he goes to sleep' he dreams about it.

l. 28. **πόσους δρόμους**, 'how many rounds will the war-chariots run?' So *τὰ πολεμιστήρια ἅρματα* Hdt. 5. 113. For the intransitive use of **ἐλαύνειν** cp. Eur. Bacch. 853 *ἔξω ἐλαύνων τοῦ φρονεῖν*. Others render **ἐλᾷ** transitively, and join it with **πολεμιστήρια**, 'how many rounds will he drive in the war-chariot race?' The accusatival construction would then be like *νικᾶν 'Ολύμπια*.

l. 30. **τί χρέος ἔβα;** 'what obligation hath come?' with a play upon *χρέος* in its meaning of 'debt;' a parody of a line of Euripides, *τί χρέος ἔβα δῶμα*; Notice the Doric form **ἔβα** retained in the quotation.

l. 32. **ἐξαλίσας** (*ἐξαλίνδω*), with long iota. Pheidippides, still asleep, bids the groom to take the horse home, 'after giving him a roll' on smooth sandy ground (*ἀλίνδηθρα* Ran. 904, or *ἐξαλίστρα*), to rub off the sweat. His father retorts, 'You have rolled me out of house and home.'

l. 35. **ἐνεχυράσασθαι**, mid., 'will get surety for the interest owing;' i.e. will put a distress in my house, and seize my goods as pledge (*ἐνέχυρα*). Here **φασίν**, in the sense of 'threatening,' gives the force of a fut. to the aor. inf.

l. 38. **δάκνει**, 'there is biting me a ——'. We expect *κόρις* ('bug') to follow, but instead of it comes 'sheriff.' The **δήμαρχοι**, introduced by Cleisthenes, were 'overseers of the hamlets' (*δῆμοι*), and were responsible for the police service, registration of citizens, valuation of property, etc.

l. 42. **γῆμ[αι] ἐπῆρε**, 'egged me on to marry.'

l. 48. **ἐγκεκοισυρωμένην** (*ἐγκοισυρόομαι*). The country bridegroom finds this niece of Megacles whom he has married, 'a very Coesyra' (a fashionable Eretrian lady who had allied herself with the family of the Alcmaeonidae). See inf. 800.

l. 52. **Κωλιάδος.** This, and the next word, are titles under which Aphrodite was worshipped by women, probably with unseemly rites. The husband brings into the bridechamber all the smells of the farm; and the lady, an atmosphere of perfume and extravagance.

l. 53. **ἐσπάθα.** The technical sense of *σπαθᾶν* is to make the web upon the loom close and thick by beating the threads of the woof together with a wooden blade (*σπάθη*); from this it easily passed into the idea of 'wastefulness.' He says, 'she *laid it on* at the loom, and I used to tell her, holding up my [ragged] cloak as an illustration [of her slatternly ways], "Madam, you *lay it on too thick*."' For **πρόφασιν** in this sense cp. *πρόφασις ἀληθεστάτη* Thuc. 1. 23.

l. 57. **πότην λύχνον**, 'a tippling lamp,' that consumes too much oil.

l. 60. **μετὰ ταῦθ'.** After the interruption he resumes the story of his married life.

l. 63. **προσετίθει**, 'wanted to add.' Notice the force of imperf. as in **'τιθέμην** inf. 65.

l. 65. **Φειδωνίδην**='Thriftison.' His grandfather's name was **Φείδων**, 'Thrifty,' inf. 134.

l. 69. **ὅταν σύ.** We must supply the apodosis—('How grand it will be) when you are grown up, and drive a chariot to the Acropolis!' Cp. Thuc. 2. 15 *καλεῖται ἡ ἀκρόπολις μέχρι τοῦδε ἔτι ὑπ' Ἀθηναίων* **πόλις.** Pheidippides might have a chance of doing this as a victor at the Panathenaea.

l. 71. **φελλέως** seems to be a general word for 'rough ground;' though some write **Φελλέως**, and describe **Φελλεύς** as a mountain-district in Attica. Notice **μὲν οὖν**='nay rather.'

l. 72. **ἐνημμένος** (*ἐνάπτω*). So *παρδαλᾶς ἐνημμένους* Av. 1250.

l. 73. **ἵππ-ερος** is, literally, 'a passion for horses,' but it is humorously modelled on the form *ἴκτ-ερος* 'jaundice.' Perhaps we might render 'horse-pox,' on the analogy of 'chicken-pox.' For **καταχεῖν** with gen. in the sense of 'shed over' cp. Hom. Il. 23. 282 *ἔλαιον χαιτάων κατέχευεν.*

l. 77. **τουτονί**, sc. the sleeping Pheidippides.

l. 82. ἰδού, 'there you are,' an expression of assent, as inf. 255, 635, 825.

l. 83. τουτονί, 'yonder.' There must have been a statue or picture of Poseidon in the room. Poseidon was called ἵππιος, because, according to an old legend, he was the creator of the horse.

l. 84. μή μοί γε, sc. εἴπῃς, as inf. 433. Cp. Acharn. 345 *μή μοί γε πρόφασιν.*

l. 88. ἔκστρεψον, 'turn off,' like a discarded suit of clothes.

l. 94. φροντιστήριον, modelled after *δικαστήριον, ἐργαστήριον*, etc. Translate 'the Reflectory,' like 'refectory,' 'manufactory.' Strepsiades has brought his son out of the room into the street, where he points out to him the door of Socrates' school.

l. 96. πνιγεύς. A sneer at the physical science of the Ionic philosophers. The sky is compared to a 'muffle,' i.e. a cover put on the fire to extinguish it; and, to carry out the notion, men are to be called, not ἄνθρ-ωποι, but ἄνθρ-ακες, 'coals,' or rather 'young sparks!' So Meton says (Av. 1001) *ἀήρ ἐστι τὴν ἰδέαν ὅλος | κατὰ πνιγέα μάλιστα*, and a similar verbal jingle occurs in Av. 1546 (speaking of Prometheus) *μόνον θεῶν γὰρ διά σ' ἀπανθρακίζομεν.* Cp. Eur. Cycl. 374 *ἀνθρώπων θέρμ' ἀπ' ἀνθράκων κρέα.*

l. 98. ἀργύριον. Here Socrates, who *μισθὸν οὐδένα ἐπράξατο* (Diog. Laert. 2. 27), is unfairly mixed up with sophists like Protagoras or Gorgias, who charged exorbitant fees for instruction (Xen. Symp. 1. 5).

l. 99. Join νικᾶν δίκαια κἄδικα, 'to win a just or unjust cause.' So *νικᾶν* 'Ὀλύμπια, cp. also inf. 115, 432, 1087, 1211, 1335.

l. 101. καλοί τε κἀγαθοί. He gives the name of 'honest gentlemen' to these 'minute philosophers,' intending thereby to rank them among the conservative and aristocratical party in Athens.

l. 104. Χαιρεφῶν, from the Attic dême of Sphettus, is described as a cadaverous-looking man (inf. 504), with bushy eyebrows, black hair, and a squeaking voice, for which reason he had the nickname of *νυκτερίς*, or 'bat.' His excitability and enthusiasm is noticed in Plato, Apol. 21 a *σφοδρὸς ἐφ' ὅ τι ὁρμήσειε.*

l. 107. σχασάμενος, lit. 'having cut,' and so, 'having cut short' or 'put a stop to.' Cp. *κώπαν σχάσον* Pind. Pyth. 10. 51.

l. 108. οὐκ ἄν, sc. *τοῦτο ποιοίην.* Pheasants, like peacocks, were in great request among the wealthy men of Athens.

l. 112. εἶναι παρ' αὐτοῖς. It is unfair to represent Socrates as 'keeping on the premises' the worse and the better argument. It was the sophist Protagoras who professed *τὸν ἥττω λόγον κρείττω ποιεῖν* (Arist. Rhet. 2. 24); and Cicero mentions (Brut. 8. 30) Gorgias, Thrasymachus, Prodicus, and Hippias, as claiming to be able to do the same.

l. 113. ὅστις ἐστί, 'quisquis is est.' The words may have a sceptical tone about them, as if the *κρείττων λόγος* has become obsolete and 'improved off the earth,' like the ancient gods. Aristophanes may be parodying the phrase of Aeschylus (Agamemnon 160) Ζεύς, *ὅστις ποτ' ἐστί*, but more likely he means to represent the dulness of Strepsiades, speaking of the 'better what's-his-name.'

l. 120. **διακεκναισμένος**, lit. 'with my colour all scraped off;' and so, no longer looking healthy but cadaverous (*ὠχριῶν* sup. 103).

l. 121. **ἔδει**, 'shalt eat' (*ἐσθίω*). The **ζύγιος**, or 'wheeler,' is distinguished from the *σειραφόρος* (inf. 1300). For **σαμφόρας** see sup. 23. Megacles was too thorough a patron of racing to be willing to see his nephew left without a horse.

l. 124. **θεῖος** is accurately here 'great uncle;' see sup. 46. In saying **εἴσειμι**, Pheidippides threatens to go back into the house, which he had left when his father took him into the street to show him the 'Reflectory,' sup. 92.

l. 126. **πεσών γε.** Strepsiades has 'had a knock-down blow,' in this refusal of his son, but instead of lying prostrate he will go and 'get taught for himself.'

l. 131. **τί ταῦτα στραγγεύομαι;** 'why am I thus loitering?' **ἔχων** expresses 'persistent action,' as we say, 'to keep loitering;' as inf. 509, or *τί δῆτα διατρίβεις ἔχων*; Eccles. 1151: *ἔχων φλυαρεῖς* Plato, Euthyd. 295 c.

l. 134. **Κικυννόθεν**, 'from *Κίκυννα*,' a dême of the Acamantid tribe.

l. 137. **ἐξήμβλωκας** (*ἀμβλόω*), 'hast caused to miscarry.' The phrase has a comic reference to Socrates, who used to boast that he was the son of a notable midwife (*μαῖα*) Phaenarete; and that in teaching young men to bring out their power of thinking, he was practising his mother's art; **μαιεύεσθαί** *με ὁ θεὸς ἀναγκάζει, γεννᾶν δὲ ἀπεκώλυσεν* Plat. Theaet. 150 c.

l. 138. **τηλοῦ γὰρ οἰκῶ**, 'my home is far away in the country;' **τῶν ἀγρῶν**, local genitive. He had been forced to sojourn in the city because of the war in Attica, cp. Thuc. 2. 52.

l. 145. The notion of measuring the distance of a flea's leap by so many times the length of its own foot has an allusion to the celebrated dictum of Protagoras, *πάντων μέτρον ἄνθρωπος*. This saying represented every one as 'a law to himself,' and denied any fixed principle of truth. Here the flea supplies its own scale for measurement. Perhaps the joke is maintained in only assigning 'two feet' (v. 150) to the flea, as if it were a 'human biped.' The process is ridiculously mysterious, for, after these 'yellow slippers' of bee's-wax have formed round the feet of the creature 'when it has cooled down,' we may ask how they were taken off, and what the **χωρίον** is that was measured, and how the slippers made the measurement easier.

l. 158. ἐμπίδας. The next subtlety was the decision as to which end of the gnat produced the hum. It was caused by the violent passage of the air 'right for the vent' (εὐθὺ τοῦ ὀρροπυγίου); the gnat being a sort of animated trumpet, namely, a long straight tube expanding at the farther end into a wide orifice, like the κώδων at the end of the σάλπιγξ. The order of the words is τὸν πρωκτὸν προσκείμενον κοῖλον ('being attached as a hollow') πρὸς στενῷ, ἠχεῖν.

l. 165. διεντερεύματος. He congratulates him for his 'power of examining the ἔντερον' of the gnat. The word is a comic parody upon διερεύνημα, from διερεύνασθαι, 'investigate;' transl. 'his insight inside.'

l. 166. φεύγων, 'as defendant;' the prosecutor was said διώκειν, as, in Scotch legal phraseology, the prosecutor is called the 'pursuer.'

l. 170. This account of Socrates bespattered by a lizard as he was star-gazing is probably modelled on the story of Thales's fall into a well while similarly engaged, Plato, Theaet. 174 a. Socrates is unfairly reckoned among the students of astronomy; a science to which he confessedly gave no attention. Cf. Xen. Mem. 4. 7. § 6 ὅλως δὲ τῶν οὐρανίων, ᾗ ἕκαστα ὁ θεὸς μηχανᾶται, φροντίστην γίγνεσθαι ἀπέτρεπεν.

l. 174. ἥσθην, 'I like the notion of.' The aorist of the instantaneous expression of feeling like ἐπῄνεσα, καλῶς ἔλεξας, etc.

l. 179. θυμάτιον. This conjecture of Hermann for the reading of the MSS. θοἰμάτιον restores good sense to the passage. Socrates is supposed to be standing in the wrestling school, close by the altar of Hermes ἐναγώνιος. He spreads a thin coating of ashes over the altar, or perhaps the 'carving board' (τράπεζα), with the avowed intention of exhibiting some geometrical problem. For this purpose he takes a skewer (ὀβελίσκος), and 'having bent it in the middle, and having so got a pair of compasses, he steals away a bit of sacrificial meat.' That is, while he is flourishing his extemporised compasses and everybody's eyes are fixed upon his right hand, he slily conveys away a piece of meat with the other. The reading θοἰμάτιον, 'the cloak,' seems impossible to explain; for the theft of a cloak in the presence of bystanders could not easily be managed, nor would it suit with δεῖπνον and τἄλφιτα, sup.

l. 180. ἐκεῖνον, 'that notable' Thales; so ἐκείνην, inf. 534.

l. 181. ἀνύσας, 'with despatch,' lit. 'having completed [your work];' see inf. 635; so βοηθησάτω τις ἀνύσας Ach. 570; νῦν οὖν ἀνύσαντε φροντίσωμεν Eqq. 71.

l. 183. μαθητιῶ, 'I want to be a disciple.' Similar desideratives in -ιάω are στρατηγιάω Xen. Anab. 7. 1. 33; κλαυσιάω Aristoph. Plut. 1099; κορυβαντιάω Vesp. 8. The interior of the School is exhibited by means of the ἐκκύκλημα bringing the interior of the building forward upon the stage. In the foreground are various pupils in grotesque attitudes; placed about the School are sundry philosophical instruments, such as some sort of celestial globe to designate *Astronomy*, an *abacus* to represent *Geometry*; while in the background, slung to the roof in a basket, Socrates is seen engaged in contemplation.

l. 186. The ghastly pallor and skinny frames of the μαθηταί remind Strepsiades of the half-starved Lacedaemonian prisoners taken at Sphacteria (B.C. 425) by Cleon and Demosthenes, Thuc. 4. 27–41.

l. 188. **τὰ κατὰ γῆς.** The disciples are not looking for 'truffles' as Strepsiades innocently supposes, but are engaged in 'original research,' in true Socratic style. Cp. Plato, Apol. 19 b *Σωκράτης ἀδικεῖ καὶ περιεγάζεται ζητῶν τά τε ὑπὸ γῆς καὶ οὐράνια.*

l. 195. **εἴσιθ'**, i.e. *εἴσιτε*, addressed to the disciples. Socrates would not be pleased to find them exposed to the sun and air, for fear they might lose the philosophic paleness.

l. 203 **ἀναμετρεῖσθαι** means 'to measure,' and 'to apportion.' Strepsiades gets hold of the latter—the wrong meaning here—and is naturally delighted at hearing of a science which is 'to apportion' to his countrymen the whole of the world; and not merely such 'allotment land' (**κληρουχική**) as might be assigned to Athenian citizens in conquered countries. See Dict. Ant. s. v. *Colonia*, and cp. Thuc. 3. 50; Hdt. 6. 100.

l. 206. **περίοδος**, 'map.' So Aristagoras exhibits to Cleomenes *χάλκεον πίνακα ἐν τῷ γῆς ἁπάσης περίοδος ἐνετέτμητο καὶ θάλασσά τε πᾶσα καὶ ποταμοὶ πάντες* Hdt. 5. 49.

l. 208. **δικαστάς.** Athens without the law-courts was not to be recognised, *οὐδὲν γὰρ ἄλλο δρᾶτε πλὴν δικάζετε* Pax 505.

l. 209. **ὡς τοῦτ'.** Supply *πείθεσθαί σε δεῖ*, '[you must believe notwithstanding] *since* this really is,' etc. Cp. inf. 326, 427, 507.

l. 210. **Κικυννῆς**, nom. plur. from *Κικυννεύς*, 'a man of *Κίκυννα*,' sup. 134.

l. 211. **παρατέταται.** The disciple next points to Euboea on the map, 'stretching its long line of coast' to the east of Attica. But Strepsiades takes *παρατείνειν* in its derived sense of 'torture,' and adds, 'yes, it got a pretty good stretching.' For the severe treatment of Euboea by Pericles, B.C. 445, see Thuc. 1. 114.

l. 215. **τοῦτο πάνυ φροντίζετε**, 'give this your best consideration.' Strepsiades, not understanding the scale of the map, is horrified to find that Sparta is only a few inches distant from Athens, and begs to have it removed further away.

l. 218. **κρεμάθρας.** The basket in which Socrates swings is intended to be a parody upon the machine by which the gods were represented on the stage as descending from heaven.

αὐτός, emphatic, 'the master himself.' So the common phrase of the disciples of Pythagoras, *αὐτὸς ἔφα.*

l. 220. ἴθ' οὗτος, 'come you, sir,' addressed to the disciple, who has however 'no time' to shout, and returns to his studies.

l. 223. ὦ 'φήμερε. Socrates quite 'assumes the god' in this form of address to Strepsiades.

l. 225. περιφρονῶ has a double meaning; 'to contemplate,' as inf. 741, and 'to despise,' as *περιφρονοῦντες αὐτοὺς ὡς δυνατώτεροι* Thuc. 1. 25. Transl. Socrates, 'I am walking the air and fixing my thoughts down on the sun.' Strepsiades, 'So then it is from a basket that you look down upon the gods, if you're obliged to do so!' After εἴπερ supply *δεῖ ὑπερφρονεῖν τοὺς θεούς*, as in Ran. 76, 77 *εἶτ' οὐ Σοφοκλέα πρότερον ὄντ' Εὐριπίδου | μέλλεις ἀνάγειν, εἴπερ γ' ἐκεῖθεν δεῖ σ' ἄγειν*; The jingle between *περιφρονεῖν* and *ὑπερφρονεῖν* may, perhaps, be given by 'contemn' and 'contem-plate.'

l. 229. εἰ μὴ κρεμάσας, sc. *ἐζήτουν*, 'unless I had made my research by suspending my thought on high, and blending my intellect with its kindred atmosphere.' This parodies the saying of Anaximenes, *ἡ ψυχὴ ἡ ἡμετέρα, ἀὴρ οὖσα, συγκρατεῖ ἡμᾶς*. Anaxagoras too called the soul *ἀεροειδής*.

l. 232. οὐ γὰρ ἀλλά, i.e. *οὐ γὰρ [οὕτως οἷόν τ' ἐστὶν] ἀλλ' ἡ γῆ*, 'for thus we should never effect our purpose, but the earth attracts powerfully to itself the moisture of the intellect: and cress has just the same property.' He means to say, 'you know that the cress has a natural affinity for water, and drains the moisture away from the surrounding soil. The earth too has just such a natural affinity and would draw away all the subtle moisture from the human intellect, leaving it dry and sterile. Therefore we rise above the earth to keep our intellect from being sucked dry.' No wonder that Strepsiades made a muddle of all this, and asked if 'the intellect attracts moisture to the cress!'

l. 237. ὡς ἐμέ, 'to me.'

l. 240. χρήστων (*χρήστης*). Notice the paroxytone accent, distinguishing it from *χρηστῶν*, gen. of *χρηστός*.

l. 241. ἄγομαι, φέρομαι. So joined in Eur. Troad. 1310. The first word implies, properly, the removal of a man's live stock; the second, of his goods. 'I'm being cleared out and plundered and having my goods seized for debt.' The accus. χρήματα is used with the passive verb as in sup. 169 *γνώμην ἀφῃρέθη*.

l. 244. δεινὴ φαγεῖν, 'terribly consuming.' See sup. 74.

l. 246. πράττῃ (2nd pers.), 'you exact;' so with double accusative, as *Σωκράτης τοὺς ἑαυτοῦ ἐπιθυμοῦντας οὐκ ἐπράττετο χρήματα* Xen. Join ὀμοῦμαι τοὺς θεούς.

l. 248. νόμισμ' οὐκ ἔστι, 'don't pass current;' νόμισμα, cp. *νομίζειν θεούς*, stands for any established belief or institution: Strepsiades limits it to the narrower meaning of 'current coin.'

τῷ [= τίνι] γὰρ ὄμνυτε. The verb *ὀμνύναι* is regularly followed by the *accus.* of the thing sworn by. Perhaps the words of Strepsiades are designedly muddled, while he is ringing the changes on *τί γὰρ ὄμνυτε*; and *τίνι χρῆσθε νομίσματι*; Byzantium being a Doric colony, the word *σιδαρέοισιν* is quoted in the native dialect.

l. 251. **εἴπερ ἔστι γε**, 'if indeed it is possible.'

l. 254. **σκίμποδα**, 'pallet-bed,' a surprise for *τρίποδα*, the sacred tripod of the Pythian priestess.

l. 257. **ὅπως μὴ θύσετε**, 'mind you don't sacrifice me like Athamas.' When Strepsiades found himself seated on the *σκίμπους*, crowned like a victim for sacrifice, and going to be introduced to the **Νεφέλαι**, it is no wonder that he remembered the story of Athamas, who had married Nephele, and had come to terrible misfortune. Athamas had been unfaithful to his wife, and sought to slay Phrixus his son by her; for which he was condemned to be sacrificed to Zeus, and was only rescued by Heracles as he was actually standing at the altar.

l. 261. **ἔχ' ἀτρεμεί.** Socrates has promised him that he shall become 'subtle as fine meal' at talking, and, as it were, suiting the action to the word, he dredges him liberally with flour, as though pouring the *οὐλοχύται* over a victim's head. At this Strepsiades winces, and cries out, 'certainly you mean to be as good as your word; for if I am dredged like this I *shall* actually turn into meal.'

l. 264. **μετέωρον**, predicative with **ἔχεις**, 'that holdest suspended.' Socrates is assuming the tone and style of a hierophant.

l. 267. **τουτὶ πτύξωμαι**, 'before I fold this [sc. my cloak] across me.' He thinks if the Clouds are coming, rain must come with them.

l. 268. **τὸ δὲ . . ἐλθεῖν**, 'to think that I came from home without so much as a cap on!' For this use cp. *τὸ δὲ μὴ πατάξαι σ' ἐξελεγχθέντ' ἀντίκρυς* Ran. 741, so Av. 5, Vesp. 835.

l. 269. **τῷδ' εἰς ἐπίδειξιν**, 'to display yourselves before this man.' Socrates calls the Clouds from all the quarters of heaven, for Olympus reckons as north of Athens; the gardens of father Oceanus, where live the Hesperid nymphs, lie far west; the mouths of the Nile to the south; while the sea of Azov and the promontory of Mimas (on the Ionian coast, opposite Chios) represent the east.

l. 271. **Νύμφαις**, 'for the nymphs,' i.e. in their honour.

l. 272. **εἴτ' ἄρα**, 'or whether at the outfall of the Nile ye are drawing up his waters [**ὑδάτων**, partitive genitive] in golden pitchers.'

l. 275. Thunder is heard behind the scenes, and then the song of the Clouds, who do not actually appear on the stage before inf. 328. They are represented as rising from the ocean to the top of the wooded heights, from which they see the whole landscape spread before them. The horizon is bounded by lofty peaks, and in the mid-distance are fruitful plains, through which rivers run murmuring to the sea. In the Antistrophe (vv. 299-313) the Clouds propose to visit the land of Attica.

l. 276. Join **φανεραὶ . . φύσιν**, 'making display of our dewy, mobile, nature.' **εὐάγητον** seems to be the Doric form (cp. *δροσεράν*) of *εὐήγητον* (*ἡγεῖσθαι*), lit. 'easily drawn.'

l. 282. **καρπούς τ' ἀρδομέναν**, lit. 'that has her fruits watered.' No other use of *ἄρδεσθαι* in a middle sense being found, many editions follow the reading *καρποὺς τ' ἀρδομέναν θ'*, i.e. '*and* the fruits, *and* the well-watered sacred soil.'

l. 285. **ὄμμα αἰθέρος**, sc. the sun. The meaning is, 'it is high time to be moving, as the sun is up.'

l. 289. **ἰδέας**, gen. after **ἀποσεισάμεναι**, used here of bodily form, as in Plat. Protag. 315 e (*'Αγάθων*) *τὴν ἰδέαν πάνυ καλός*. It will be noticed that the language of this song of the Clouds, an evident imitation of some familiar form of sacred poetry, is overlaid with epithets, and repetitions of words.

l. 295. Join **θεῶν σμῆνος**, 'a swarm of deities,' like *ἑσμὸς γυναικῶν*, Lysist. 353. **'Αοιδαῖς** (if the reading be correct) must mean 'with singing.'

l. 296. **οὐ μὴ σκώψεις**, lit. 'wilt thou not not-jeer?' etc. Translate 'Refrain from jeering, and from doing what those scurvy burlesquers do.' **τρυγοδαίμονες** is a sort of concentrated comic form, from *τρύξ*, the wine-lees with which the players' faces were stained in the early days of comedy, while the whole form of the word has an echo of *κακοδαίμονες*.

l. 300. **λιπαράν**, 'splendid;' lit. 'shining,' 'sleek.' This favourite epithet of Athens was first used by Pindar, and became so hackneyed as to form a frequent butt for the wit of comic poets. Aristophanes (Ach. 639) declares that it suits 'sardines in oil,' better than his city.

l. 302. **οὗ σέβας**, 'where reverence is paid to unutterable mysteries, where the temple [of Demeter and Cora at Eleusis] that receives the initiated opens wide its gates (so *πύλας ἀναδεικνύναι* Soph. El. 1458) at the holy rites; and where there are,' etc.

l. 307. **πρόσοδοι**, 'processions,' as in Pax 397, and Xen. Anab. 6, 1. (5, 9). Such processions were seen at the Panathenaea.

l. 311. **Βρομία χάρις**. The 'festivity of Bromios at the incoming of spring' is the 'great' or 'city' Dionysia, the celebration of which began on the 9th of Elaphebolion; i.e. towards the end of March.

l. 312. **ἐρεθίσματα**, 'provocatives.' Critias is said to have called Anacreon *συμποσίων ἐρέθισμα*.

l. 316. **ἀργοῖς**, 'lazy,' comes in at the end of the line as a surprise, where some word like *εὐσεβής* or *ἁγνός* might have been expected.

l. 318. The moral value of the gifts degenerates as the list proceeds.

'Sententiousness and logic and intellect' are very well; but 'humbug and circumlocution and bamboozling and over-mastering' are of a more doubtful character. Phaeax (Eqq. 1377 foll.) is called *γνωμοτυπικὸς καὶ σαφὴς, καὶ* **κρουστικός**, | **καταληπτικός** *τ' ἄριστα τοῦ θορυβητικοῦ*, 'sententious and intelligible and bamboozling, and masterful over the noisy mob.' The words have a sort of semi-philosophical colouring.

l. 319. **ταῦτ' ἄρα**, 'therefore it is that;' in fuller form, viz. *διὰ ταῦτ' ἄρα*, Av. 486. See inf. 335, 353.

l. 320. **καπνοῦ**. A regular word for what is 'unsubstantial,' joined with *φλυαρία*, Plato, Rep. 9. 581 d. Cp. *καπνοῦ σκιά*, Soph. Ant. 1170.

l. 321. **γνωμιδίῳ**, 'and having pricked wit with a witticism to counterargue the opponent's argument.' In other words, he wants to figure as one of the 'dialectici qui ipsi se compungunt suis acuminibus' Cic. Orat. 2. 38, 158.

l. 323. **Πάρνηθα**. The theatre being open to the sky, Socrates was able to direct the gaze of Strepsiades towards Mount Parnes, on the Boeotian frontier, and to pretend that the Clouds were to be seen 'coming softly down' the hill side, 'trailing aslant through the hollows and the thickets,' on their way to the theatre. It may be doubted whether Parnes was actually visible to the spectators. Probably the Acropolis hid the view. Now they have come 'close to the entrance' (**παρὰ τὴν εἴσοδον**), the regular door by which the chorus trooped in upon the stage; and at last Strepsiades sees them—as they come in faster and faster, and he hails them with reverent words.

l. 331. **οὐ γὰρ μὰ Δί'**, i.e. ['yes, no doubt you did,] for, verily, you don't know that it is they who.' The word **σοφιστής** originally implied no dispraise, but merely meant 'a man of wisdom and skill.' Orpheus is so called, (Eur. Rhes. 924); and Herodotus gives the name to the Seven Sages (1. 29), and to Pythagoras (4. 95). The word first began to suggest the idea of dishonesty or immorality when applied to paid teachers of logic and rhetoric. Cp. Xen. Mem. 1. 6, 13 *τὴν σοφίαν τοὺς ἀργυρίου τῷ βουλομένῳ πωλοῦντας* **σοφιστὰς** *ἀποκαλοῦσιν*. It seemed indecorous to make merchandise of true wisdom, and there was a suspicion that the article so offered for sale was itself a sham.

l. 332. **θουριομάντεις**. In 'Thurian prophets' there is a sneer at the Athenian soothsayer Lampon, who had worked himself into high favour, and had been appointed to conduct a colony to Thurii, 444 B.C. The 'medicine-men' probably allude to Hippocrates and Herodicus, who may be supposed to have given themselves airs on the strength of their medical skill. Plato, Rep. 405, speaks with something of contempt of the *κομψοὶ 'Ασκληπιάδαι* of his day, and complains that Herodicus introduced the system of doctoring invalids who had better have been left to the chances of nature. The 'idle fops (*ἀργο-κομή-*

τας) have signet rings and fine trimmed nails,' or, as others say, 'rings right up to the nails,' or 'rings set with onyxes.' 'The song-twisters of cyclic choruses' are the 'dithyrambic poets of the day.' The dithyrambic choruses stood or danced 'in a ring' round the altar of Bacchus; the tragic choruses were arranged in a square (*τετράγωνοι*). They are all lumped together as 'astrological quacks,' perhaps with special allusion to the astronomical studies of Anaxagoras and Hippias of Elis, and the mathematics of Meton, who is made to say (Av. 995) *γεωμετρῆσαι βούλομαι τὸν ἀέρα.*

l. 334. Join **βόσκουσ' ἀργούς**, 'keep in idleness, because they write poetry about them.'

l. 335. **ταῦτ' ἄρα**, see sup. 319, 'Therefore it was that they kept celebrating in poetry.' The dithyrambic poets used such fine similes and synonyms to describe shapes and movements of the Clouds.

l. 337. **εἶτ' ἀερίας, διεράς**, 'next they described them as [sc. *νεφέλας ἐποίουν*] atmospheric, liquid; as air-floating birds with hooked talons.' There seems something wrong about this pair of epithets, slipped in between nouns substantive. Reisig would omit the commas and read *ἀερίας διερᾶς*, 'of the moist atmosphere.' The fem. adj. *ἀερία* may be used as a substantive, as in Homer *ὑγρή, ζεφυρίη, ἠοίη*, etc. Notice the Doric dialect in these dithyrambic specimens, as e.g. **ἑκατογκεφάλα** for *ἑκατογκεφάλου.*

l. 338. **ἀντ' αὐτῶν**, 'in recompense for these [compliments] they gulped down slices of fine big conger, and bird-flesh of thrushes.' Soc. 'Well but wasn't it all very deservedly [enjoyed] because of [their praise of] these goddess-Clouds?' These dainties would be enjoyed by the dithyrambic poets at the table of the Choragus, while the chorus was training.

l. 340. **τί παθοῦσαι** means properly 'under what pressure?' referring to external influences. The contrasted phrase **τί μαθών**, inf. 402, implies 'on what inducement?' 'what made you *think* of doing it?' The former might be rendered '*qua de caussa*;' the latter '*qua de ratione*.'

l. 341. **εἴξασι**, a form of the 3rd pers. plur. of *ἔοικα*, found here and in ver. 343, Av. 96, 383, Eur. Hel. 497, I. A. 848. We may suppose that the Chorus wore loose and floating drapery and female masks with long noses (*ῥῖνας* 344): this astonishes Strepsiades, who says, 'yonder clouds,' **ἐκεῖναί γ'** [sc. in the sky visible over his head], 'are not like that.'

l. 347. **Κενταύρῳ**. Porson compares Shakespeare, Hamlet, 3. 2; Antony and Cleopatra, 4. 12.

l. 348. **γίγνονται πάνθ' ὅ τι**, 'they turn into anything they please.' Cp. Homer, Od. 4. 17, of the transformation of Proteus, **πάντα δὲ γιγνόμενος** *πειρήσεται.* Notice the curious combination of **πάνθ' ὅ τι** instead of *πᾶν ὅ τι*, comparing Eur. Ion 233 *πάντα θεᾶσθ' ὅ τι καὶ θέμις ὄμμασι.*

l. 349. **ἄγριόν τινα**, 'a brutal specimen of those shaggy fellows.' The son of Xenophantes is Hieronymus the dithyrambic poet, of whom the Schol. says, *ἐκωμῳδεῖτο ὡς πάνυ κομῶν*, the wearing of long hair being considered at Athens a mark of conceit and haughtiness in grown men. By **μανίαν** is meant 'lewduess;' specially characteristic of the Centaurs. **ᾔκασαν**, aor. of custom.

l. 351. **Σίμωνα** (reckoned along with *Κλεώνυμος* among the *ἐπιόρκοι* inf. 399) is called by the Schol. 'a sophist;' and Eupolis accuses him of downright theft, *ἐξ Ἡρακλείας ἀργύριον ὑφείλετο.*

l. 353. **ταῦτ' ἄρα.** See sup. 319. **Κλεωνύμος**, 'the Falstaff of Aristophanes,' is as fat and as cowardly as that hero. He tried to shirk military service (Eqq. 1369 foll.), and, when in the field, he fled 'relicta non bene parmula' (**ῥίψασπις**). Cp. Vesp. 19, foll., Av. 1473. In Vesp. 592 he is called *Κολακώνυμος ἀσπιδαβολῆς.*

l. 354. **ἔλαφοι**, sc. the 'timidi dammae cervique fugaces.'

l. 355. **Κλεισθένης ὁ Σιβυρτίου** is represented as smooth-faced as an eastern Eunuch, Acharn. 118. His effeminacy is a constant butt of Aristophanes, who sometimes gives his name a feminine termination, sc. *Κλεισθένη* Thesm. 763.

l. 360? **εἴπερ τινὶ κἄλλῳ . . κἀμοί**, 'if ye have ever done it for anyone else . . . utter also for me,' etc. The expression **ῥῆξατε φωνήν**, 'give vent to your voice,' occurs in Hdt. 1. 85; cp. Eur. Suppl. 710 *ἔρρηξε δ' αὐδήν*, and Virgil, Aen. 2. 129 'rumpit vocem.'

l. 361. Prodicus of Ceos, who is numbered here among the transcendental philosophers (**μετεωροσοφισταί**), was known for an etymological treatise *περὶ ὀρθότητος ὀνομάτων*, his pedantic accuracy in which respect is often playfully alluded to in Plato's dialogues. From his treatise called *Ὧραι* comes the famous story of the 'Choice of Heracles,' Xen. Mem. 2. 1. 21 foll. He is said to have charged extortionate fees to his pupils (Cratyl 384 b), and Socrates laughingly says that he often hands over to the training of Prodicus those of his hearers 'who are so barren as never to be pregnant with a thought of their own' (Theaet. 151 b).

l. 362. **βρενθύει.** This description of the 'lofty gait' and 'sidelong glances' of Socrates is pleasantly reproduced by Alcibiades in Plato's Symp. 221 b. Cp. also Phaedo 117 b *ὁ Σωκράτης . . ὥσπερ εἰώθει ταυρηδὸν ὑποβλέψας πρὸς τὸν ἄνθρωπον.*

l. 363. **κἀφ' ἡμῖν**, 'and relying on us;' cp. Acharn. 330 *ἦ 'πὶ τῷ θρασύνεται;*

l. 370. **ὕοντα**, sc. *τὸν Δία.*

l. 371. **αἰθρίας**, so *κονία* Ach. 18; *αἰκία* Eccles. 663; 'in fine weather;' a genitive expressing point of time, as *νυκτός*, *χειμῶνος*, and inf. 721, *φρουρᾶς*. For the sentiment cp. Lucr. 6. 400 'denique cur nunquam caelo iacit undique puro Iupiter in terras fulmen?' **ταύτας δ' ἀποδημεῖν**, under the government of *χρῆν*, 'and that these [Clouds] should be far away.'

l. 372. **προσέφυσας**, 'this [illustration] you have admirably adapted to your present argument.' *προσφύειν*, lit. 'to make to grow to,' cp. Aesch. Suppl. 276 *καὶ ταῦτ' ἀληθῆ πάντα προσφύσω λόγῳ.*

l. 375. **ὦ πάντα σὺ τολμῶν**, he means, 'you man of reckless daring,' as in Soph. O. C. 761. Strepsiades is shocked at the rationalism of Socrates.

l. 376. **φέρεσθαι**, 'to sweep along.'

l. 377. **κατακρημνάμεναι**, 'hanging downwards,' from *κατακρήμναμαι*, another form of *κρέμαμαι*. So of the grapes hanging from a vine, *κατεκρημνῶντο δὲ πολλαὶ βότρυες* Hymn Hom. 7. 39. **ἀνάγκη** was used by the physical philosophers of the day to express what we now call 'natural laws,' such as 'gravitation;' Democritus affirming that *πάντα κατ' ἀνάγκην γίγνεσθαι*. The views enunciated by Socrates are like those of Anaxagoras who called 'thunder' *σύγκρουσις νεφῶν*, and 'lightning' *ἔκτριψις νεφῶν*. Cp. also Lucret. 6. 96 'tonitru quatiuntur caerula caeli, | propterea quia concurrunt sublime volantes | aetheriae nubes contra pugnantibus ventis.'

l. 380. **δῖνος**. This 'aetherial whirl' must not be identified with the 'vortex' theory of Democritus, which represented the impalpable atoms as setting to various centres, and thus creating all sensible objects. Aristophanes seems rather to allude to the 'rotation of the heavens,' *οὐρανοῦ φοράν* (or *δίνην*), which (according to Empedocles) regulated the motion of the earth. This notion had been popularized by Euripides, who speaks of *οὐράνιαι δῖναι νεφέλας δρομαίου* Alcest. 244; and *αἰθέριος ῥύμβος* ('rotation') in Frag. Pirith. 2. Aristophanes prefers the rarer masculine form *δῖνος*, from its resemblance to *Διός*, and from its sounding more like a proper name. Cp. Lucret. 5. 622 'cum caeli *turbine* ferri.' The Scholiast says that Strepsiades understands here another meaning of **δῖνος**, viz. 'a round-bellied pitcher or pot;' which falls in with the interpretation of the word inf. 1473.

l. 381. **ὁ Ζεὺς οὐκ ὤν**, 'the fact of Zeus being non-existent,' in apposition to **τουτί**.

l. 385. **τῷ = τίνι**, sc. 'quo argumento,' as *τῷ τοῦτο κρίνεις*; Plut. 48; Transl. 'How may one be convinced of this?'

l. 386. **ἀπὸ σαυτοῦ**, 'by an illustration from yourself.'

l. 388. **δεινὰ ποιεῖ γ' εὐθύς μοι**, 'it (sc. *ἡ γαστήρ*) at once lets me know (**μοι**) its distress and disturbance.' So Thuc. 5. 42 *'Αθηναῖοι* **δεινὰ ἐποίουν** (*indignabantur*) *νομίζοντες ἀδικεῖσθαι.*

l. 389. **ζωμίδιον**, 'the drop of broth;' the diminutive intensifying by contrast the loudness of the noise produced.

l. 390. **ἐπάγει**, sc. *ἡ γαστήρ*, 'subjungit.'

l. 396. **καὶ καταφρύγει.** The antithesis is loosely put. It would be more clearly expressed *τοὺς μὲν καταφρύγει, τοὺς δὲ περιφλύει*, 'some of us it burns to ashes, and others, that survive, it singes.'

l. 399. **Κρόνια** are 'old-world notions,' belonging to the primaeval times of Cronus. **βεκκεσέληνε** is modelled on the word *προσέληνος*, 'pre-lunar,' an epithet chosen for themselves by the Arcadians to express their early origin. The prefix *βεκκε-* recalls the experiment of Psammetichus II (Hdt. 2. 2), who shut two babies up with a she-goat, and waited to hear their first utterances, expecting thereby to learn what was the primitive language. Their first cry was *βεκ* (imitating the bleat of their foster-mother), and the king having learned that *βεκός* was the Phrygian word for bread, felt that he had established a science of Comparative Philology. The whole word may be rendered 'antediluvian.'

l. 400. **Θέωρος**, a different character to the one mentioned in Eqq. 608, is described as a flatterer Vesp. 42 foll., ib. 418 *Θεώρου θεοισεχθρία.* His perjury is probably in connection with his embassy to Sitalces, Ach. 134 foll.

l. 401. **'Αθηνέων**, quoted in Homeric dialect, from Od. 3. 278. Cp. Lucret. 6. 417 'postremo cur sancta deum delubra suasque | discutit infesto praeclaras fulmine sedes? . . . . | altaque cur plerumque petit loca plurimaque eius | montibus in summis vestigia cernimus ignis?' and ib. 387 'quodsi Iuppiter atque alii divi . . . iaciunt ignem, cur quibus incautum scelus aversabile cumquest | non faciunt icti flammas ut fulguris halent?'

l. 402. **τί μαθών;** see on sup. 340. Some MSS. read *τί παθών* here.

l. 404. **ἄνεμος.** Cp. Lucret. 6. 124 foll. 'cum subito validi venti conlecta procella | nubibus intorsit sese conclusaque ibidem | turbine versanti magis ac magis undique nubem | cogit uti fiat spisso cava corpore circum, | post, ubi comminuit vis eius et impetus acer, | tum perterricrepo sonitu dat scissa fragorem;' ib. 276 foll. 'insinuatus ibi vortex versatur in arto, | et calidis acuit fulmen fornacibus intus; | nam duplici ratione accenditur; ipse sua cum | mobilitate calescit, et e contagibus ignis.'

l. 406. **πυκνότητα** is, then, the 'compression' of this wind which has swollen the cloud.

l. 408. **ἀτεχνῶς** = 'exactly;' distinguished in meaning from *ἀτέχνως*, paroxytone. The **Διάσια** is described by Thucydides (1. 126) as *Διὸς ἑορτὴ Μειλιχίου μεγίστη, ἔξω τῆς πόλεως, ἐν ᾗ πανδημεὶ θύουσι, πολλοὶ οὐχ ἱερεῖα, ἀλλὰ θύματα ἐπιχώρια*, these *θύματα* generally being cakes or biscuits in the form of animals. Comparing inf. 864 we see the

Διάσια was kept as a sort of fair, where toys were bought for the children.

l. 409. **ὤπτων** (*ὀπτάω*), 'I was roasting a haggis for my kinsmen, and in my carelessness I did not slit it (**ἔσχων**, imperf. from *σχάω*, a collateral form of *σχάζω*).' This 'haggis' was a sheep's paunch filled with minced liver, fat, etc.: in roasting it a slit or hole had to be made in it, as a vent for the confined air. A similar haggis is described in Odyssey 20. 24 foll.

l. 414. **τὸ ταλαίπωρον.** This list of virtues that the Chorus commends to Strepsiades represents just those that his *contemporaries* assigned to Socrates, *ἀφροδισίων καὶ γαστρὸς πάντων ἀνθρώπων ἐγκρατέστατος ἦν, εἶτα πρὸς χειμῶνα καὶ θέρος καὶ πάντας πόνους καρτερικώτατος* Xen. Mem. 1. 2, 1; so Plato. Symp. 220 a, b. Here **ἀνοήτων** is parallel to the *ἀφροδισίων* in Xenophon; cp. Eur. Troad. 989 *τὰ μωρὰ γὰρ πάντ' ἐστὶν Ἀφροδίτη βροτοῖς.* But Socrates could hardly have been thought of as **γυμνασίων ἀπέχων**, which fact suggests the possibility that the true reading is preserved in the quotation of the lines by Diog. Laert. 2. 5, 27 *οἴνου τ' ἀπέχει* **κάδηφαγίας**, 'and gluttony.'

l. 419. **πράττων** refers to 'political action,' as its connection with **βουλεύων** and **τῇ γλώττῃ πολεμίζων** further shows.

l. 420. **ἕνεκέν γε.** Strepsiades is ready to guarantee all these requirements, saying gaily, 'Well, as far as a stubborn heart goes, be quite at ease: I can cheerfully offer myself in those respects [as an anvil for one] to hammer on.' For **παρέχοιμ' ἄν** without the reflexive *ἐμαυτόν* cp. Soph. Aj. 1146 *πατεῖν παρεῖχε τῷ θέλοντι ναυτίλων.*

l. 423. **ἄλλο τι δῆτ' οὐ νομιεῖς**, 'in full,' *ἄλλο τι δῆτα* [*ποιήσεις ἢ*] *οὐνομιεῖς*, lit. 'will you do anything else than refuse to believe?' In Plato this elliptic use of *ἄλλο τι* has passed into a regular formula with the sense of '*nonne*,' as *ἄλλο τι ὁμολογοῖ ἄν* = 'nonne confitebitur?' Symp. 200 d. Transl. here 'will you not refuse to believe?'

l. 425. **οὐδ' ἂν ἀπαντῶν** (*ἀπαντάω*), 'I wouldn't do it even if I met them, [much less would I seek their company].'

l. 427. **ὅ τι σοι δρῶμεν**, conjunctive, 'what we are to do for thee.'

l. 430. **ἑκατὸν σταδίοισιν**, 'to be best of all the Greeks in oratory by a hundred furlongs.' A similar hyperbole occurs in Ran. 91 *Εὐριπίδου πλεῖν ἢ σταδίῳ λαλίστερα.*

l. 432. **ἐν τῷ δήμῳ**, 'in the public assembly,' sc. the *ἐκκλησία*. Cp. Plato, Euthyd. 284 b *οἱ ῥήτορες ὅταν λέγωσιν ἐν τῷ δήμῳ.* Translate **γνώμας νικήσει**, here (and in Vesp. 594) 'shalt carry resolutions.' See note on sup. 99, and cp. Plato, Gorg. 456 a *οἱ νικῶντες τὰς γνώμας περὶ τούτων.*

l. 433. **μή μοί γε**, sc. *εἴπητε*, to which **λέγειν** is object, 'don't talk to me of my moving important resolutions.' So *μή μοι* sup. 84; Vesp. 1179 *μή μοί γε μύθους.*

l. 434. **ὅσα**, 'only so much as to,' like Lat. 'tantum.' Cp. *οὐδὲν ἄρ' ἐμοῦ μέλον ὅσον δὲ μόνον εἰδέναι* Vesp. 1288. **ἐμαυτῷ**, 'in my own interest.'

l. 436. **προπόλοισι**, 'our attendants,' sc. Socrates and his followers.

l. 437. **κοππατίας**, see sup. 23.

l. 438. **χρήσθων** (1st aor. imperat.), 'let them deal with me just as they please, I hand over this body of mine to them for beating, for hunger, thirst, squalor, cold, for flaying into a wine-bottle.' Cp. Eqq. 370 *δερῶ σε θύλακον κλοπῆς*, 'I'll flay you into a bag for stolen goods.' Grammatically, the subject of **τύπτειν** and **δείρειν** is *ὑμᾶς*; and *ἐμέ* the subject of the other infinitives. **ῥιγῶν**, as in Ach. 1146; Av. 935; Vesp. 446, the Attic form of infin. for the common form **ῥιγοῦν**.

l. 448. **κύρβις**, 'a walking statute-book,' 'a *corpus iuris*.' The *κύρβεις* were triangular pyramids of wood revolving on a pivot, whereon were written the laws of Solon. Cp. Av. 1354 *ἐστὶν ἡμῖν τοῖσιν ὄρνισιν νόμος | παλαιὸς ἐν ταῖς τῶν πελαργῶν κύρβεσιν.* **τρύμη** is properly 'a hole,' but from the idea of a hole making its way through anything, it is used here for a 'sharper.' **μάσθλης**, 'a supple-jack,' lit. a strap of soft-dressed leather. **γλοιός**, 'a slippery knave.' He is to unite in himself the two opposite qualities of the **εἴρων** and **ἀλάζων**, the former being a 'dissembler,' understating the truth about himself; the latter an 'impostor,' who overstates it. **ἀργαλέος** seems to mean what we call an 'awkward customer.' **ματιολοιχός** is the MS. reading, an uncertain word, for which most editions adopt *ματτυολοιχός*, Bentley's emendation from Athenaeus 14. 663 c, who gives the word *ματτύη* as a 'dainty dish.'

l. 452. **ἀπαντῶντες**, i.e. *οἱ ἀπαντῶντες*, 'they that meet me.'

l. 455. **ἔκ μου**, i.e. 'made of my flesh;' so Eqq. 372 *περικόμματ'* ('mincemeat') *ἔκ σου σκευάσω.*

l. 457. **τῷδέ γε.** The Chorus talks admiringly of Strepsiades and his courage. With the words **ἴσθι θ' ὡς** the Choreutes turns to him and addresses him. Join **παρ' ἐμοῦ . . . ἕξεις.**

l. 461. **πείσομαι** (*πάσχω*), 'what will be my case?'

l. 465. **ἆρά γε τοῦτ' ἄρ'.** The coincidence of the interrogatival **ἆρα** and the inferential **ἄρα** is unusual, but the meaning is simple enough, 'Shall I then ever behold this with my eyes?'

l. 466. **βουλομένους**, 'wishing to impart their views to you, and to come to a conference, ready to consult with you about claims and counterpleas involving many talents, subjects meet for a mind like yours.' Cf. *ἄξιον γὰρ Ἑλλάδι* Ach. 8; *τῇ πόλει γὰρ ἄξιον* ib. 204. This rendering makes **πράγματα** depend on **συμβουλευσομένους**, as Thuc. 8. 68 *ὅστις ξυμβουλεύσαιτό τι.* Here **ἀντιγραφαί** are the demurrers and objections taken by the defendant to the plaintiff's accusation, which is especially represented by **πράγματα.** Cp. Vesp. 1426 *δικῶν γὰρ οὐ δέομ' οὐδὲ πραγμάτων.*

l. 476. **ἀλλ' ἐγχείρει.** 'take in hand;' addressed to Socrates. **προδιδάσκειν** seems to mean, 'to *carry on* his education,' the preposition giving the notion of advance from point to point.

l. 479. **μηχανάς.** Socrates means 'methods' or 'plans,' but Strepsiades understands the word to mean 'engines of war,' such as battering-rams; *μηχανὰς προσῆγον τῇ πόλει* Thuc. 2. 76. Perhaps we should render **μηχανάς,** 'ingenuities,' which sounds sufficiently like 'engines' to suggest the misunderstanding.

l. 483. **μνημονικός.** Cp. Plato, Rep. 486 D *ἐπιλήσμονα ἄρα ψυχὴν ἐν ταῖς ἱκανῶς φιλοσόφοις μή ποτε ἐγκρίνωμεν, ἀλλὰ μνημονικὴν αὐτὴν ζητῶμεν δεῖν εἶναι.*

l. 487. **λέγειν μέν,** 'the power of speaking is not in it, but that of cheating is.' The antithesis seems poor and meaningless. Possibly there is a feeble joke in the contrast of **λέγειν** and *ἀποστ-***ερεῖν** ('speak'), as though he had said, 'I can't *chat*, but I can *cheat*.'

l. 490. **ὑφαρπάσει,** 'snap it up;' so **προβάλωμαι**='chuck you something,' both words suggesting the **κυνηδόν.** Cp. Vesp. 916 *ἤν μή τι κἀμοί τις προβάλλῃ τῷ κυνί.* **δέει,** not *δέῃ,* 'lest you be actually in need of a flogging;' so Eur. Phoen. 93 *μή τις πολιτῶν ἐν τρίβῳ φαντάζεται,* or Plato, Lach. *ὁρῶμεν μὴ Νικίας οἴεταί τι λέγειν καὶ οὐ λόγου ἕνεκα ταῦτα λέγει.*

l. 495. **ἐπιμαρτύρομαι,** sc. *τοὺς παρόντας,* like Lat. *antestor,* for fear that the assailant should deny having given the blow; cp. inf. 1222, 1297.

l. 496. **ἀκαρῆ,** sc. *χρόνον,* lit. 'an indivisible amount of time,' i.e. 'a moment' (*ἀ-κείρω*).

l. 497. **κατάθου θοἰμάτιον.** The connection seems to be that Socrates is so well satisfied with the practical wisdom of Strepsiades, that he is ready instantly to admit him to the *φροντιστήριον,* to enter which he must leave his cloak behind. Strepsiades thinks it is the preparation for a flogging. See inf. 857. 1498, and 719.

l. 499. **φωράσων,** 'to search for stolen goods.' A man with a search-warrant had to enter the suspected premises unclad, for fear that he might convey the missing property thither, under his cloak, and then pretend to have discovered it. Cp. Ran. 1364 *Ἑκάτα παράφηνον ἐς Γλύκης, ὅπως ἂν εἰσελθοῦσα φωράσω.*

l. 502. **τῷ τῶν μαθητῶν,** 'to which of the disciples shall I become like?' By **φύσιν** Socrates means 'character,' while Strepsiades understands it of 'bodily condition,' so that he is reminded of Chaerephon's meagre and ghostlike look. See note on sup. 104.

l. 506. **ἀνύσας τι,** 'with what speed you may;' lit. 'having made some despatch.'

l. 507. **μελιτοῦτταν** (Attic contraction for *μελιτόεσσαν,* as *οἰνοῦτταν*

Plut. 1121 for *οἰνόεσσαν*), sc. *μάζαν*, 'a sweet-cake,' honey in Greece being used for all the purposes for which we now employ sugar.

l. 508. **εἰς Τροφωνίου**, sc. *ἄντρον*. This was a natural fissure in the limestone rocks of Lebadeia in Boeotia, and was celebrated as early as the time of Croesus (Hdt. 1. 46) as one of the most famous Oracles. Pausanias, who had himself visited the cave, describes (9. 39, 2–14) how the enquirer, after a course of lustral washings and sacrifices, and after drinking of the spring of Oblivion to make him forget his former thoughts, and of the spring of Remembrance to impress upon him the coming revelation, descended a ladder, carrying a cake to appease the serpents and other noisome beasts that haunted the cave. Reaching the bottom of the shaft he had to creep on hands and knees through a narrow opening to the actual place of the Oracle. There a sort of stupor came over him, during which he received such visions as were vouchsafed him; at last he woke up from his trance with a splitting headache, and in such terror that it was months before he could smile again. No wonder Strepsiades did not like the look of the entrance into the *φροντιστήριον*, if it reminded him of this awful place!

l. 509. **ἔχων**, see sup. 131.

l. 510. The Chorus wishes Strepsiades good luck as his retreating form disappears down the passage to the Reflectory. Then, while the stage is clear of all the actors, the Chorus files forward, and the leader makes an address to the spectators in the name of the author of the play. This regular address, which, because it dealt with subjects unconnected with the plot, was called the 'Digression' (*παράβασις*), is peculiar to the old comedy, but not indispensable, as it is wanting in the Eccles., Lysistr., and Plutus. It must be remembered that we are here reading the *second* edition of the 'Clouds' (see Introduction); so that the failure of which the poet speaks refers to its earlier and unsuccessful exhibition. 'I hope,' he says, 'you will receive more graciously my recast of the play: it is the best I ever wrote. And I think I can reckon on your good taste, for you took very kindly to my first youthful essay. My comedy, while full of clever novelties, introduces no obscene exhibitions on the stage, no coarse jokes, no rude horse-play, no claptrap, no cruel personalities. Therefore I hope you will show your good sense by signifying your warm approval' (vv. 518–562).

l. 519. **ἐκθρέψαντα**, i.e. 'his dramatic talent had been fostered by the theatrical representations at the Dionysia from year to year.'

l. 520. **οὕτω νικήσαιμι**, 'May I win the prize to-day and be reckoned a clever poet as surely as (**οὕτω . . . ὡς**), it was in my honest belief (**ἡγούμενος**) that you were an audience of shrewd critics (**δεξιούς**), and that it was the most cleverly constructed of all my comedies, that I chose to give a taste to you, first of all the world, of the play which caused me the greatest amount of bother. And after all that (εἶτα) I was obliged to retire, having been worsted by vulgar playwrights, though I never deserved it. That 's the grievance I have against you, so clever as you are, you for whom I took all that trouble. But, notwithstanding, I never will, if I can help it, desert the cause of the shrewd critics among you.' He is taking credit to himself for having been generous enough to exhibit the first, and unsuccessful, edition of the 'Clouds' to the Athenian people at the great Dionysia in the city (πρώτους .. ὑμᾶς), instead of representing it, as he might have done, at the theatre in the Peiraeus, or at the country Dionysia. And as he had done this with full confidence in the appreciativeness of his audience, and the intrinsic value of his play, it was doubly hard to have been beaten, as he was; Kratinus winning the first prize with his Πυτίνη, 'the flask,' and Ameipsias the second with his Κόννος. But he attributes this defeat to the ignorance of the κριταί, and not to the clever audience before whom he played; and therefore he loyally comes before them again.

l. 528. ἐξ ὅτου, 'from the time when,' answered by ἐκ τούτου, 'thenceforth,' inf. 533. ἐνθάδε, 'here,' i.e. 'in this very theatre.' ὁ σώφρων τε χὼ καταπύγων, 'my Modest Man and my Rake (characters in his early play of the Δαιταλεῖς or 'Banqueters,' 427 B.C.) were most warmly praised by men with whom it is a pleasure even to speak.' He means the judges and the spectators who approved the play.

l. 529. κἀγώ, 'and I (for I was still a maid, and it was not right for me to be a mother yet) exposed my bantling, and another girl took it and reared it, and you generously nurtured it and educated it. From that time forth I have from your hands a sure pledge of sound judgment. So to-day (νῦν), like Electra in the play (ἐκείνην), this comedy of mine has come seeking, if she may chance to meet with spectators no less clever. For if she do but catch sight of it she will recognise her brother's curl.' The intention of all this badinage is to remind the audience of their kind reception accorded to the play of the Δαιταλεῖς, which he takes as an earnest of their present approval. He had been too young in B.C. 427 to enjoy the rights of full citizenship, and so he could not ask permission to bring his own play on the stage (χορὸν αἰτεῖν). So the actor and poet Philonides (παῖς ἑτέρα) had to take up the poor unacknowledged thing and present it as his own, and the audience took to it at once with most fatherly affection. What they had done for the 'Banqueters' Aristophanes is convinced they will do for his new comedy, which will instinctively recognise the former appreciative spectators, just as Electra (in Aesch. Choeph. 164 foll.) recognises the lock of Orestes' hair hung upon Agamemnon's tomb.

l. 540. κόρδαχ' εἵλκυσεν, 'danced a Kordax;' this was an unseemly dance, accompanied by indecent gestures. With εἵλκυσεν expressing the 'trailing step' of a slow measure cp. Pax 328 ἐν τουτί μ' ἔασον ἑλκύσαι.

l. 541. ἀφανίζων. He brings on the stage no testy old man, stick in hand, 'drubbing the other actors to *conceal* the badness of the jokes;' nor makes the Furies rush torch in hand across the stage, nor introduces a noisy and shouting (ἰού, ἰού) procession.

l. 545. οὐ κομῶ. Probably the poet is making a grotesque allusion to his own premature baldness, as in Pax 769 foll., and playing upon the double meaning of κομᾶν, 'to be proud,' and 'to wear long hair.' One may translate, 'I don't give myself (h)airs.'

l. 549. μέγιστον ὄντα, 'at the height of his power,' sc. after his success at Sphacteria, 425 B.C. The allusion is to the attack he had made upon Cleon in the 'Knights,' which was exhibited in the same year as Cleon's victory. With γαστέρα cp. Eqq. 454 παῖ' αὐτὸν . . . καὶ γάστριζε.

l. 550. κοὐκ ἐτόλμησα, 'I wasn't hard enough to jump on him again when he was down.' κειμένῳ is probably equivalent to τεθνηκότι, seeing that Cleon never experienced any political 'downfal,' but died in 422, the year after the exhibition of the 1st edition of the 'Clouds.' This Parabasis, which belongs to the 2nd edition only, must of course have been later than B.C. 421, as it alludes to the Maricas of Eupolis, which was brought out in that year. But Aristophanes did not altogether spare the memory of Cleon, as we see from the 'Wasps' and the 'Peace,' and indeed from inf. 581, unless that passage remains unaltered from the 1st edition.

l. 551. οὗτοι, 'these fellows,' sc. his rival playwrights.

l. 553. τὸν Μαρικᾶν παρείλκυσεν (implying something clumsy and awkward in the representation); 'when he had, like a miserable wretch, miserably turned inside out my play of the "Knights," having foisted into his Maricas (αὐτῷ), for the sake of the Kordax, a tipsy old woman, whom Phrynicus had long ago made a character of—the old woman whom the sea-monster was going to eat.' Eupolis had borrowed the general scheme of the 'Knights' from Aristophanes; and in order to ridicule the mother of Hyperbolus, had plagiarised on Phrynicus' burlesque of the 'Andromeda' or 'Cassiopeia.' We may suppose that the place of the princess, bound to the rock, was supplied by this drunken hag; who, probably, ends by dancing a vulgar 'break-down,' to express her joy at being rescued from the monster.

l. 556. ἐποίησεν ἐς, 'wrote in ridicule of.' Hermippus, a dramatist of the time of Pericles, had made fun of Hyperbolus and his mother in his play of Ἀρτοπωλίδες. By ἐρείδουσιν he means 'they are ever bringing all their weight down upon him.' Perhaps, 'peg away at Hyperbolus.'

l. 559. **τῶν ἐγχέλεων.** Cleon is compared (Eqq. 864 foll.) to an eel-catcher, who stirs up the mud that he may get more fish, *ὅπερ γὰρ οἱ τὰς ἐγχέλεις θηρώμενοι πέπονθας, | ὅταν μὲν ἡ λίμνη καταστῇ, λαμβάνουσιν οὐδέν, | ἐὰν δ' ἄνω τε καὶ κάτω τὸν βόρβορον κυκῶσιν, | αἱροῦσι· καὶ σὺ λαμβάνεις ἢν τὴν πόλιν ταράττῃς.*

l. 562. **ἐς τὰς ὥρας τὰς ἑτέρας,** lit. 'for the next set of seasons [and so on to the next],' i.e. 'for all time to come,' as Eur. I. A. 122 *ἐς τὰς ἄλλας ὥρας*, Theocr. 15. 74 *κεἰς ὥρας κἤπειτα*, Thesmoph. 950 *ἐκ τῶν ὡρῶν ἐς τὰς ὥρας.*

l. 563. **ὑψιμέδοντα.** This hymn of invocation by the chorus seems to ignore the deposition of Zeus and the reign of Dinos.

l. 567. **μοχλευτήν,** 'upheaver,' referring to Poseidon as *ἐννοσίγαιος* and *ἐνοσίχθων.*

l. 571. **ἱππονώμαν,** 'charioteer,' as in Eur. Hippol. 1399.

l. 579. **ἔξοδος,** 'military expedition with no sense about it.' The Clouds could stop proceedings in the *ἐκκλησία* by letting rain fall, which reckoned for an evil omen. So Dicaeopolis (Acharn. 169) *ἀλλ' ἀπαγορεύω μὴ ποιεῖν ἐκκλησίαν . . . διοσημία 'στι, καὶ ῥανὶς βέβληκέ με.*

l. 581. **εἶτα,** 'then again, when you were choosing as your general that accursed Paphlagonian Tanner (Cleon is so called in Eqq. 44), we knitted our brows, and we made a terrible to-do.' This passage, unaltered from the 1st edition (see Introduction, p. xi.), seems most naturally to refer to Cleon's first *στρατηγία* at Pylos (Thuc. 4. 28); Aristophanes implies that his success as general there was something undeserved; the grace of the gods 'giving a turn for the good' (589) to the folly of the Athenians.

l. 583. **βροντὴ .. ἀστραπῆς,** 'the thunder burst through the rift cloven by the lightning:' the words are from the 'Teucer' of Sophocles. **ἐξέλειπε τοὺς ὁδούς** does not seem here to describe a lunar eclipse, but only a continuance of bad weather, 'when neither sun nor stars for many days appeared.'

l. 587. **φασὶ γάρ,** cp. Eccles. 475 *λόγος γέ τοί τίς ἐστι τῶν γεραιτέρων, | ὅσ' ἂν ἀνόητ' ἢ μῶρα βουλευσώμεθα, | ἅπαντ' ἐπὶ τὸ βέλτιον ἡμῖν ξυμφέρειν.*

l. 589. **ταῦτα μέντοι,** explained by the following words **ἅττ' ἄν,** *κ.τ.λ.*

l. 591. **ἢν Κλέωνα,** 'if having convicted Cleon the cormorant of bribery and peculation you shall then pin his neck in the pillory.' Cleon is represented in the 'Knights' (956) as having a signet ring with the device of **λάρος** *κεχηνὼς ἐπὶ πέτρας δημηγορῶν.*

l. 593. **αὖθις ἐς τἀρχαῖον,** 'coming back once more to the old state of things, you shall find that, even though you did make a mistake, the affair shall turn out with the best result for our city:' cp. *πειθομένοισι δὲ ἄμεινον συνοίσεται* Hdt. 4. 15.

l. 595. **ἀμφί μοι αὖτε** With this reading we must supply ἴσθι or rather the Doric ἔσο. 'Be about me, O king!' i. e. vouchsafe thy presence. But the regular phrase is construed with an accusative, as in Terpander's *ὄρθιος νόμος*, which opens *ἀμφί μοι αὖθις ἄναχθ' ἑκατηβόλον ᾀδέτω ἁ φρήν*. Similar openings are found to four Homeric hymns; e. g. 5. 18 *ἀμφί μοι Ἑρμείαο φίλον γόνον ἔννεπε μοῦσα*, and Eur. Troad. 511 *ἀμφί μοι Ἴλιον, ὦ μοῦσα . . ἄεισον*. On these analogies we might better read *ἀμφί μοι αὖ σε* (sc. *ᾀδέτω φρήν*). This regular prelude was so thoroughly established that the verb *ἀμφιανακτίζειν* was used as an equivalent for *προοιμιάζεσθαι*.

l. 597. **ὑψικέρᾱτα πέτραν**, a phrase borrowed from Pindar. The epithet is a heteroclite accus., the ordinary nominat. being *ὑψίκερως*, cp. *χρυσοκέρατ' ἔλαφον* Eur. Hel. 382.

l. 599. **οἶκον**, the old temple of Artemis in Ephesus, built by Chersiphron of Gnossus, Ol. 45. It was burned by Herostratus, B.C. 356.

l. 602. **αἰγίδος ἡνίοχος**, probably means 'wielder of the aegis,' as *κιθάρας ἡνίοχος*. Green renders it 'charioted on thine aegis,' and compares Aesch. Eum. 403 *ἔνθεν διώκουσ' ἦλθον ἄτρυτον πόδα, | πτερῶν ἄτερ ῥοιβδοῦσα κόλπον αἰγίδος, | πώλοις ἀκμαίοις τόνδ' ἐπιζεύξασ' ὄχον*. But the meaning there is rather that the movement of the goddess swelled out the folds of the Aegis than that she used the Aegis like a sail to increase her speed.

l. 604. **σελαγεῖ**, 2 pers sing., from *σελαγεῖσθαι* (cp. Acharn. 924 *σελαγοῖντ' ἂν εὐθύς*), 'sparklest.' With **σὺν πεύκαις**, sc. 'the torches' carried by the Delphic Bacchanals, cp. Eur. Bacch. 306 *κἀπὶ Δελφίσιν πέτραις πηδῶντα σὺν πεύκαισι*.

l. 609. **χαίρειν**, 'greeting,' the regular beginning of a letter, as often in Demosth. *βασιλεὺς Μακεδόνων Φίλιππος Ἀθηναίων τῇ βουλῇ καὶ τῷ δήμῳ* **χαίρειν**. Cleon is said to have been the first to introduce this language of friendly correspondence into an official despatch from Sphacteria. **τοῖς συμμάχοις** are added because the play is acted at the Dionysia, where 'the allies' are present as spectators; cp. Acharn. 502 foll.

l. 612. **δραχμήν**, cognate accus. with **ὠφελοῦσα**, 'to the amount of a drachma,' so *ὠφελεῖν ὠφέλειαν* Plato, Euthyd. 275 c. **εἰς δᾷδα**, 'to save torch-light.'

l. 615. This amusing picture of the sufferings of the gods through the inaccuracies of the Athenian calendar may have been happily timed, because the astronomer Meton had been endeavouring, only a few years before, to improve the current system of reckoning, and Aristophanes may have wished to make a passing hit at the 'new-fangled' change. The difficulty, which was a very old one, lay in the attempt to make the solar year (regulated by the sun's apparent crossing of the tropics) harmonize with the lunar year, which settled all the religious festivals in Athens. The solar year consists roughly of 365¼ days; the lunar month of 29½ days, so that 12 lunar months = 354 days. The common system in vogue at Athens, since Solon's time, for harmonizing these two methods of reckoning, was by arranging a cycle of 8 years (ὀκταετηρίς), five of which consisted of the ordinary number of 354 days, while the other three were each raised to the number of 384, by the insertion of a month of 30 days. Now 354 × 5 = 1770, and 384 × 3 = 1152, which gives a sum of 2922, identical in amount with 8 solar years of 365¼ days. But as the three inserted months in the ὀκταετηρίς consisted of 30 days instead of 29½ (the true lunar month), there was an error in excess at the end of the cycle of 1½ day—a very appreciable quantity. The gods might well grumble, as this would be sufficient to disarrange the whole calendar. We might illustrate it by supposing Shrove Tuesday pushed forward to Ash Wednesday, or vice versa.

l. 620. **στρεβλοῦτε**, i.e. extort evidence from slaves by torture; whereas on a festival the law-courts ought to be closed.

l. 621. Join **ἡμῶν τῶν θεῶν**. Memnon, son of Tithonus and Eos, and Sarpedon, son of Zeus, were special favourites of the Gods, and fell in the Trojan war.

l. 623. The meetings of the Amphictyonic council were held in the autumn of each year near Thermopylae (whence the name **Πυλαία** for the meeting), and in the spring at Delphi. The council was composed of two classes of representatives, **Πυλαγόραι** and **Ἱερομνήμονες**. Athens sent three of the former, elected by show of hands (**χειροτονία**) and one Hieromnemon, elected by lot (**λαχών**), who was the highest commissioner.

l. 625. **ἀφῃρέθη**. Probably his official garland was blown off by a puff of wind; and the Clouds may be supposed to have sent it.

l. 627. Socrates comes out from the Reflectory, grumbling at his aged pupil's incorrigible dulness. He swears by Respiration, Void, and Atmosphere. In sup. 424 he had declared there were no gods but 'Void, Clouds, and the Tongue.'

l. 630. **σκαλαθυρμάτια**, 'deep-dug quibbles,' apparently from *σκαλ-*, as in *σκαλεύω*, *σκάλπω*, and *ἀθυρμάτιον*, a diminutive of *ἄθυρμα*, 'child's play,' 'amusement.' **ἅττα**, Attic for *τινά* (*ἄτινα*).

l. 632. **θύραζε πρὸς τὸ φῶς**, 'out into the daylight,' for part at least of the *φροντιστήριον* was undergound.

l. 633. **ἔξει**, from *ἐξιέναι*, 'come forth.'

l. 635. **ἀνύσας τι**, see sup. 181.

l. 638. **περὶ μέτρων**. The question of 'measures' (which Strepsiades understands as 'dry measures,' and not as poetical *metres*) is considered in vv. 639–646; that of 'rhythm' in vv. 647–656. By περὶ ἐπῶν is meant the science of ἡ ὀρθοέπεια, of which Protagoras and Prodicus were considered masters. Protagoras also advocated a strict division of the genders of nouns, cp. Arist. Rhet. 3. 5 Πρωταγόρας τὰ γένη τῶν ὀνομάτων διῄρει, ἄρρενα καὶ θήλεα καὶ σκεύη. Such studies as these, and the etymological attempts of Cratylus, were of course the new things of the day.

l. 639. ἔγωγε, sc. βούλομαι μανθάνειν.

l. 640. διχοινίκῳ, 'I was cheated of two choenices;' the dat. is strange, but it is really instrumental, as the amount *by which* the cheating was done.

1 Medimnus = 6 ἑκτεῖς = 12 ἡμιεκτέα = 48 χοίνικες, so Strepsiades is able to say, 'wager me (περίδου) if the "semi-sixth" be not a measure of 4,' because the 'semi-sixth' is ½ of ⅙ of 48 choenices, = 4 choenices. Walsh renders neatly, 'Soc. I don't ask that, but what *poetic* measure You like the best—the triple or quadruple? Strep. I think the gallon measure beats them all. Soc. Pooh, nonsense, fellow! Strep. Will you bet me, then, That gallon's not "quadruple" of the quart?'

l. 647. ταχύ γ' ἂν δύναιο, said ironically, 'short work you would make in learning about rhythms!'

l. 649. συνουσίᾳ, 'a party;' cp. Vesp. 1209 προσμάνθανε συμποτικὸς εἶναι καὶ συνουσιαστικός.

l. 651. κατ' ἐνόπλιον, 'suited to the war-tune,' as we might say, 'to the time of a march.' This rhythm was generally based on the anapaest ⏑⏑–, and so distinguished from the rhythm κατὰ δάκτυλον, –⏑⏑. The dactyl was so called because of the one long and two short joints of the finger (δάκτυλος) represented by the one long and two short feet. Strepsiades, mistaking δάκτυλος, as he had mistaken μέτρα, holds up one finger after another, and makes vulgar gestures with them.

l. 655. ᾠζυρέ. The penult. is always long in Homer; but short in Attic; as Arist. Av. 1641; Vesp. 1504; Lysist. 948.

l. 658. πρότερα τούτων, 'before these;' τούτων referring to the difficult lessons of the ἄδικος λόγος.

l. 659. τετραπόδων, a class of animals to which ἀλεκτρύων certainly does not belong.

l. 662. τήν τε θήλειαν, 'you are calling the female and the male alike ἀλεκτρύων.' The word is of common gender, as 'fowl' with us; so for correctness' sake (ὀρθῶς) he proposes to distinguish them as ἀλέκτωρ and ἀλεκτρύαινα, just as we might suggest 'turker' and 'turkess' as a way of distinguishing between cock and hen turkey.

l. 670. τὴν κάρδοπον. The next anomaly is that a noun, shown to be feminine by the gender of the article, should have a masculine termination. In rendering, we must retain the Greek word, otherwise the anomaly disappears in translation; 'you call it ἡ κάρδοπος' (emphasising the last syllable) 'masculine, when it is feminine.' Strep. 'How do I make κάρδοπος masculine?' Soc. 'Of course you do, just as you make Κλεώνυμος.' Strep. 'How is that? tell me.' Soc. 'According to you, κάρδοπος and Κλεώνυμος are identical.' [In gender, that is, as shown by the termination -ος; but Strepsiades does not understand this, and is surprised to hear that the two are identical; so he answers,] 'But, my good sir, Κλεώνυμος [so far from being a κάρδοπος] hadn't got a κάρδοπος at all, but he did his kneading in a round mortar.' We must suppose his kitchen to have been very poorly furnished.

l. 680. ἐκεῖνο δ' ἦν ἄν, 'so it would run then, καρδόπη, Κλεωνύμη.' Strepsiades, having got right as to the termination and gender of καρδόπη, gets into a mess again by turning Κλεώνυμος into Κλεωνύμη, so that he must, as Socrates says, have a lesson about the genders and terminations of proper names (ὀνομάτων).

l. 688. οὐκ ἄρρεν' ὑμῖν ἐστιν; 'are they not masculine in your view?' So Od. 4. 569 καί σφιν γαμβρὸς Διός ἐσσι, 'and *in their eyes* thou art son-in-law of Zeus.'

l. 690. 'Αμυνία. Here the vocative of 'Αμυνίας is identical in termination with a feminine nominative.

l. 693. ἀτὰρ τί ταῦτα, 'but why am I learning these things, which we all know?' Soc. 'That isn't the case at all.' The words οὐδὲν μὰ Δί' seem a strange answer to Strepsiades' question. Perhaps they mean οὐδὲν μανθάνεις ὧν πάντες ἴσμεν, 'you are not learning what everybody knows, but a piece of rare new science.'

l. 696. ἐνταῦθά γε, sc. on the ἀσκάντης, sup. 633. With μὴ δῆθ' supply ἐκφροντίσαι με κέλευσον.

l. 698. οὐκ ἔστι παρὰ ταῦτα ἄλλα, 'there is no other way besides this;' so Plat. Phaedo 107 a οὐκ ἔχω παρὰ ταῦτ' ἄλλο τι λέγειν.

l. 700. σαυτόν, is governed both by στρόβει and πυκνώσας, 'twist yourself in every way, gathering yourself together.' The next words are intended as a sneer at the *desultory* method of the Sophists.

l. 710. Κορίνθιοι is, of course, a surprise for κόρεις. Perhaps we might say 'Bulgarians,' for the sake of the sound.

l. 712. ψυχὴν ἐκπίνουσιν, 'are drinking up my life-blood;' so Soph. El. 785 τοὐμὸν ἐκπίνουσ' ἀεὶ | ψυχῆς ἄκρατον αἷμα.

l. 718. καὶ πῶς; sc. οὐ βαρέως ἀλγεῖν δεῖ;

l. 719. χροιά, 'my complexion;' cp. sup. 504 and inf. 1171. On ἐμβάς see inf. 858, and cf. sup. 103.

l. 721. φρουρᾶς, 'whilst singing at my post,' the gen., like χειμῶνος Av. 1089, or τῆς ἐκκλησίας Plut. 725. With ᾄδων cp. Aesch. Ag. 16, where the sentinel says ἀείδειν ἢ μινύρεσθαι δοκῶ, | ὕπνου τόδ' ἀντίμολπον ἐντέμνων ἄκος. He means here that instead of sleeping he cries out as he is bitten by the κόρεις.

l. 722. **ὀλίγου**, 'almost;' probably a shortened form of the phrase *ὀλίγου* or *μικροῦ δεῖ*, 'it wants little.'

l. 726. **ἀπόλωλα.** Strepsiades says, 'your threat of **ἀπολεῖ** is out of date; I am already destroyed.'

l. 727. **οὐ μαλθακιστέα**, 'you must not be a coward, but must wrap yourself up,' i.e. he must face the *κόρεις*, and tuck himself up in the bedding of the *ἀσκάντης*, so as to concentrate his attention.

l. 729. **τίς ἂν ἐπιβάλοι**, 'who will be so kind as to throw over me a cheating notion out of the sheepskin rugs?' But as **ἀρνακίδων** is intended to suggest *ἀρνεῖσθαι* = 'to repudiate,' we might render 'a dodge for *fleecing*, out of these sheepskins.' Then follow a few moments of silence, during which Strepsiades is supposed to be thinking. After a while, Socrates proposes to peep at him, and see how he is going on.

l. 733. **ἔχεις τι;** in the sense of *ἐξεύρηκάς τι;* The Schol. says it is the regular question put to hunters or fishers, 'have you got anything?'

l. 737. **αὐτός**, emphatic, 'tu ipse primus aliquid inveni, idque mihi expone.' This is the principle of the Socratic method of instruction, to evolve thought from the pupil, rather than to impart knowledge.

l. 740. **σχάσας.** It is difficult to settle the meaning; for *σχάζω* signifies 'to cut,'—sometimes in the sense of 'cutting loose,' sometimes of 'cutting across,' and so 'stopping' or 'checking.' Perhaps the best is 'checking the play of your subtle thought,' like **πυκνώσας** sup. 701. Walsh takes *σχάσας* closely with **λεπτήν**, and renders 'slicing small;' but see sup. 107. **διαιρῶν** is the technical word for logical 'division.'

l. 744. **τὴν γνώμην**, 'in your mind.' An easier reading would be *τῇ γνώμῃ*. 'Then once again set it going in your mind, and lock it up there.' *ζύγωθρον* is the 'bar of a door,' or the 'tongue of a balance;' so the verb *may* mean, as the Schol. suggests, 'to weigh.'

l. 749. **εἰ.** The proper apodosis follows in v. 755 **οὐκ ἂν ἀποδοίην.** With **Θετταλήν** cp. Hor. Epod. 5. 45 'Quae sidera excantata voce Thessala, | lunamque caelo deripit.'

l. 755. **ὁτιὴ τί δή;** This is equivalent to 'quia . . quid?' The idiom arises from the eager desire to anticipate what another is going to say, but, as one does not really know what is coming, the clause has to end in a question. As if we might say, 'Yes, yes, of course, because you would do —— what?' cp. Plut. 135 foll. ΧΡΕΜ. *οὔκουν οὐδ' ἔστιν αἴτιος, καὶ ῥᾳδίως | παύσει' ἄν, εἰ βούλοιτο, ταῦθ';* ΠΛΟ. *ὁτιὴ τί δή;* ΧΡΕΜ. *ὅτι οὐδ' ἂν εἷς θύσειεν ἀνθρώπων ἔτι*, cp. inf. 784.

l. 758. **γράφοιτο**, 'were inscribed' or 'registered.' The first step in a private law-suit was the lodging with the Archon a written complaint, *λῆξις δίκης*. If no objection appeared on the face of the declaration, it was written out on a tablet of wax, or other material, and hung on the wall of the court, as part of the cause-list. It was to this tablet that Strepsiades proposed to apply the burning-glass.

l. 761. **εἶλλε**, 'centre,' 'keep in narrow round.' Here Socrates suggests that Strepsiades must not confine himself to one uniform method of thinking. Join **λινόδετον τοῦ ποδός** as *ἐρύειν τινὰ ποδὸς* Od. 17. 479.

l. 770. **ὁ γραμματεύς**, sc. the Archon's clerk. Here **γράφοιτο** is used in the middle voice, but in sup. 758 in the passive.

l. 771. **ὧδε**, 'like this.' He throws himself into the posture of a man holding a burning-glass.

l. 774. **διαγέγραπται**, 'has been erased;' properly of drawing the pen or style *across* the writing; here he should properly have said, 'obliterated' or 'melted out.'

l. 776. **ἀντιδικῶν** (particip. *ἀντιδικέω*). 'How, as defendant, you would rebut the indictment, when you were going to be cast in the suit, because you had no witnesses on your side.'

l. 779. **ἐνεστώσης** (*ἐνίστημι*, so *ἑστώς* Soph. Aj. 87; *ἑστῶσα* Eccles. 64 for *ἑστηκώς, ἑστηκυῖα*), 'one case still on the list before mine.' With **καλεῖσθ'** cp. Vesp. 1441 *ἕως ἂν τὴν δίκην ἄρχων καλῇ*.

l. 781. **ἔγωγ'**, sc. *λέγω τι*, 'am talking sense;' in answer to sup. **οὐδὲν λέγεις**, 'you are talking nonsense.' Nicias (Eqq. 80 foll.) similarly proposes suicide as a way of escape from trouble.

l. 783. **διδαξαίμην**. The use of the middle voice is peculiar, except in the sense of 'getting some one else taught;' but cp. Plato, Rep. 421 c *χυτρεὺς . . . τοὺς υἱεῖς ἢ ἄλλους οὓς ἂν διδάσκῃ χείρους δημιουργοὺς διδάξεται*. So there is no need to repeat **ἄν**, and to read *οὐκ ἂν διδάξαιμ' ἄν σ' ἔτι*.

l. 784. **ὁτιὴ τί**; see on sup. 755.

l. 785. **ἅττ' ἂν καὶ μάθῃς**, 'whatever you *have* learnt.'

l. 786. **νῦν δή**, as we say, 'just now.' See inf. 825.

l. 788. **ματτόμεθα**. He is trying to recollect his *κάρδοπος* or *καρδόπη*.

l. 789. **οὐκ ἐς κόρακας ἀποφθερεῖ**; a condensed way of saying *οὐκ ἀποφθερούμενος ἐς κόρακας ἄπει*; so in Eqq. 892; cp. Pax 72 *ἐκφθαρεὶς οὐκ οἶδ' ὅποι*, and Demosth. 560. 10 *φθείρεσθαι πρὸς τοὺς πλουσίους*, 'to rush headlong to join the wealthy.'

l. 792. **ἀπὸ γὰρ ὀλοῦμαι**, tmesis for *ἀπολοῦμαι γάρ*, as inf. 1440.

l. 798. **ἀλλ' οὐκ ἐθέλει γάρ**, 'but *since* he does not choose to learn, what am I to be at?' 'what! do you permit [such insubordination]?' 'Yes, for he's vigorous and lusty, and sprung from those high-flown dames of Coesyra's lot.' See on sup. 48.

l. 803. This verse, which bears a suspicious resemblance to inf. 843, must be addressed to Socrates, bidding him to go indoors again and wait a while. This he certainly does not immediately do, as he has to wait while the Chorus address the *ἀντιστροφή* to him, recommending him 'to strike while the iron is hot.' If we might read εἰσελθεῖν, we could construe, 'wait a minute for me to go indoors,' as in Soph. Trach. 1176 καὶ μὴ 'πιμεῖναι τοὐμὸν ὀξῦναι στόμα. But the song of the Chorus seems inconsistent with the context. Socrates had rudely dismissed Strepsiades, who had shown neither readiness nor obedience. Possibly in the first, or acted, edition of the Clouds, Socrates had bidden Strepsiades to fetch his son, and he had joyfully obeyed.

l. 811. γνούς must stand alone, = 'now you know all about it you must lose no time (ταχέως) in sucking out of the man, in his amazement and evident excitement, all the advantage you can.'

l. 814. οὔτοι μὰ τὴν 'Ομίχλην. Strepsiades here adds a fourth deity, 'Mist,' to the three by whom Socrates swore sup. 627. He comes from the house on to the stage with Pheidippides, threatening to turn him out of doors, and bidding him go to the house of his poor. proud uncle, and fill his belly by eating the columns, the only remains of the former wealth and magnificence of the family.

l. 817. τὸν Δίᾱ. Probably the α is long, as in Lysistr. 24 καὶ νὴ Δίᾱ παχύ.

l. 819. τὸ . . νομίζειν, see sup. 268. τηλικουτονί may be compared with sup. 799 εὐσωματεῖ καὶ σφριγᾷ.

l. 821. φρονεῖς ἀρχαικά, 'have old-fashioned notions.' Here παιδάριον has special reference to the full-grown man' (ἀνήρ) below.

l. 824. ὅπως δέ, 'but mind you don't teach anyone this.' So said the μαθητής sup. 143.

l. 828. Δῖνος, see on sup. 380 foll.

l. 830. ὁ Μήλιος. Socrates himself was not from Melos, but the atheistic philosopher (ὁ ἄθεος) Diagoras was; so to call Socrates 'the Melian' was to call him by implication an atheist. Similarly, Amynias, who was really son of Pronapus, is called (Vesp. 1267) ὁ Σέλλου, because he was as poor as Aeschines, son of Sellus.

l. 832. μανιῶν, so the plural is used, Pax 65 παράδειγμα τῶν μανιῶν, Thesmoph. 689 μανίαις φλέγων, Eur. Heracl. 904 ἐγγὺς μανιῶν ἐλαύνει.

l. 833. χολῶσιν; According to the Schol. χολᾶν παρὰ τοῖς 'Αττικοῖς τὸ μαίνεσθαι, παρὰ δὲ τοῖς κοινοῖς τὸ θυμοῦσθαι. Similarly μελαγχολᾶν is used of madness.

l. 837. ἐς βαλανεῖον. The Socratic philosophers are here represented as abstaining from the warm bath from being too stingy to pay the trifling fee (ἐπίλουτρον). Cp. Av. 1282 ἐκόμων, ἐπείνων, ἐρρύπων, ἐσωκράτουν.

l. 838. καταλόει (2nd pers. pres. mid.). With this form cp. λόεον Od. 4. 252, λόε ib. 10. 361, and λόεσθαι Hes. Op. 747. The word is intended to have a reference back to the βαλανεῖον and its expenses, and (as suggested by ὥσπερ τεθνεῶτος) to the practice of washing a corpse; so that βίον comes in at the end of the line as a surprise; 'but you, as though I were already dead, are washing away at my —— livelihood.' Cp. Plaut. Trinum. 406 'argentum —— comessum, expotum, exunctum, *elutum in balineis.*'

l. 839. **ὑπέρ** in the sense of *ἀντί*, sup. 796.

l. 840. **καὶ μάθοι .. ἄν**, '*could* one learn?'

l. 841. **ἄληθες**; when so accented implies surprise and annoyance in the questioner, 'are you in earnest?' 'do you really mean that?' The word is frequent in Aristoph., cp. also Soph. O. R. 350; Ant. 758.

l. 844. Strepsiades runs indoors to fetch a cock and a hen, while Pheidippides soliloquizes on his father's craziness.

l. 845. **εἰσαγαγών**, 'having brought the case into court.' The full term is *εἰσάγειν δίκην* or *γραφήν*. Join **παρανοίας** **ἕλω**, 'am I to convict him of madness?' So sup. 591 *δώρων ἑλόντες*. Cp. Xen. Memor. I. 2, 49 *φάσκων κατὰ νόμον ἐξεῖναι* **παρανοίας ἑλόντι καὶ τὸν πατέρα δῆσαι.** 'Or am I to take for granted that he is near his end,' says Pheidippides, 'and to order him a coffin?'

l. 853. **παρὰ τοὺς γηγενεῖς**, 'to join those Sons of Earth.' Comparing Eur. Ion 987 foll. *οἶσθα γηγενῆ μάχην; .... οἶδ' ἣν γίγαντες ἔστησαν θεοῖς*, we may suppose that Pheidippides meant to describe these philosophers as *θεομάχοι* and *ἄθεοι*. But very likely there is a further reference to the subterranean *φροντιστήριον* where they dwelt. Cp. sup. 507.

l. 855. **ἐπελανθανόμην ἄν**. For this use of the imperf. indic. with *ἄν* to denote repeated occurrences cp. sup. 54, Vesp. 268 *οὐ μὴν πρὸ τοῦ γ' ἐφολκὸς ἦν, ἀλλὰ πρῶτος ἡμῶν* | **ἡγεῖτ' ἂν** *ᾄδων* **Φρυνίχου**, Aves 520 **ὤμνυ** *τ' οὐδεὶς τότ'* **ἂν** *ἀνθρώπων θεόν.*

l. 856. **θοἰμάτιον**, see sup. 497, inf. 1498.

l. 857. **καταπεφρόντικα**, 'have thought it away.' Cp. *χρῆσθαι ταῖς φιλίαις οὐ* **καταχρῆσθαι**, Synes. 206 a, = 'misuse.'

l. 858. **ποῖ τέτροφας**; 'to what purpose have you turned?' We must refer the form to *τρέπω*, not *τρέφω*, as in Soph. Trach. 1008 *ἀνατέτροφας ὅ τι καὶ μύσῃ*, where the Schol. interprets by *ἀνέτρεψας*. Cf. Vesp. 665 **ποῖ τρέπεται** *τὰ χρήματα τἄλλα*; For **ἐμβάδας** cp. sup. 718.

l. 859. **ὥσπερ Περικλέης**, 'like Pericles, for a "necessary purpose" I have —— lost them.' Pericles was said to have induced Cleandridas, the counsellor of the Lacedaemonian king Pleistoanax, to withdraw his army from Attica (in B.C. 445), by a bribe of ten talents. The only account he gave to the people of the transaction was *ἐς τὸ δέον ἀνήλωσα*, which phrase Strepsiades adopts, substituting as a surprise **ἀπώλεσα** for *ἀνήλωσα*.

l. 860. **εἶτα τῷ πατρί**, 'and then, when you've once complied with your father, be as naughty as you like. I know very well how I complied with your wishes when you were a lisping child of six years old.' This punctuation joins **οἶδα** directly with **πιθόμενος**, but we may stop οἶδ' off between commas, 'I too once (I know) complying with you, bought you, etc.'

l. 863. Ἡλιαστικόν. The fee to each Ἡλιαστής for his day's service was at this time three obols. It had originally been only one obol, but had been augmented by Cleon. Cp. Plut. 329 *τριωβόλου μὲν οὕνεκα | ὠστιζόμεσθ' ἑκάστοτ' ἐν τἠκκλησίᾳ.*

l. 869. κρεμαθρῶν. Socrates would naturally have said *οὐ τρίβων* ('not versed in') τῶν μαθημάτων, but substitutes for it κρεμαθρῶν, referring to his own 'baskets' or 'hoists,' sup. 217. The word suggests to Pheidippides the being 'hoisted up' for a flogging; and he plays upon the word τρίβων, which means 'a well-worn cloke.' Perhaps we might render, 'he hasn't yet learned to rub along with our hoists.' PHEID. 'You'd have the nap well rubbed off you, if you were hoisted up.'

l. 872. ἰδοὺ κρέμαι', 'hark at his "were hoi-i-isted!"' The sneer is at his pronunciation of κρέμαιο, in which he appears to have given the diphthong *αι* full and broad, instead of toning it down to something more like *α*. So the Attics preferred to write *κλάειν* for *κλαίειν*, *κάειν* for *καίειν*.

l. 874. ἀπόφευξιν. The would-be orator is regarded from three points of view: if he is a defendant, he must understand the principles of 'Acquittal;' if a plaintiff, the right method of the 'Summons;' if an advocate, the art of 'convincing Nullification.' In the last bombastic expression χαύνωσις means the invalidation or dissolution of the arguments on the other side, put in such a convincing shape as to carry the judges with it.

l. 876. καί τοι, i.e. even Hyperbolus, though he was such a dullard; so that after all there is hope for Pheidippides.

l. 881. πῶς δοκεῖς, properly = 'how think you?' But as an idiom it has lost its interrogatival force, and means only here 'you can't think how [prettily].' So Acharn. 24 *ὠστιοῦνται πῶς δοκεῖς*, Eur. Hippol. 446 *τοῦτον λαβοῦσα* (sc. *Κύπρις*) *πῶς δοκεῖς καθύβρισεν*. Cp. Ran. 54 *πόθος τὴν καρδίαν ἐπάταξε πῶς οἴει σφόδρα ;*

l. 883. = sup. 113.

l. 885. πάσῃ τέχνῃ, 'by all manner of means.'

l. 888. While the actors who are representing Strepsiades and Socrates retire behind the scenes to change their dresses, and to reappear in the characters of Just and Unjust Argument, the Chorus would naturally address themselves to Pheidippides, so as to fill up the interval. But even in the time of the Scholiast the passage was wanting; having probably been left incomplete, when the author was preparing the second edition of the play for the stage. The scene of the two *Λόγοι* touting for young Pheidippides, is like the competition between Εὐδαιμονία (or Κακία) and Ἀρετή in the story of the Choice of Heracles (Xen. Mem. 2. 1, 21 foll.). Δίκαιος Λόγος, in the plain dress of a simple old man, represents the Morality of the Good Old Times; Ἄδικος, got up as a fop of the period, serves to picture Immorality, as shown in the modern style. Similarly, in the lost Antiope of Euripides, Zethus represented the spirit of the early days of Hellas, and Amphion the habits a later age.

l. 892. ἐν τοῖς πολλοῖσι, 'before this large audience.' So Eur. Hipp. 610 *τά τοι κάλ' ἐν πολλοῖσι κάλλιον λέγειν.*

l. 894. σε νικῶ, 'I'm your master.'

l. 897. διὰ τουτουσί, 'thanks to those gentry yonder;' pointing to the spectators in the theatre, whose want of sense has led to this craze for novelties.

l. 901. αὔτ', i.e. *αὐτά*, sc. *τὰ δίκαια*. The accent is thrown back by the elision.

l. 903. παρὰ τοῖσι θεοῖς, cp. Soph. O. C. 1381 *ἡ παλαίφατος | Δίκη ξύνεδρος Ζηνὸς ἀρχαίοις νόμοις.*

l. 905. πατέρα. Cp. Aesch. Eum. 641 *αὐτὸς δ' ἔδησε πατέρα, πρεσβύτην Κρόνον.*

l. 907. χωρεῖ, 'advances,' 'spreads;' so sup. 18. Cp. *οὐ χωρεῖ τοὔργον* Pax 472. λεκάνην, he wants to be sick: cp. Acharn. 585 *τῆς κεφαλῆς νύν μου λαβοῦ, | ἵν' ἐξεμέσω· βδελύττομαι γὰρ τοὺς λόφους.*

l. 910. ῥόδα μ' εἴρηκας, so the double accus. in Eur. Alc. 954 *ἐρεῖ δέ μ' ὅστις ἐχθρὸς ὢν κυρεῖ τάδε.*

l. 912. χρυσῷ. In a similar sense *εὐθὺς κατεχρύσου πᾶς ἀνὴρ Εὐριπίδην* Eccles. 826. Cp. Plaut. Asin. 1. 3, 3 'quae tu in nos dicis aurum atque argentum merumst.'

l. 913. ἀλλὰ μολύβδῳ, sc. *ἔπαττόν σε*, 'ay! but it wasn't gold but lead that I dusted thee with a while ago.' It is commonly assumed that as lead is a base metal it only serves here to mark the contrast to gold, as though he had said—'Well, such words as this used to be looked upon as something very unlike praise.' But if there is sufficient ground for believing that refractory slaves were beaten with a lash loaded with lead, it will make it more pointed for the *Δίκαιος Λόγος* to say (with reference to the days when he was paramount, and the Ἄδικος was kept well in control), 'Ay, but in bygone days I used to dust you with the loaded lash;' to which the upstart Ἄδικος Λόγος answers, 'Yes, and all that redounds the more to my glory now.'

l. 915. πολλοῦ, 'exceedingly;' like *ὀλίγου, μικροῦ.*

l. 916. φοιτᾶν, in the technical sense of 'going to school;' so Eqq. 1235 *ἐφοίτας ἐς τίνος διδασκάλου;*

l. 921. εὖ πράττεις, 'art in good case.'

l. 920. πρότερον. 'In the good old days you had no occupation, but you went about cadging with a beggar's wallet on your back, like Telephus, nibbling from it, not broken victuals, but maxims worthy of the sycophant Pandeletus.' Telephus king of Mysia had been wounded by the spear of Achilles, and as only the same weapon could work the cure, he had to wander about in disguise till he fell in with Achilles, who healed him. Telephus was a stock character with Euripides, and a favourite butt for the wit of Aristophanes.

l. 925. **ὤμοι σοφίας.** Both the *Λόγοι* cry out in the same breath. The *Ἄδικος* says (with a fond regret), 'Ah me, for that cleverness (sc. of Telephus) which you have called to mind!' The *Δίκαιος* (with stern indignation), 'Ah me, for that madness of thine and of the city which is rearing thee as a curse to our growing lads!'

l. 929. **τοῦτον**, sc. Pheidippides.

l. 932. **δεῦρ' ἴθι.** The *Ἄδικος* is about to draw Pheidippides to his side; but the *Δίκαιος* hinders him, and they nearly come to blows.

l. 937. **ὅπως ἂν ἀκούσας.** 'that when he has listened to you both he may make his choice and attend his master.'

l. 945. **ἢν ἀναγρύξῃ.** 'if he do but mutter a syllable,' Eqq. 294 *διαφορήσω σ', εἴ τι γρύξει.* The order of the next words is *ὥσπερ ὑπ' ἀνθρηνῶν κεντούμενος . . ἀπολεῖται ὑπὸ τῶν γνωμῶν.*

l. 954. **λέγων**, 'in wordy warfare.'

l. 955. **νῦν γὰρ ἅπας**, 'for now on this very stage (**ἐνθάδε**) there is set going every form of danger to wisdom, on whose behalf the sorest contest is being engaged in by my friends.' This meaning of the passive **ἀνεῖται** comes through such phrases as *ἀνιέναι τὰς κύνας* Xen. Cyn. 7. 7. Cp. Ran. 882 *νῦν γὰρ ἀγὼν σοφίας ὁ μέγας χωρεῖ πρὸς ἔργον ἤδη.*

l. 960. **ῥῆξον φωνήν**, cp. sup. 357.

l. 962. **ἐνενόμιστο**, 'was believed in,' analogous to the phrase *νομίζειν θεούς.*

l. 963. **παιδός.** Compare the old saying, 'Little boys should be seen and not heard.' So Xen. de Rep. Lac., of the young Spartans, *ἐκείνων ἧττον ἂν φωνὴν ἀκούσαις ἢ τῶν λιθίνων.*

l. 964. **ἐν ταῖς ὁδοῖς.** So Plato, Charm. 159 b *σωφροσύνη εἶναι . . τὸ ἡσυχῇ ἔν τε ταῖς ὁδοῖς βαδίζειν καὶ διαλέγεσθαι.* The Athenian boys would learn reading and writing from the *γραμματιστής* till the age of 13, when the *κιθαριστής* would take up their education. Plat. Legg. 7. 809 e. There were no public schools, but the youths from the same quarter or ward (**κωμήτας**) would naturally attend the same masters; and when they had reached the class-room, there was the same orderly 'standing at attention,' without fidgetting or crossing the legs; while they learned such fine old 'national anthems' as the 'Pallas' of Lamprocles (476 B.C.); or the 'Loud strain of the Lyre,' by Cydides.

l. 969. **ἐντειναμένους τὴν ἁρμονίαν** seems to mean 'keeping up the key.' **ἁρμονία** is not equivalent to the modern use of 'harmony,' but rather to the 'style' or 'key.' The national *ἁρμονία* here referred to is the Doric (ἡ Δωριστί), the calmest and most serious style (*σταστιμωτάτη οὖσα καὶ μάλιστ' ἦθος ἔχουσα ἀνδρεῖον . . . φανερὸν ὅτι τὰ Δώρια μέλη πρέπει παιδεύεσθαι μᾶλλον τοῖς νεωτέροις* Arist. Pol. 8. 7, 8). The Phrygian mode (ἡ Φρυγιστί) was a more passionate and excited style (*ὀργιαστικὰ καὶ παθητικά* ib.); the Lydian (ἡ Λυδιστί) was the most plaintive and tender, and suited to soprano and treble voices (*πρέπει τῇ τῶν παίδων ἡλικίᾳ* ib). Plato, Lach. 188 d, calls ἡ Δωριστί the only true Ἑλληνικὴ ἁρμονία.

l. 970. **εἰ δέ τις αὐτῶν**, 'but if any one of them should play the buffoon, or start any of those flourishes, such as musicians now-a-days affect, those intricate flourishes *à la* Phrynis, he got well drubbed, being beaten with many stripes, for spoiling good music.' Phrynis of Mitylene is represented as having ruined the fine old music of Terpander by introducing a florid and effeminate style.

l. 982. **τῶν πρεσβυτέρων ἁρπάζειν**, 'to snatch it away before their elders (could get it).' The genitive follows the common construction with verbs of overcoming, forestalling, etc., so *προλαβεῖν τί τινος* in Lucian: cp. Soph. Ant. 297 *οὔποτ' ἔκ γ' ἐμοῦ | τιμὴν προέξουσ' οἱ κακοὶ τῶν ἐνδίκων*, i. e. 'rather than the just.'

l. 983. **κιχλίζειν** (from *κίχλη*, 'a thrush') is variously rendered—'to eat dainties,' the thrush being a delicacy; or 'to giggle,' with reference to the chuckling note of the bird.

l. 984. The **Διπόλια** was an ancient festival in honour of **Ζεὺς Πολιεύς**, the **Βουφόνια**, or 'slaughter of the ox,' was a part of the ceremonial. With **τεττίγων ἀνάμεστα** cp. Eqq. 1331 *τεττιγοφόρας, ἀρχαίῳ σχήματι λαμπρός*, Thuc. 1. 6 *οἱ πρεσβύτεροι τῶν εὐδαιμόνων* (sc. Ἀθηναίων) *οὐ πολὺς χρόνος ἐπειδὴ . . ἐπαύσαντο . . χρυσῶν τεττίγων ἐνέρσει κρώβυλον ἀναδούμενοι τῶν ἐν τῇ κεφαλῇ τριχῶν*. They chose the Cicada as their symbol, because they believed it to be, like themselves, indigenous to the soil (*αὐτόχθων*). **Κηκείδης** was an old dithyrambic poet.

l. 986. **ἱματίοισι**, contrasted with **γυμνούς**, sup. 965.

l. 992. **φλέγεσθαι**, 'to flare up.'

l. 993. **ὑπανίστασθαι**, cp. *ὑπαναστάσεις*, 'rising up from one's seat to make room for another,' Plato, Rep. 425 b.

l. 995. **ὅτι τῆς Αἰδοῦς**, 'because thou art going to model anew the pattern of Honour,' sc. by exemplifying it in thy life. Cp. Plat. Symp. 228 *εὑρήσει* (*τοὺς λόγους*) *θειοτάτους καὶ πλεῖστ' ἀγάλματα ἀρετῆς ἐν αὐτοῖς ἔχοντας*. Another reading is *ὅ τι τῆς Αἰδοῦς μέλλει τἄγαλμ' ἀναπλήσειν*, 'which is likely to corrupt the pattern of Honour.' So *ἀναπλέως*, 'infected,' Plat. Phaedo 83 d.

l. 997. **μήλῳ βληθείς**, cp. Virg. Ecl. 3. 64 'malo me Galatea petit, lasciva puella.' **ἀποθρανσθῇς**, as though the apple had given you a 'knock-down blow.'

l. 998. **Ἰαπετόν**, brother of *Κρόνος*, sup. 929; we may say, 'Methuselah.' This seems to settle the meaning of **ἡλικίαν** in the next line; cp. Il. 22. 419 *ἤν πως ἡλικίην αἰδέσσεται ἠδ' ἐλεήσῃ γῆρας*. You are not 'to spite your father for his years,' though they make him unsympathetic with you now; for the years that have made *him* old, were those that he spent in rearing *you* from childhood upwards.

l. 1001. **υἱέσιν**. There is said to be an intentional pun between this form and *ὑσίν*, 'hogs,' the sons of Hippocrates being swinishly dull. **καλοῦσιν** is the contracted future, parallel to **εἴξεις**, 'thou wilt be like.'

l. 1003. **τριβολ-εκτράπελα**, perhaps = 'far-fetched subtleties.' As specimens of the conversation of the *jeunesse dorée* in the days of Aristophanes cp. Eqq. 1375 foll. *τὰ μειράκια ταυτὶ λέγω, τἀν τῷ μύρῳ* (perfumers' shops), *ἃ στωμυλεῖται τοιαδὶ καθήμενα· | σοφός γ' ὁ Φαίαξ δεξιῶς τ' οὖν ἀπέθανε. | συνερκτικὸς γάρ ἐστι καὶ περαντικός, | καὶ γνωμοτυπικὸς καὶ σαφὴς καὶ κρουστικός, | καταληπτικός τ' ἄριστα τοῦ θορυβητικοῦ.*

l. 1004. **ἑλκόμενος**, 'getting dragged into court.'

l. 1005. The grounds of the **Ἀκαδήμεια** were on the Cephisus, a mile north of Athens. Cimon had laid out the walks and planted them. Round the altar of Athena that stood there was the group of sacred olive trees (**μορίαι**). The white reed formed the regular garland of the twin Dioscuri, the types of manly vigour; the **μῖλαξ** may be our 'convolvulus.' The list of leaves and flowers is amusingly interrupted by **ἀπραγμοσύνης**, 'idleness.' Some would make it the name of a flower, e. g. 'hearts-ease,' but cp. Vesp. 1059 *ὀζήσει δεξιότητος*. Similarly, Tennyson, Maud, 6. 6 'smelling of musk and of insolence.'

l. 1007. **λεύκη**, the 'white-poplar,' is the tree sacred to Heracles. The epithet is doubtful; perhaps it is 'that tosses its leaves,' a characteristic of the aspens; or 'that sheds its leaves (lovingly) over you;' cp. Hor. Od. 3. 18, 14 'Spargit agrestes tibi silva frondes.'

l. 1012. **χροιὰν λευκήν**, 'a clear skin.'

l. 1018. **ψήφισμα μακρόν**, comes in as a surprise in the list of personal qualities, 'a long-winded bill.'

l. 1019. **ἀναπείσει**, the subject is *ὁ Ἄδικος Λόγος*, as also to **ἀναπλήσει** inf.

l. 1022. The Schol. speaks of Antimachus as a scoundrel, 'femininely fair, and dissolutely pale.'

l. 1025. **καλλίπυργον**, 'lofty.' So Aesch. Supp. 96 *ἐλπίδες καλλίπυργοι*.

l. 1031. **σε**, sc. *τὸν Ἄδικον Λόγον*, who must now produce something to cap the excellent remarks of the *Δίκαιος*.

l. 1032. **ἔοικε δεῖν σοι**, 'it looks as if you wanted.' **ὑπερβαλεῖ**, 2 sing. fut. mid.

l. 1036. **ἐπνιγόμην τὰ σπλάγχνα**, 'my heart was like to choke.'

l. 1040. **νόμοι** and **δίκαι** are the equivalents of *leges* and *iura*.

l. 1041. καὶ τοῦτο πλεῖν [Attic for πλέον], 'and this is worth more than 10,000 staters, that a man though choosing the worse arguments should after all [ἔπειτα] win.' The Athenian gold στατήρ was worth 20 drachmae. But the allusion may be to the silver στατήρ, worth four drachmae.

l. 1043. σκέψαι, addressed to Pheidippides; but ψέγεις inf. refers to the Δίκαιος. The return to πρῶτον is at εἶτα 1055.

l. 1047. εὐθὺς γάρ σε, 'for there at once I've got you round the waist, having caught you so that you can't escape.' Cp. Ach. 571 ἐγὼ γὰρ ἔχομαι μέσος.

l. 1051. Ἡράκλεια λουτρά; The story ran that Athene made the hot springs at Thermopylae burst forth to refresh Heracles, when exhausted with his labours, as Peisander tells, τῷ δ' ἐν Θερμοπύλῃσι θεὰ γλαυκῶπις Ἀθήνη | ποίει θερμὰ λοετρὰ παρὰ ῥηγμῖνι θαλάσσης. In after times natural hot springs went by the general name of Ἡ. λ.

l. 1058. ἀγορητήν. It is necessary to keep the play upon ἀγορᾷ, so we may say 'public places' and 'public speaker.' Cp. Hom. Il. 1. 247 τοῖσι δὲ Νέστωρ | ἡδυεπὴς ἀνόρουσε, λιγὺς Πυλίων ἀγορητής. By σοφούς he means such men as Odysseus, who are famed in Homer for their eloquence.

l. 1063. πολλοῖς, sc. διὰ τὸ σωφρονεῖν ἀγαθὸν ἐγένετο. For the case of Πηλεύς cp. Hor. Od. 3. 7. 17 'narrat paene datum Pelea Tartaro | Magnessam Hippolyten dum fugit abstinens.' Peleus had been rewarded by the Gods, for his chastity in resisting the advances of Hippolyte, with the present of the famous sword (τὴν μάχαιραν), that could cut through everything. But, like Potiphar's wife, Hippolyte slandered Peleus to her husband Acastus, who stole the sword, and left the man defenceless in the midst of dangers.

l. 1064. ἀστεῖον, ironically, as χρηστός, sup. 8, 'fine,' 'pretty.'

l. 1065. οὐκ [ὁ ἐκ] τῶν λύχνων, 'the man from the lampmarket.' Cp. Eqq. 1315 Ὑπέρβολος . . ἐπώλει τοὺς λύχνους. With τὰ λύχνα, 'lamp-market,' cp. τὰ ὄρνεα, 'bird-market,' Av. 13; οἱ ἰχθύες, 'fish-market,' Vesp. 789.

l. 1072. ἅνεστιν, i. e. ἃ ἔνεστιν.

l. 1076. ἐμοίχευσάς τι. The addition of τι seems to treat the escapade very lightly, as we say, 'a bit of' so and so.

l. 1078. χρῶ, i. e. 'indulge,' as Hdt. 1. 137 τῷ θυμῷ χρᾶται.

l. 1079. πρὸς αὐτόν, 'to the injured husband.'

l. 1080. ἐπανενεγκεῖν, with the force of an imperative, 'refer to Zeus;' cp. Eur. Ion 827 ἀλοὺς μὲν ἀνέφερ' ἐς τὸν δαίμονα, '[saying] how he too is the slave of love,' etc.

l. 1103. ἡττήμεθα. The Δίκαιος Λόγος is fairly beaten. The theatre is all on the side of Ἄδικος. There is nothing left to do, but to toss his cloak to the audience, and spring down as if to join them, and run off at a side door.

l. 1105. We must suppose that Socrates returns on the stage and undertakes the education of Pheidippides. But the scene comes in very awkwardly. If, as is commonly held, the contest between the two Λόγοι belongs to the second edition only of the play, we may suppose that the right place for l. 1105 is immediately after 881, from which it has been severed by the insertion of the scene of the Λόγοι, the final harmonising of the whole having never been completed.

l. 1108. **στομώσεις.** The technical meaning of *στομοῦν* is to 'give an edge to,' see inf. 1160; here too it has of course a reference to powers of talk; 'sharpen him on the one side (**ἐπὶ τὰ ἕτερα**) to be fit for petty suits;' with **οἷαν δικιδίοις** cp. Thuc. 6. 12 *τὸ πρᾶγμα μέγα εἶναι καὶ μὴ οἷον νεωτέρῳ*, Plat. Euthyd. 272 a *λόγους οἵους εἰς τὰ δικαστήρια*. The commoner construction after *οἷος* is the infinitive.

l. 1112. **ὠχρὸν μὲν οὖν.** This is better written as an 'aside' of Pheidippides than put into the mouth of Strepsiades. 'Nay rather, you'll get (your son) back a ghastly and miserable creature.' Cp. sup. 103, 120, inf. 1171.

l. 1115. **τοὺς κριτάς,** 'the judges,' who had to decide on the merits of the rival poets. The accusative, in strict grammar, is the object to **φράσαι.** 'We wish to point out to the judges, viz. what advantages they will gain, if they support this our chorus, as justice demands.' This anticipation of the accusative, as object in the main clause, instead of subject in the subordinate, is a frequent idiom with verbs of 'perceiving' or 'telling.' Cp. inf. 1148, Soph. Aj. 118 *ὁρᾷς Ὀδυσσεῦ τὴν θεῶν ἰσχὺν ὅση*, Eur. Temen. frag. 9. *γνῶναι τὸν ἐχθρὸν ᾗ μάλισθ' ἁλώσιμος.*

l. 1125. **σφενδόναις,** sc. with the 'flail of the flashing hail.'

l. 1126. Join **τὸν κέραμον τοῦ τέγους αὐτοῦ,** 'the tile-work of his roof.'

l. 1129. **ὕσομεν τὴν νύκτα.** Such heavy rain would mar the bridal procession and extinguish the torches, so that the ill-advised judge would in his despair wish his home was in Egypt, where at any rate there was no rain.

l. 1131. Strepsiades, true to his promise, sup. 669, reappears on the stage with a sack of meal (**τουτονί** 1146) upon his shoulders. Then he stands and anxiously reckons up on his fingers the few last days of the month—26th, 27th, 28th, 29th, etc. The days of the third decade of the Athenian month might be reckoned backwards, viz. the last day = *ἕνη καὶ νέα*, 29th = *δευτέρα φθίνοντος* [sc. *μηνός*, 'of the waning month], 28th = *τρίτη φ.*, 27th = *τετράς φ.*, 26th = *πέμπτη φ.* The name ἕνη (cp. Lat. *sen-ex*) **καὶ νέα** = 'old-and-new,' was given by Solon to the last day of the month, because the first half of it was reckoned as belonging to the end of an old month, and the latter half to the beginning of the new. The next day was called **νουμηνία,** marking not the actual astronomical conjunction of sun and moon, but the day on which the thin edge of the new moon was first visible in the evening sky.

l. 1135. ὀμνύς (rather than ὄμνυσ', the commoner reading), goes directly with φησί, 'iurans dicit se me perditurum esse deposito sacramento.' The πρυτανεῖα are the sums deposited by either party before the law-suit began; 'staking his deposits against me.' 'And when I make a modest and fair request, "my good sir, there's a part of my debt you mustn't take now; and part you must defer my payment of; and part you must remit altogether," they declare they shall never get their money back like that, but they revile me, on the ground that I am dishonest, and they say they'll have the law of me!' δικάσασθαι, with the MSS., and not δικάσεσθαι, as sup. 35; cp. Od. 2. 137 φημὶ τελευτηθῆναι, not τελευτήσεσθαι.

l. 1146. τουτονί. See sup. 1131.

l. 1147. ἐπιθαυμάζειν, 'to compliment:' give a 'honorarium;' a sort of euphemism for μισθὸν δοῦναι.

l. 1148. καί μοι τὸν υἱόν, see on sup. 1115, 'and tell me of that son of mine whom you just took indoors, whether he has learned that famous argument.' The antecedent to ὅν is υἱόν, and not λόγον, cp. Plat. Symp. 177 a οὐκ ἐμὸς ὁ μῦθος ἀλλὰ Φαίδρου τοῦδε ὃν μέλλω λέγειν.

l. 1154. βοάσομαι τἄρα, a parody from the Πηλεύς of Euripides. Strepsiades in his wild delight breaks into tragic metre and dialect.

l. 1156. τὰ ἀρχαῖα, 'the original sum,' i.e. the capital. To claim τόκοι τόκων (i.e. ἀνατοκισμός or 'compound interest') was not forbidden by Athenian law, but it was looked upon as mean and grasping.

l. 1158. οἷος, with the force of ὅτι τοῖος, 'seeing that so clever a son is being reared for me.'

l. 1164. ὡς ἐμέ, 'to me.' Join κάλεσον ἔνδοθεν.

l. 1170. ἰοῦ. The Schol., on Pax 316, makes ἰοῦ a shout of joy; and ἰού (oxytone) a cry of woe.

l. 1171. Strepsiades dances round his son, shouting 'huzza,' to see the true philosophic pallor (χροιάν) on his face; 'and now,' he says, 'you have for the first time in your life, a repudiative and contradictious look, and there is positively in full bloom upon you that true native boldness [that seems to ask] "what's that you say?" and the appearance of being cheated while you are the cheat and the knave.—I know that right well; and on your face is the real Attic look.' By τὸ τί λέγεις σύ; he refers to the characteristic captiousness of the Athenians, who would wrangle and dispute on every question. οἶδ' ὅτι stands out of the construction, like πῶς δοκεῖς sup. 881. With Ἀττικὸν βλέπος cp. Horace's 'frons urbana' Ep. 1. 9, 11.

l. 1177. νῦν οὖν, 'now then, see that you save me, since *you it was* (καί) that destroyed me.'

l. 1179. Pheidippides, of course, knows all about the ἕνη τε καὶ νέα, but he at once begins to air his sophistries, and to ask, 'What, can there be an "old-and-new"?' 'Yes,' his father answers, 'a certain day so-called, against which my creditors declare that they will lodge me their deposits.' 'All right,' says Pheidippides, 'then the depositors will lose them, for it is impossible for one day to become two days;' and so his argument is that the depositors will be found not to have lodged their money for *any one definite* day; so that their whole action will be invalid.

l. 1187. **ὁ Σόλων.** When Pheidippides makes the general remark that 'Solon was the people's friend,' his father naturally says, 'this has nothing to do so far (πω) with the "Old-and-New."' 'Yes it has,' says the son, 'and so he put the summons for a brace of days, viz. for the "Old-and-New," so that the deposits might be lodged on the New Moon.' 'Why,' asks Strepsiades, 'did he add that back-day (**τὴν ἕνην**) instead of having it all settled on the **νουμηνία**?' 'O,' says the youth, 'to give a *locus poenitentiae* to the defendants.' They would have a whole day to think over their position after the issuing of the summons, because the *real* work of the case did not begin till the *θέσεις* were lodged on the *νουμηνία*: 'so that they might voluntarily make a compromise one day sooner, or, failing that, might begin their bother the first thing in the morning on the New Moon.' With **ἵνα δὴ τί** sc. *γένοιτο*; lit. 'in order that what might happen?' cp. Pax 409 *ἵνα τί δὲ τοῦτο δρᾶτον*; Plat. Apol. 26. c *ἵνα τί ταῦτα λέγεις*;

l. 1196. **ἀρχαί,** i.e. *αἱ ἀρχαί = οἱ ἄρχοντες.* 'Why then do the magistrates refuse to take the deposits on the New Moon, but [insist on having them] on the Old-and-New?' 'Why, they seem to me to act like the forestallers: in order that they may bag the fees as soon as possible, they therefore forestalled them by one day.' Whether by the **προτένθαι** is here meant only 'gourmands,' who buy up dainties before they come into the open market; or whether the allusion is to a board at Athens whose duty was to taste and pronounce satisfactory the meats to be offered in sacrifice, it makes no difference to the illustration. The whole pretended argument is intentionally ridiculous.

l. 1201. **εὖ γ',** 'bravo!' Then Strepsiades turns to the impassive audience and rates them soundly for not sharing in his triumph.

l. 1202. **ἡμέτερα κέρδη τῶν σοφῶν,** where *ἡμέτερα* is equivalent to *ἡμῶν*, with which *τῶν σοφῶν* may be regarded in apposition. So in Plato, *ἡ ὑμετέρα τῶν σοφιστῶν τέχνη ἐπιδέδωκεν*, and the common Latin usage, *mea ipsius sententia*, etc.

l. 1203. **ἀριθμός,** 'a string of units, merely a drove of sheep;' cp. Eur. Troad. 476 *ἀριστεύοντ' ἐγεινάμην τέκνα, οὐκ ἀριθμὸν ἄλλως*: Hor. Ep. 1. 2, 27 'nos numerus sumus.' With **ἄλλως** cp. Eur. Hec. 489 *δόξαν ἄλλως*. By **ἀμφορῆς νενησμένοι** he means that the audience, rising motionless row behind row, look like a lot of 'wine-jars stacked up.'

l. 1205. **μοὐγκώμιον,** i.e. *ᾀστέον μοι ἐγκώμιον*, 'I must sing a song of triumph over this good luck.'

l. 1211. Join νικᾷς δίκας, 'win your suits by power of speaking.'

l. 1214. Exeunt Strepsiades and Pheidippides. Enter Pasias (sup. 81), a pot-bellied (inf. 1237) usurer, accompanied by a witness (1218), who however takes no part in the dialogue (κωφὸν πρόσωπον).

l. 1215. τότε, 'long ago,' referring back to the time when Strepsiades first asked for a loan, 'then it would have been better to have unblushingly refused, than to get all this trouble, while I am dragging you here to give evidence about my money, and besides this I am going to be disagreeable to a man of my own hamlet,' sc. Strepsiades.

l. 1221. καλοῦμαι = προσκαλοῦμαι, 'in ius voco,' 'summons.' He raises his voice, and Strepsiades hears him within the house, and comes out crying, 'who is this?' thus interrupting Pasias, who goes on—'summons him, I say, for the "Old-and-New."'

l. 1223. τοῦ χρήματος; sup. 22.

l. 1226. ὅν. The antecedent, unexpressed, is ἐμέ, sc. ὠνήσασθαι ἵππον, 'that *I* bought a horse, *I*, who,' etc.

l. 1228. The natural order is οὐ γάρ πω τότ' ἐξηπίστατο Φ., μὰ τὸν Δία, τὸν λόγον.

l. 1232. καὶ ταῦτ', 'and will you choose to adjure the gods to witness this refusal?'

l. 1235. κἂν προσκαταθείην, 'Yes, I'd add threepence more to my deposit for the pleasure of swearing.' He would enjoy the solemn humbug of adjuring gods in whom he did not believe.

l. 1237. ἁλσὶν διασμηχθείς. Strepsiades coolly changes the subject, and looking with a critical eye at Pasias' 'fair round belly,' thinks what a capacious bottle it would make—if properly tanned—'this fellow would be all the better for a rubbing of salt.'

l. 1240. ἐμοῦ καταπροίξει = προῖκα ἐμοῦ καταφρονήσεις, 'flout me for nothing.'

l. 1241. Join γελοῖος τοῖς εἰδόσιν, 'is a good joke to knowing hands.'

l. 1245. Strepsiades runs back into the house to fetch the κάρδοπος, meanwhile Pasias steps across the stage to ask his witness (as we see by the question ποῦ 'σθ' οὗτος;) whether he thinks that Strepsiades means to pay.

l. 1251. κάρδοπον is the predicate; 'who should call καρδόπη κάρδοπος.'

l. 1252. οὐχ ὅσον γε, the equivalent of the slang phrase 'not if I know it!' With the infin. cp. ὅσα γ' ὧδ' ἰδεῖν Pax 856.

l. 1256. πρὸς ταῖς δώδεκα, sc. μναῖς, 'as well as your twelve minae,' sup. 21, 1224.

l. 1258. τὴν κάρδοπον, i. e. so foolish as to use the expression ἡ (fem.) κάρδοπος (masc. termination). Exit Pasias.

l. 1259. Enter Amynias, another money-lender (sup. 31), in pitiable plight, with a tragical story of his upset from a carriage.

l. 1260. δαιμόνων. The tragic poet Carcinus, and his son Xenocles, are favourite butts for the comic writers (as Vesp. 1482–1537). Here the allusion is to the *Λικύμνιος* of Xenocles, which represents the slaying of Licymnius, brother of Alcmena, by his nephew Tlepolemus, son of Heracles. The cry of Amynias reminded Strepsiades of the lamentations of some of these demi-gods or heroes. In the play, Tlepolemus must have damaged a chariot and upset the rider by reckless driving or intentional malice.

l. 1269. **ἄλλως τε μέντοι**, i. e. '*especially* as I am in a disaster,' and want the money sorely. Literally, 'on other grounds, of course, and also,' etc.

l. 1271. **εἶχες**. The tense looks back to the time when the loan was contracted—'You really did get into a mess, then.'

l. 1272. **ἵππους ἐλαύνων**. 'It was through driving horses, so help me heaven! that I got my tumble.' 'Why are you playing the fool then, as though you had been thrown from an ass?' **ἀπ' ὄνου πεσεῖν** is said to have been a cant phrase to describe an act of stupid clumsiness. But it is thought that a pun is intended between **ἀπ' ὄνου** and **ἀπὸ νοῦ**, 'not off your Ned!' but 'off your head.'

l. 1275. **αὐτός**, emphatic, 'whatever may be the state of your chariot, and the chances of your money, "you, certainly can't be right in yourself."' 'How so?' 'You give me the idea of having had concussion of the brain.' '*You* give me the idea of having been as good as summoned already.' This spiteful re-iteration of the very form of the sentence seems better than the reading *προσκεκλήσεσθαί γέ μοι*.

l. 1278. **κάτειπέ μοι**. He puts him through an examination to see if he understands **τὰ μετέωρα** (1284).

l. 1285. **τόκος**. Strepsiades pretends not to know the technical sense of *τόκος*, sc. 'interest,' and to think only of the ordinary sense 'offspring' or 'produce.' Transl. 'Pay me the interest that the money bears.' 'What sort of a creature is it that it bears?' Plato, Rep. 555 e, plays upon the same double meaning, where he speaks of *οἱ χρηματισταὶ* . . **τοῦ πατρὸς** [i. e. *τοῦ ἀργυρίου*] **ἐκγόνους τόκους** *πολλαπλασίους κομιζόμενοι*.

l. 1289. **ὑπορρέοντος**, 'slipping away,' i. e. unnoticed.

l. 1290. **θάλατταν**. Cp. Lucr. 6. 608 foll. 'Mare mirantur non reddere maius | naturam, quo sit tantus decursus aquarum, | omnia quo veniant ex omni flumina parte.'

l. 1296. **ἀποδιώξεις σαυτόν**, 'stir your stumps;' perhaps the word is intentionally used to sneer at Amynias as an intending prosecutor (*διώκων*).

l. 1299. **ᾄξεις** (*ἀίσσω*), 'will you trot?' **ἐπιαλῶ**, fut. from **ἐπ-ιάλλω**, 'I will lay it on,' sc. *τὸ κέντρον*.

l. 1301. **ἔμελλόν σ' ἄρα**, 'Ah! I was pretty sure to stir you, with your pair of wheels and your teams and all!' see on sup. 31, 15. Exit Strepsiades to resume his interrupted feast.

l. 1305. ἐρασθείς. The corresponding word in the Antistrophe (1312) is ἐζήτει in most MSS. Perhaps ἐπῄτει (ἐπαιτέω) is the simplest emendation.

l. 1321. Enter Strepsiades in an agony of terror, pursued by his son.

l. 1323. Join ἀμυνάθετε πάσῃ τέχνῃ, 'by every means in your power.'

l. 1329. πόλλ' ἀκούων καὶ κακά, 'hearing this lot of epithets, abusive though they are.' So πολλοῖς τοῖς ῥόδοις, 'with your roses in plenty.'

l. 1339. ἐδιδαξάμην μέντοι, 'I have managed indeed to get you taught how to controvert justice.' Cp. παῖδας περισσῶς ἐκδιδάσκεσθαι σοφούς Eur. Med. 297.

l. 1344. ὅ τι καὶ λέξεις, 'what you *will* say.'

l. 1347. εἰ μή τῳ (τινί) 'πεποίθειν, 'unless he had had something to trust in .. but there is something on the strength of which he shows a bold front;' cp. Soph. O. C. 1031 ἀλλ' ἔσθ' ὅτῳ σὺ πιστὸς ὢν ἔδρας τάδε.

l. 1352. πάντως δέ, 'and of course you'll do so.' The Chorus takes for granted that he will comply.

l. 1356. τὸν Κριόν, ὡς ἐπέχθη. We do not know the subject of this song of Simonides of Ceos, about 'master Ram, how he was sheared;' but it probably alludes to Κριός (Κρῖος?) a famous wrestler of Aegina, who had found his match at last.

l. 1358. ἀλοῦσαν. Among the women's 'songs at the mill' one is preserved, that runs ἄλει, μύλα, ἄλει· καὶ γὰρ Πίττακος ἀλεῖ, μεγάλας Μιτυλάνας βασιλεύων.

l. 1360. ἑστιῶντα, 'entertaining a lot of grasshoppers,' who could only chirrup and didn't care to drink, cp. Plut. Symp 4. 1, 1 ἐν ἀέρι καὶ δρόσῳ καθάπερ οἱ τέττιγες σιτούμενον.

l. 1364. ἀλλά, 'at any rate,' as inf. 1369; so Eur. Hec. 391 ὑμεῖς δέ μ' ἀλλὰ θυγατρὶ συμφονεύσατε. When songs were introduced at a banquet, it was customary for the singer to hold, while he sang, a branch of myrtle (μυρρίνη) or bay, and to pass it on to the next singer. Here the practice was to be extended to recitations.

l. 1366. ἐγὼ γὰρ Αἰσχύλον, 'why, I consider Aeschylus far ahead among the poets for being full of sound, incoherent, bombastic, precipice-writing.' For this use of πρῶτος cp. Eur. El. 82 foll. σὲ πρῶτον ἀνθρώπων . . πιστὸν νομίζω. ἀξύστατος (ἀ-σύστατος, συνίσταμαι), properly 'having no cohesion,' γῆ, Plat. Tim. 61 a, so 'irregular,' 'uneven.' By κρημνοποιόν he means using rugged, break-neck phrases, such as Euripides calls (Ran. 929) ῥήμαθ' ἱππόκρημνα.

l. 1369. θυμὸν δακών, 'suppressing my anger;' the phrase is an extension of δάκνειν στόμα Soph. Trach. 49, or δάκνειν ἑαυτόν Ran. 43.

l. 1371. ἐκίνει, 'violated.' The allusion is to the story of the incestuous connection of Macareus with his sister Canache, in the Aeolus of Euripides. ὦ ἀλεξίκακε is a horrified appeal to 'Απόλλων *ἀποτρόπαιος*, we may render, 'God save the mark!' The emphasis lies on **ὁμομητρίαν**, i.e. 'half-sister by the mother's side,' as marriage with a half-sister by the father's side was not considered at Athens within the prohibited degrees of relationship.

l. 1375. **ἠρειδόμεσθα**, 'we planted word against word,' taking the middle voice with active force; or **ἔπος πρὸς ἔπος** may be an adverbial accusative, 'we pegged away—word against word.'

l. 1379. **ἐν δίκῃ γ' ἄν**, sc. *τύπτοιο*.

l. 1392. **πηδᾶν ὅ τι λέξει**, 'are leaping with anxiety [to know] what he will say.'

l. 1396. **ἀλλ' οὐδ' ἐρεβίνθου**, 'no, not at the price of a pea;' it will be so terribly cudgelled. Cp. Pax 1223 *οὐκ ἂν πριαίμην οὐδ' ἂν ἰσχάδος μιᾶς*, Plaut. Mil. Glor. 316 'non ego tuam empsim vitam vitiosa nuce.'

l. 1407. **τρέφειν τέθριππον**. See note on sup. 13.

l. 1415. **κλάουσι παῖδες**. Parodied from the Alcestis of Euripides, 691, *χαίρεις ὁρῶν φῶς, πατέρα δ' οὐ χαίρειν δοκεῖς*;

l. 1416. **τοῦτο**, sc. *τὸ τύπτεσθαι* or *κλάειν*. There is an emphasis on **σύ** in contrast to **ἐγὼ δέ γ'** in the next line.

l. 1420. **τὸν πατέρα**. Strepsiades is half persuaded of the general truth of the argument, as far as regards **γέροντες**, but he does not see how it can be extended to 'fathers.'

l. 1421. **ἀνήρ** is here used like *ἄνθρωπος*, as on Soph. Aj. 77 *πρόσθεν οὐκ ἀνὴρ ὅδ' ἦν*; for Pheidippides wants to show (as a Sophist would) that **νόμος** is a thing of human creation, a convention or compromise for mutual convenience. That being granted, he may ask, 'Is it then a bit the less allowable for me too to lay down a new law for sons, to serve for all time to come, that they should beat their fathers in retaliation?'

l. 1426. **ἀφίεμεν**, 'we excuse,' 'remit.' The subject (unexpressed) of **συγκεκόφθαι** is *ἡμᾶς*.

l. 1429. **ψηφίσματα**, sup. 1018.

l. 1431. **ἐπὶ ξύλου**, 'on a perch.'

l. 1432. **Σωκράτει**. It is amusing to see how Pheidippides, when he is hard pressed with an argument, takes refuge in 'authority.'

l. 1433. **εἰ δὲ μή**, 'otherwise.' Cp. Ran. 628 *ἀγορεύω τινὶ | ἐμὲ μὴ βασανίζειν, ἀθάνατον ὄντ', εἰ δὲ μή, | αὐτὸς σεαυτὸν αἰτιῶ.*

l. 1434. **δίκαιός εἰμ'**, 'I have the right to chastise you; and so will you have the right to chastise your son, if you get one.' 'But suppose I don't: then all my tears will have gone for nothing, and you will die of laughing at me!'

l. 1437. **ὦνδρες ἥλικες**. He addresses the older portion of the audience; **τούτοισι** represents the younger generation. **συγχωρεῖν τἀπιεικῆ**, 'to make reasonable concessions.'

l. 1440. **ἀπὸ γὰρ ὀλοῦμαι**, 'yes, for I shall be destroyed if I don't.' The tmesis as in sup. 792.

l. 1441. **καὶ μὴν ἴσως γ' οὐκ.** Pheidippides implies that his father will count his recent drubbing as nothing, in his joy at hearing that the extravagant wife and foolishly fond mother is going to 'catch it' too. But Strepsiades is not 'educated up' to that Euripidean view, which lowered the dignity of a mother, and made her merely the mechanical agent of the child's existence (Eurip. Orest. 552). It must be remembered that Socrates (Xen. Mem. 2. 2), so far from countenancing such an idea, enjoined the duty of the tenderest filial love even to a harsh mother.

l. 1448. **τί δ' ἄλλο ἤ.** The resumption of the question **τί δ'**, 1445, as in sup. 1287, inf. 1496; lit. 'what else could there be than that, if you do this, nothing will stand in the way of your hurling yourself and the worse argument into the Gulf, along with Socrates?' The **βάραθρον** was a chasm behind the Acropolis, into which criminals convicted on a capital charge were thrown.

l. 1455. **στρέψας** is intended as a pun upon the name *Στρεψιάδης*.

l. 1457. **ἐπῄρετε**, imperf. *ἐπαίρω* (not aor. *ἐπήρατε*), 'kept egging on.' Here the Chorus suddenly takes a high moral line, and declare that they have visited Strepsiades with 'judicial blindness' for his arrogance and dishonesty.

l. 1464. **ὦ φίλτατε**, addressed to Pheidippides, 'see that you destroy C. and S., pursuing them with your vengeance.' **μετελθών**, as in Eur. I. T. 14 *τοὺς θ' ὑβρισθέντας γάμους | Ἑλένης μετελθεῖν.*

l. 1468. **καταιδέσθητι**, the verse is parodied from some tragedy.

l. 1471. = sup. 828.

l. 1473. **διὰ τουτονὶ τὸν Δῖνον**, 'thanks to this Dinos here; ah! miserable fool that I was, when I actually thought you, though made of pottery as you are, to be a god.' If the last line be genuine, we have no alternative but to take the interpretation of the Scholiast, who says that a **δῖνος** is an earthenware jar broader above than at bottom, so that it looked something like a top. *δῖνος* seems used for a wine-jar in Vesp. 618. Of course Strepsiades is playing on the name.

l. 1475. **ἐνταῦθα**, 'stand yonder [and] keep your folly and your chatter for yourself.' Exit Pheidippides.

l. 1477. **ἐξέβαλλον**, imperf., 'sought to turn out.'

l. 1478. **Ἑρμῆ.** A bust of Hermes is standing in the street near the house of Strepsiades. He goes up to it and asks the god's advice whether he shall bring an action against Socrates and his friends (*γραφὴ ἀσεβείας*), or anything else the god likes to suggest. He puts his ear to the mouth of the statue, and pretends to have heard its counsel (**ὀρθῶς παραινεῖς**).

l. 1495. **ὅ τι ποιῶ**; 'you ask what I am doing, why nothing more than chopping logic with the beams of your house.'

l. 1498. **θοἰμάτιον.** See sup. 497 and 856.

l. 1503. **ἀεροβατῶ . . . . ἥλιον**, the very words of Socrates, sup. 225.

INDEX

Of Proper Names and the Principal Words and Phrases explained in the Notes.

The references are generally to the lines in the *Text*.

October, 1888.

The Clarendon Press, Oxford,

LIST OF SCHOOL BOOKS,

PUBLISHED FOR THE UNIVERSITY BY

HENRY FROWDE,

AT THE OXFORD UNIVERSITY PRESS WAREHOUSE,

AMEN CORNER, LONDON.

*** *All Books are bound in Cloth, unless otherwise described.*

LATIN.

Allen. *An Elementary Latin Grammar.* By J. BARROW ALLEN, M.A. *Fifty-seventh Thousand* . . . . Extra fcap. 8vo. 2s. 6d.

Allen. *Rudimenta Latina.* By the same Author. Extra fcap. 8vo. 2s.

Allen. *A First Latin Exercise Book.* By the same Author. *Fourth Edition.* . . . . Extra fcap. 8vo. 2s. 6d.

Allen. *A Second Latin Exercise Book.* By the same Author. Extra fcap. 8vo. 3s. 6d.

[*A Key to First and Second Latin Exercise Books: for Teachers only.*]

Jerram. *Anglice Reddenda; or Extracts, Latin and Greek, for Unseen Translation.* By C. S. JERRAM, M.A. *Fourth Edition.* Extra fcap. 8vo. 2s. 6d.

Jerram. *Anglice Reddenda.* SECOND SERIES. By C. S. JERRAM, M.A. Extra fcap. 8vo. 3s.

Jerram. *Reddenda Minora; or, Easy Passages, Latin and Greek, for Unseen Translation.* For the use of Lower Forms. Composed and selected by C. S. JERRAM, M.A. . . . . Extra fcap. 8vo. 1s. 6d.

Lee-Warner. *Hints and Helps for Latin Elegiacs.* Extra fcap. 8vo. 3s. 6d.

[*A Key is provided: for Teachers only.*]

Lewis and Short. *A Latin Dictionary*, founded on Andrews' Edition of Freund's Latin Dictionary. By CHARLTON T. LEWIS, Ph.D., and CHARLES SHORT, LL.D. . . . . 4to. 25s.

Nunns. *First Latin Reader.* By T. J. NUNNS, M.A. *Third Edition.* Extra fcap. 8vo. 2s.

Papillon. *A Manual of Comparative Philology* as applied to the Illustration of Greek and Latin Inflections. By T. L. PAPILLON, M.A. *Third Edition.* Crown 8vo. 6s.

Ramsay. *Exercises in Latin Prose Composition.* With Introduction, Notes, and Passages of graduated difficulty for Translation into Latin. By G. G. RAMSAY, M.A., Professor of Humanity, Glasgow. *Second Edition.* Extra fcap. 8vo. 4s. 6d.

Sargent. *Easy Passages for Translation into Latin.* By J. Y. SARGENT, M.A. *Seventh Edition.* . . . . Extra fcap. 8vo. 2s. 6d.

[*A Key to this Edition is provided: for Teachers only.*]

Sargent. *A Latin Prose Primer.* . . . Extra fcap. 8vo. 2s. 6d.

Caesar. *The Commentaries* (for Schools). With Notes and Maps. By CHARLES E. MOBERLY, M.A.
The Gallic War. Second Edition . . . . . Extra fcap. 8vo. 4*s.* 6*d.*
The Gallic War. Books I, II. . . . . . Extra fcap. 8vo. 2*s.*
The Civil War . . . . Extra fcap. 8vo. 3*s.* 6*d.*
The Civil War. Book I. *Second Edition.* . . Extra fcap. 8vo. 2*s.*

Catulli Veronensis *Carmina Selecta*, secundum recognitionem ROBINSON ELLIS, A.M. . . . . Extra fcap. 8vo. 3*s.* 6*d.*

Cicero. *Selection of interesting and descriptive passages.* With Notes. By HENRY WALFORD, M.A. In three Parts. *Third Edition.* Extra fcap. 8vo. 4*s.* 6*d.*
Part I. *Anecdotes from Grecian and Roman History.* . *limp*, 1*s.* 6*d.*
Part II. *Omens and Dreams; Beauties of Nature.* . . *limp*, 1*s.* 6*d.*
Part III. *Rome's Rule of her Provinces.* . . . . . *limp*, 1*s.* 6*d.*

Cicero. *De Senectute.* With Introduction and Notes. By LEONARD HUXLEY, B.A. *In one or two Parts* . . . . Extra fcap. 8vo. 2*s.*

Cicero. *Pro Cluentio.* With Introduction and Notes. By W. RAMSAY, M.A. Edited by G. G. RAMSAY, M.A. *Second Edition.* Extra fcap. 8vo. 3*s.* 6*d.*

Cicero. *Selected Letters* (for Schools). With Notes. By the late C. E. PRICHARD, M.A., and E. R. BERNARD, M.A. *Second Edition.* Extra fcap. 8vo. 3*s.*

Cicero. *Select Orations* (for Schools). *First Action against Verres; Oration concerning the command of Gnaeus Pompeius; Oration on behalf of Archias; Ninth Philippic Oration.* With Introduction and Notes. By J. R. KING, M.A. *Second Edition.* . . . . . Extra fcap. 8vo. 2*s.* 6*d.*

Cicero. *In Q. Caecilium Divinatio* and *In C. Verrem Actio Prima.* With Introduction and Notes. By J. R. KING, M.A. Extra fcap. 8vo. *limp*, 1*s.* 6*d.*

Cicero. *Speeches against Catilina.* With Introduction and Notes. By E. A. UPCOTT, M.A. *In one or two Parts.* . . . Extra fcap. 8vo. 2*s.* 6*d.*

Cicero. *Philippic Orations.* With Notes, &c. by J. R. KING, M.A. *Second Edition.* . . . . 8vo. 10*s.* 6*d.*

Cicero. *Select Letters.* With English Introductions, Notes, and Appendices. By ALBERT WATSON, M.A. *Third Edition.* . . . . 8vo. 18*s.*

Cicero. *Select Letters.* Text. By the same Editor. *Second Edition.* Extra fcap. 8vo. 4*s.*

Cornelius Nepos. With Notes. By OSCAR BROWNING, M.A. *Third Edition.* Revised by W. R. INGE, M.A. . . . Extra fcap. 8vo. 3*s.*

Horace. With a Commentary. Volume I. *The Odes, Carmen Seculare*, and *Epodes.* By EDWARD C. WICKHAM, M.A., Head Master of Wellington College. *New Edition. In one or two Parts.* Extra fcap. 8vo. 6*s.*

Horace. *Selected Odes.* With Notes for the use of a Fifth Form. By E. C. WICKHAM, M.A. *In one or two Parts.* . . . Extra fcap. 8vo. 2*s.*

Juvenal. *XIII Satires.* Edited, with Introduction, Notes, etc., by C. H. PEARSON, M.A., and H. A. STRONG, M.A. . . . . Crown 8vo. 6*s.*
Or separately, Text and Introduction, 3*s.*; *Notes*, 3*s.* 6*d.*

Livy. *Selections* (for Schools). With Notes and Maps. By H. LEE-WARNER, M.A. . . . . Extra fcap. 8vo
Part I. *The Caudine Disaster.* . . . . . . *limp*, 1*s.* 6*d.*
Part II. *Hannibal's Campaign in Italy.* . . . . . *limp*, 1*s.* 6*d.*
Part III. *The Macedonian War.* . . . . *limp*, 1*s.* 6*d.*

Livy. *Book I.* With Introduction, Historical Examination, and Notes. By J. R. SEELEY M.A. *Second Edition.* . . . . 8vo. 6*s.*

Livy. *Books V—VII.* With Introduction and Notes. By A. R. CLUER, B.A. *Second Edition.* Revised by P. E. MATHESON, M.A. *In one or two parts.* . . . . Extra fcap. 8vo. 5*s.*

Livy. *Books XXI—XXIII.* With Introduction and Notes. By M. T. TATHAM, M.A. . . . . Extra fcap. 8vo. 4*s.* 6*d.*

Livy. *Book XXII.* With Introduction and Notes. By the same Editor. . . . . Extra fcap. 8vo. 2*s.* 6*d.*

Ovid. *Selections* (for the use of Schools). With Introductions and Notes, and an Appendix on the Roman Calendar. By W. RAMSAY, M.A. Edited by G. G. RAMSAY, M.A. *Third Edition.* . Extra fcap. 8vo. 5*s.* 6*d.*

Ovid. *Tristia*, Book I. Edited by S. G. OWEN, B.A. Extra fcap. 8vo. 3*s.* 6*d.*

Persius. *The Satires.* With Translation and Commentary by J. CONINGTON, M.A., edited by H. NETTLESHIP, M.A. *Second Edition.* 8vo. 7*s.* 6*d.*

Plautus. *Captivi.* With Introduction and Notes. By W. M. LINDSAY, M.A. *In one or two Parts.* : . . . . . Extra fcap. 8vo. 2*s.* 6*d.*

Plautus. *Trinummus.* With Notes and Introductions. By C. E. FREEMAN, M.A. and A. SLOMAN, M.A. . . . . . Extra fcap. 8vo. 3*s.*

Pliny. *Selected Letters* (for Schools). With Notes. By the late C. E. PRICHARD, M.A., and E. R. BERNARD, M.A. *New Edition. In one or two Parts.* . . . . Extra fcap. 8vo. 3*s.*

Sallust. *Bellum Catilinarium* and *Jugurthinum.* With Introduction and Notes, by W. W. CAPES, M.A. . . . . Extra fcap. 8vo. 4*s.* 6*d.*

Tacitus. *The Annals.* Books I—IV. Edited, with Introduction and Notes for the use of Schools and Junior Students, by H. FURNEAUX, M.A. Extra fcap. 8vo. 5*s.*

Tacitus. *The Annals.* Book I. By the same Editor. Extra fcap. 8vo. *limp*, 2*s.*

Terence. *Adelphi.* With Notes and Introductions. By A. SLOMAN, M.A. . . . . Extra fcap. 8vo. 3*s.*

Terence. *Andria.* With Notes and Introductions. By C. E. FREEMAN, M.A., and A. SLOMAN, M.A. . . . . Extra fcap. 8vo. 3*s.*

Terence. *Phormio.* With Notes and Introductions. By A. SLOMAN, M.A. . . . . Extra fcap. 8vo. 3*s.*

Tibullus and **Propertius.** Edited, with Introduction and Notes, by G. G. RAMSAY, M.A. *In one or two Parts.* . . . . Extra fcap. 8vo. 6*s.*

Virgil. With Introduction and Notes, by T. L. PAPILLON, M.A. In Two Volumes. . . . Crown 8vo. 10*s.* 6*d.*; Text separately, 4*s.* 6*d.*

Virgil. *Bucolics.* With Introduction and Notes, by C. S. JERRAM, M.A. *In one or two Parts.* Extra fcap. 8vo. 2*s.* 6*d.*

Virgil. *Aeneid I.* With Introduction and Notes, by C. S. JERRAM, M.A. Extra fcap. 8vo. *limp*, 1*s.* 6*d.*

Virgil. *Aeneid IX.* Edited with Introduction and Notes, by A. E. HAIGH, M.A. . . . Extra fcap 8vo. *limp* 1*s.* 6*d.* *In two Parts.* 2*s.*

GREEK.

Chandler. *The Elements of Greek Accentuation* (for Schools). By H. W. CHANDLER, M.A. *Second Edition.* . Extra fcap. 8vo. 2*s*. 6*d*.

Liddell and Scott. *A Greek-English Lexicon*, by HENRY GEORGE LIDDELL, D.D., and ROBERT SCOTT, D.D. *Seventh Edition.* . 4to. 36*s*.

Liddell and Scott. *A Greek-English Lexicon*, abridged from LIDDELL and SCOTT's 4to. edition, chiefly for the use of Schools. *Twenty-first Edition.* Square 12mo. 7*s*. 6*d*.

Veitch. *Greek Verbs, Irregular and Defective:* their forms, meaning, and quantity; embracing all the Tenses used by Greek writers, with references to the passages in which they are found. By W. VEITCH, LL.D. *Fourth Edition.* Crown 8vo. 10*s*. 6*d*.

Wordsworth. *Graecae Grammaticae Rudimenta in usum Scholarum.* Auctore CAROLO WORDSWORTH, D.C.L. *Nineteenth Edition.* . 12mo. 4*s*.

Wordsworth. *A Greek Primer, for the use of beginners in that Language.* By the Right Rev. CHARLES WORDSWORTH, D.C.L., Bishop of St. Andrew's. *Seventh Edition.* . . . . . Extra fcap. 8vo. 1*s*. 6*d*.

Wright. *The Golden Treasury of Ancient Greek Poetry;* being a Collection of the finest passages in the Greek Classic Poets, with Introductory Notices and Notes. By R. S. WRIGHT, M.A. . . *New edition in the Press.*

Wright and Shadwell. *A Golden Treasury of Greek Prose;* being a Collection of the finest passages in the principal Greek Prose Writers, with Introductory Notices and Notes. By R. S. WRIGHT, M.A., and J. E. L. SHADWELL, M.A. . . . . Extra fcap. 8vo. 4*s*. 6*d*.

A SERIES OF GRADUATED READERS.—

Easy Greek Reader. By EVELYN ABBOTT, M.A. *In one or two Parts.* . . . . Extra fcap. 8vo. 3*s*.

First Greek Reader. By W. G. RUSHBROOKE, M.L., Second Classical Master at the City of London School. *Second Edition.* Extra fcap. 8vo. 2*s*. 6*d*.

Second Greek Reader. By A. M. BELL, M.A. Extra fcap. 8vo. 3*s*. 6*d*.

Fourth Greek Reader; being Specimens of Greek Dialects. With Introductions and Notes. By W. W. MERRY, D.D., Rector of Lincoln College. . . . . Extra fcap. 8vo. 4*s*. 6*d*.

Fifth Greek Reader. Selections from Greek Epic and Dramatic Poetry, with Introductions and Notes. By EVELYN ABBOTT, M.A. Extra fcap. 8vo. 4*s*. 6*d*.

THE GREEK TESTAMENT.—

Evangelia Sacra Graece. . . . . Fcap. 8vo. *limp*, 1*s*. 6*d*.

The Greek Testament, with the Readings adopted by the Revisers of the Authorised Version. Fcap. 8vo. 4*s*. 6*d*.; or on writing paper, with wide margin, 15*s*.

Novum Testamentum Graece juxta Exemplar Millianum. 18mo. 2*s*. 6*d*.; or on writing paper, with large margin, 9*s*.

Novum Testamentum Graece. Accedunt parallela S. Scripturae loca, necnon vetus capitulorum notatio et canones Eusebii. Edidit CAROLUS LLOYD, S.T.P.R., necnon Episcopus Oxoniensis.
18mo. 3*s.*; or on writing paper, with large margin, 10*s.* 6*d.*

A Greek Testament Primer. An Easy Grammar and Reading Book for the use of Students beginning Greek. By REV. E. MILLER, M.A.
Extra fcap. 8vo. 3*s.* 6*d.*

Outlines of Textual Criticism applied to the New Testament. By C. E. HAMMOND, M.A. *Fourth Edition.* . . Extra fcap. 8vo. 3*s.* 6*d.*

Aeschylus. *Agamemnon.* With Introduction and Notes, by ARTHUR SIDGWICK, M.A. *Third Edition. In one or two Parts* . Extra fcap. 8vo. 3*s.*

Aeschylus. *Choephoroi.* With Introduction and Notes, by the same Editor. . . . . Extra fcap. 8vo. 3*s.*

Aeschylus. *Eumenides.* With Introduction and Notes, by the same Editor. *In one or two Parts.* . . . . Extra fcap. 8vo. 3*s.*

Aeschylus. *Prometheus Bound.* With Introduction and Notes, by A. O. PRICKARD, M.A. *Second Edition.* . . . . Extra fcap. 8vo. 2*s.*

Aristophanes. *The Clouds.* With Introduction and Notes, by W. W. MERRY, D.D. *Second Edition.* . . . . . . Extra fcap. 8vo. 2*s.*

Aristophanes. *The Acharnians.* By the same Editor. *Third Edition. In one or two Parts.* . . . . . . Extra fcap. 8vo. 3*s.*

Aristophanes. *The Frogs.* By the same Editor. *New Edition. In one or two Parts.* . . . . Extra fcap. 8vo. 3*s.*

Aristophanes. *The Knights.* By the same Editor. *In one or two Parts.* . . . . Extra fcap. 8vo. 3*s.*

Cebes. *Tabula.* With Introduction and Notes, by C. S. JERRAM, M.A.
Extra fcap. 8vo. 2*s.* 6*d.*

Demosthenes. *Orations against Philip.* With Introduction and Notes. By EVELYN ABBOTT, M.A., and P. E. MATHESON, M.A., Vol. I. *Philippic I* and *Olynthiacs I—III. In one or two Parts.* . . . Extra fcap. 8vo. 3*s.*

Euripides. *Alcestis.* By C. S. JERRAM, M.A. Extra fcap. 8vo. 2*s.* 6*d.*

Euripides. *Hecuba.* By C. H. RUSSELL. *Immediately.*

Euripides. *Helena.* By the same Editor. . Extra fcap. 8vo. 3*s.*

Euripides. *Heracleidae.* By the same Editor. Extra fcap. 8vo. 3*s.*

Euripides. *Iphigenia in Tauris.* With Introduction and Notes. By the same Editor. . . . . Extra fcap. 8vo. 3*s.*

Euripides. *Medea.* With Introduction, Notes and Appendices. By C. B. HEBERDEN, M.A. *In one or two Parts.* . . . Extra fcap. 8vo. 2*s.*

Herodotus. Book IX. Edited with Notes, by EVELYN ABBOTT, M.A. *In one or two Parts.* . . . . Extra fcap 8vo. 3*s.*

Herodotus. *Selections.* Edited, with Introduction, Notes, and a Map, by W. W. MERRY, D.D. . . . . Extra fcap. 8vo. 2*s.* 6*d.*

Homer. *Iliad,* Books I–XII. With an Introduction, a brief Homeric Grammar, and Notes. By D. B. MONRO, M.A. Extra fcap. 8vo. 6*s.*

Homer. *Iliad,* Book I. By the same Editor. *Third Edition.*
Extra fcap. 8vo. 2*s.*

Homer. *Iliad,* Books VI and XXI. With Notes, &c. By HERBERT HAILSTONE, M.A. . . . . Extra fcap. 8vo. 1*s.* 6*d.* each.

Homer. *Odyssey*, Books I–XII. By W. W. MERRY, D.D. *New Edition. In one or two Parts.* . . . . . . Extra fcap. 8vo. 5*s.*

Homer. *Odyssey*, Books XIII–XXIV. By the same Editor. *Second Edition.* . . . . Extra fcap. 8vo. 5*s.*

Homer. *Odyssey*, Books I and II. By the same Editor.
Extra fcap. 8vo. each 1*s.* 6*d.*

Lucian. *Vera Historia.* By C. S. JERRAM, M.A. *Second Edition.*
Extra fcap. 8vo. 1*s.* 6*d.*

Plato. *The Apology.* With Introduction and Notes. By ST. GEORGE STOCK, M.A. *In one or two Parts.* . . . . . Extra fcap. 8vo. 2*s.* 6*d.*

Plato. *Meno.* With Introduction and Notes. By ST. GEORGE STOCK, M.A. *In one or two Parts.* . . . . . . Extra fcap. 8vo. 2*s.* 6*d.*

Sophocles. (For the use of Schools.) Edited with Introductions and English Notes by LEWIS CAMPBELL, M.A., and EVELYN ABBOTT, M.A. New and Revised Edition. 2 Vols. . . . . . Extra fcap. 8vo. 10*s.* 6*d.*
Sold separately, Vol. I. Text, 4*s.* 6*d.* Vol. II. Notes, 6*s.*

☞ *Also in single Plays. Extra fcap. 8vo. limp,*
Oedipus Tyrannus, Philoctetes. New and Revised Edition, 2*s.* each.
Oedipus Coloneus, Antigone. 1*s.* 9*d.* each.
Ajax, Electra, Trachiniae. 2*s.* each.

Sophocles. *Oedipus Rex:* Dindorf's Text, with Notes by W. BASIL JONES, D.D., Lord Bishop of S. David's. . Extra fcap. 8vo. *limp*, 1*s.* 6*d.*

Theocritus. Edited, with Notes, by H. KYNASTON, D.D. (late SNOW). *Fourth Edition.* . . . . . . Extra fcap. 8vo. 4*s.* 6*d.*

Xenophon. *Easy Selections* (for Junior Classes). With a Vocabulary, Notes, and Map. By J. S. PHILLPOTTS, B.C.L., Head Master of Bedford School, and C. S. JERRAM, M.A. *Third Edition.* . Extra fcap. 8vo. 3*s.* 6*d.*

Xenophon. *Selections* (for Schools). With Notes and Maps. By J. S. PHILLPOTTS, B.C.L. *Fourth Edition.* . . . Extra fcap. 8vo. 3*s.* 6*d.*

Xenophon. *Anabasis*, Book I. With Notes and Map. By J. MARSHALL, M.A., Rector of the High School, Edinburgh. . . Extra fcap 8vo. 2*s.* 6*d.*

Xenophon. *Anabasis*, Book II. With Notes and Map. By C. S. JERRAM, M.A. . . . . Extra fcap. 8vo. 2*s.*

Xenophon. *Anabasis*, Book III. By J. MARSHALL, M.A.
Extra fcap. 8vo. 2*s.* 6*d.*

Xenophon. *Vocabulary to the Anabasis.* By J. MARSHALL, M.A.
Extra fcap. 8vo. 1*s.* 6*d.*

Xenophon. *Cyropaedia*, Book I. With Introduction and Notes. By C. BIGG, D.D. . . . . Extra fcap. 8vo. 2*s.*

Xenophon. *Cyropaedia*, Books IV, V. With Introduction and Notes, by C. BIGG, D.D. . . . . Extra fcap. 8vo. 2*s.* 6*d.*

Xenophon. *Hellenica*, Books I, II. With Introduction and Notes. By G. E. UNDERHILL, M.A. . . . . Extra fcap. 8vo. 3*s.*

EARLY AND MIDDLE ENGLISH, &c.

Mayhew and Skeat. *A Concise Dictionary of Middle English.* By A. L. MAYHEW, M.A., and W. W. SKEAT, Litt. D. . . Crown 8vo. 7*s.* 6*d.*

Skeat. *A Concise Etymological Dictionary of the English Language.* By W. W. SKEAT, Litt. D. *Third Edition.* . . . Crown 8vo. 5*s.* 6*d.*

Tancock. *An Elementary English Grammar and Exercise Book.* By O. W. TANCOCK, M.A., Head Master of King Edward VI's School, Norwich. *Second Edition.* . . . . Extra fcap. 8vo. 1*s.* 6*d.*

Tancock. *An English Grammar and Reading Book,* for Lower Forms in Classical Schools. By O. W. TANCOCK, M.A. *Fourth Edition.* Extra fcap. 8vo. 3*s.* 6*d.*

Skeat. *The Principles of English Etymology. First Series.* By W. W. SKEAT, Litt. D. . . . . Crown 8vo. 9*s.*

Earle. *The Philology of the English Tongue.* By J. EARLE, M.A., Professor of Anglo-Saxon. *Fourth Edition.* . . . Extra fcap. 8vo. 7*s.* 6*d.*

Earle. *A Book for the Beginner in Anglo-Saxon.* By the same Author. *Third Edition.* . . . . Extra fcap. 8vo. 2*s.* 6*d.*

Sweet. *An Anglo-Saxon Primer, with Grammar, Notes, and Glossary.* By HENRY SWEET, M.A. *Third Edition.* . . . Extra fcap. 8vo. 2*s.* 6*d.*

Sweet. *An Anglo-Saxon Reader.* In Prose and Verse. With Grammatical Introduction, Notes, and Glossary. By the same Author. *Fourth Edition, Revised and Enlarged.* . . . . . Extra fcap. 8vo. 8*s.* 6*d.*

Sweet. *A Second Anglo-Saxon Reader.* By the same Author. Extra fcap. 8vo. 4*s.* 6*d.*

Sweet. *Anglo-Saxon Reading Primers.*

I. *Selected Homilies of Ælfric.* Extra fcap. 8vo. *stiff covers,* 1*s.* 6*d.*

II. *Extracts from Alfred's Orosius.* Extra fcap. 8vo. *stiff covers,* 1*s.* 6*d.*

Sweet. *First Middle English Primer, with Grammar and Glossary.* By the same Author. . . . . Extra fcap. 8vo. 2*s.*

Sweet. *Second Middle English Primer.* Extracts from Chaucer, with Grammar and Glossary. By the same Author. . . Extra fcap. 8vo. 2*s.*

Morris and Skeat. *Specimens of Early English.* A New and Revised Edition. With Introduction, Notes, and Glossarial Index.

Part I. From Old English Homilies to King Horn (A.D. 1150 to A.D. 1300). By R. MORRIS, LL.D. *Second Edition* . . Extra fcap. 8vo. 9*s.*

Part II. From Robert of Gloucester to Gower (A.D. 1298 to A.D. 1393). By R. MORRIS, LL.D., and W. W. SKEAT, Litt. D. *Third Edition* Extra fcap. 8vo. 7*s.* 6*d.*

Skeat. *Specimens of English Literature,* from the 'Ploughmans Crede' to the 'Shepheardes Calender' (A.D. 1394 to A.D. 1579). With Introduction, Notes, and Glossarial Index. By W. W. SKEAT, Litt. D. *Fourth Edition.* Extra fcap. 8vo. 7*s.* 6*d.*

Typical Selections from the best English Writers, with Introductory Notices. *Second Edition.* In Two Volumes Vol. I Latimer to Berkeley. Vol. II. Pope to Macaulay. . . Extra fcap. 8vo. 3*s.* 6*d.* each.

A SERIES OF ENGLISH CLASSICS.

Langland. *The Vision of William concerning Piers the Plowman,* by WILLIAM LANGLAND. Edited by W. W. SKEAT, Litt. D. *Fourth Edition.* Extra fcap. 8vo. 4*s.* 6*d.*

Chaucer. I. *The Prologue to the Canterbury Tales; The Knightes Tale; The Nonne Prestes Tale.* Edited by R. MORRIS, LL.D. *Fifty-first Thousand.* . . . . Extra fcap. 8vo. 2*s.* 6*d.*

Chaucer. II. *The Prioresses Tale; Sir Thopas; The Monkes Tale; The Clerkes Tale; The Squieres Tale, &c.* Edited by W. W. SKEAT, Litt. D. *Third Edition.* . . . . Extra fcap. 8vo. 4*s.* 6*d.*

Chaucer. III. *The Tale of the Man of Lawe; The Pardoneres Tale; The Second Nonnes Tale; The Chanouns Yemannes Tale.* By the same Editor. *New Edition, Revised.* . . . . . Extra fcap. 8vo. 4*s.* 6*d.*

Gamelyn, The Tale of. Edited by W. W. SKEAT, Litt. D. Extra fcap. 8vo. *stiff covers,* 1*s.* 6*d.*

Minot. *The Poems of Laurence Minot.* Edited, with Introduction and Notes, by JOSEPH HALL, M.A. . . . . Extra fcap. 8vo. 4*s.* 6*d.*

Wycliffe. *The New Testament in English,* according to the Version by JOHN WYCLIFFE, about A.D. 1380, and Revised by JOHN PURVEY, about A.D. 1388. With Introduction and Glossary by W. W. SKEAT, Litt. D. Extra fcap. 8vo. 6*s.*

Wycliffe. *The Books of Job, Psalms, Proverbs, Ecclesiastes, and the Song of Solomon:* according to the Wycliffite Version made by NICHOLAS DE HEREFORD, about A.D. 1381, and Revised by JOHN PURVEY, about A.D. 1388. With Introduction and Glossary by W. W. SKEAT, Litt. D. Extra fcap. 8vo. 3*s.* 6*d.*

Spenser. *The Faery Queene.* Books I and II. Edited by G. W. KITCHIN, D.D.

Book I. *Tenth Edition.* . . . . . Extra fcap. 8vo. 2*s.* 6*d.*
Book II. *Sixth Edition.* . . . . Extra fcap. 8vo. 2*s.* 6*d.*

Hooker. *Ecclesiastical Polity,* Book I. Edited by R. W. CHURCH, M.A., Dean of St. Paul's. *Second Edition.* . . . . Extra fcap. 8vo. 2*s.*

Marlowe and Greene.—MARLOWE'S *Tragical History of Dr. Faustus,* and GREENE'S *Honourable History of Friar Bacon and Friar Bungay.* Edited by A. W. WARD, M.A. *New Edition.* . . . Extra fcap. 8vo. 6*s.* 6*d.*

Marlowe. *Edward II.* Edited by O. W. TANCOCK, M.A. *Second Edition.* . . . . Extra fcap. 8vo. *Paper covers,* 2*s.* *cloth,* 3*s.*

Shakespeare. Select Plays. Edited by W. G. CLARK, M.A., and W. ALDIS WRIGHT, M.A. . . . . Extra fcap. 8vo. *stiff covers.*

The Merchant of Venice. 1*s.* *Macbeth.* 1*s.* 6*d.*
Richard the Second. 1*s.* 6*d.* *Hamlet.* 2*s.*

Edited by W. ALDIS WRIGHT, M.A.

The Tempest. 1*s.* 6*d.*
As You Like It. 1*s.* 6*d.*
A Midsummer Night's Dream. 1*s.* 6*d.*
Twelfth Night. 1*s.* 6*d.*
Julius Cæsar. 2*s.*
Coriolanus. 2*s.* 6*d.*
Richard the Third. 2*s.* 6*d.*
Henry the Fifth. 2*s.*
King John. 1*s.* 6*d.*
King Lear. 1*s.* 6*d.*

Shakespeare as a Dramatic Artist; *a popular Illustration of the Principles of Scientific Criticism.* By R. G. MOULTON, M.A. Crown 8vo. 5s.

Bacon. *Advancement of Learning.* Edited by W. ALDIS WRIGHT, M.A. *Third Edition.* . . . . Extra fcap. 8vo. 4s. 6d.

Milton. I. *Areopagitica.* With Introduction and Notes. By JOHN W. HALES, M.A. *Third Edition.* . . . . . Extra fcap. 8vo. 3s.

Milton. II. *Poems.* Edited by R. C. BROWNE, M.A. 2 vols. *Fifth Edition.* . Extra fcap. 8vo. 6s. 6d. Sold separately, Vol. I. 4s., Vol. II. 3s.

In paper covers:—

Lycidas, 3d. *L'Allegro*, 3d. *Il Penseroso*, 4d. *Comus*, 6d.

Milton. III. *Paradise Lost.* Book I. Edited with Notes, by H. C. BEECHING, M.A. . Extra fcap. 8vo. 1s. 6d. *In white Parchment*, 3s. 6d.

Milton. IV. *Samson Agonistes.* Edited with Introduction and Notes by JOHN CHURTON COLLINS. . . . Extra fcap. 8vo. *stiff covers*, 1s.

Clarendon. *History of the Rebellion.* Book VI. Edited with Introduction and Notes by T. ARNOLD, M.A. . . Extra fcap. 8vo. 4s. 6d.

Bunyan. *The Pilgrim's Progress, Grace Abounding, Relation of the Imprisonment of Mr. John Bunyan.* Edited by E. VENABLES, M.A. Extra fcap. 8vo. 5s. *In white Parchment*, 6s.

Dryden. *Stanzas on the Death of Oliver Cromwell; Astraea Redux; Annus Mirabilis; Absalom and Achitophel; Religio Laici; The Hind and the Panther.* Edited by W. D. CHRISTIE, M.A. . Extra fcap. 8vo. 3s. 6d.

Locke's *Conduct of the Understanding.* Edited, with Introduction, Notes, &c. by T. FOWLER, D.D. *Second Edition.* . . Extra fcap. 8vo. 2s.

Addison. *Selections from Papers in the 'Spectator.'* With Notes. By T. ARNOLD, M.A. . Extra fcap. 8vo. 4s. 6d. *In white Parchment*, 6s.

Steele. *Selected Essays from the Tatler, Spectator, and Guardian.* By AUSTIN DOBSON. . . Extra fcap. 8vo. 5s. *In white Parchment*, 7s. 6d.

Berkeley. *Select Works of Bishop Berkeley*, with an Introduction and Notes, by A. C. FRASER, LL.D. *Third Edition.* . . Crown 8vo. 7s. 6d.

Pope. I. *Essay on Man.* Edited by MARK PATTISON, B.D. *Sixth Edition.* . . . . Extra fcap. 8vo. 1s. 6d.

Pope. II. *Satires and Epistles.* By the same Editor. *Second Edition.* Extra fcap. 8vo. 2s.

Parnell. *The Hermit.* . . . . . . *Paper covers*, 2d.

Johnson. I. *Rasselas.* Edited, with Introduction and Notes, by G. BIRKBECK HILL, D.C.L. Extra fcap. 8vo. *limp*, 2s. *In white Parchment*, 3s. 6d.

Johnson. II. *Rasselas; Lives of Dryden and Pope.* Edited by ALFRED MILNES, M.A. . . . . Extra fcap. 8vo. 4s. 6d.

Lives of Pope and Dryden. . . . . . *Stiff covers*, 2s. 6d.

Johnson. III. *Life of Milton.* Edited, with Notes, etc., by C. H. FIRTH, M.A. . . . . Extra fcap. 8vo. *stiff covers*, 1s 6d.; *cloth*, 2s. 6d.

Johnson. IV. *Vanity of Human Wishes.* With Notes, by E. J. PAYNE, M.A. . . . . *Paper covers*, 4d.

Gray. *Selected Poems.* Edited by EDMUND GOSSE.
Extra fcap. 8vo. *Stiff covers*, 1*s*. 6*d*. *In white Parchment*, 3*s*.

Gray. *Elegy, and Ode on Eton College.* . . *Paper covers*, 2*d*.

Goldsmith. *Selected Poems.* Edited, with Introduction and Notes, by AUSTIN DOBSON. . . . . Extra fcap. 8vo. 3*s*. 6*d*. *In white Parchment*, 4*s*. 6*d*.

Goldsmith. *The Traveller.* Edited by G. BIRKBECK HILL, D.C.L.
Extra fcap. 8vo. *stiff covers*, 1*s*.

The Deserted Village. . . . . . *Paper covers*, 2*d*.

Cowper. I. *The Didactic Poems of* 1782, with Selections from the Minor Pieces, A.D. 1779–1783. Edited by H. T. GRIFFITH, B.A.
Extra fcap. 8vo. 3*s*.

Cowper. II. *The Task, with Tirocinium*, and Selections from the Minor Poems, A.D. 1784–1799. By the same Editor. *Second Edition.*
Extra fcap. 8vo. 3*s*.

Burke. I. *Thoughts on the Present Discontents; the two Speeches on America.* Edited by E. J. PAYNE, M.A. *Second Edition.*
Extra fcap. 8vo. 4*s*. 6*d*.

Burke. II. *Reflections on the French Revolution.* By the same Editor. *Second Edition.* . . . . Extra fcap. 8vo. 5*s*.

Burke. III. *Four Letters on the Proposals for Peace with the Regicide Directory of France.* By the same Editor. *Second Edition.*
Extra fcap. 8vo. 5*s*.

Keats. *Hyperion*, Book I. With Notes, by W. T. ARNOLD, B.A.
Paper covers, 4*d*.

Byron. *Childe Harold.* With Introduction and Notes, by H. F. TOZER, M.A. . . . . . Extra fcap. 8vo. 3*s*. 6*d*. *In white Parchment*, 5*s*.

Scott. *Lay of the Last Minstrel.* Edited with Preface and Notes by W. MINTO, M.A. With Map.
Extra fcap. 8vo. *stiff covers*, 2*s*. *In Ornamental Parchment*, 3*s*. 6*d*.

Scott. *Lay of the Last Minstrel.* Introduction and Canto I, with Preface and Notes by W. MINTO, M.A. . . . . *Paper covers*, 6*d*.

FRENCH AND ITALIAN.

Brachet. *Etymological Dictionary of the French Language*, with a Preface on the Principles of French Etymology. Translated into English by G. W. KITCHIN, D.D., Dean of Winchester. *Third Edition.*
Crown 8vo. 7*s*. 6*d*.

Brachet. *Historical Grammar of the French Language.* Translated into English by G. W. KITCHIN, D.D. *Fourth Edition.*
Extra fcap. 8vo. 3*s*. 6*d*.

Saintsbury. *Primer of French Literature.* By GEORGE SAINTSBURY, M.A. *Second Edition.* . . . . . . Extra fcap. 8vo. 2*s*.

Saintsbury. *Short History of French Literature.* By the same Author. . . . . Crown 8vo. 10*s*. 6*d*.

Saintsbury. *Specimens of French Literature.* . . Crown 8vo. 9*s*.

Beaumarchais. *Le Barbier de Séville.* With Introduction and Notes by AUSTIN DOBSON. . . . . Extra fcap. 8vo. 2*s.* 6*d.*

Blouët. *L'Éloquence de la Chaire et de la Tribune Françaises.* Edited by PAUL BLOUET, B.A. (Univ. Gallic.) Vol. I. *French Sacred Oratory.* Extra fcap. 8vo. 2*s.* 6*d.*

Corneille. *Horace.* With Introduction and Notes by GEORGE SAINTSBURY, M.A. . . . . Extra fcap. 8vo. 2*s.* 6*d.*

Corneille. *Cinna.* With Notes, Glossary, etc. By GUSTAVE MASSON, B.A. . . . . . . Extra fcap. 8vo. *stiff covers,* 1*s.* 6*d.* *cloth,* 2*s.*

Gautier (Théophile). *Scenes of Travel.* Selected and Edited by G. SAINTSBURY, M.A. . . . . Extra fcap. 8vo. 2*s.*

Masson. *Louis XIV and his Contemporaries;* as described in Extracts from the best Memoirs of the Seventeenth Century. With English Notes, Genealogical Tables, &c. By GUSTAVE MASSON, B.A. Extra fcap. 8vo. 2*s.* 6*d.*

Molière. *Les Précieuses Ridicules.* With Introduction and Notes by ANDREW LANG, M.A. . . . . Extra fcap. 8vo. 1*s.* 6*d.*

Molière. *Les Femmes Savantes.* With Notes, Glossary, etc. By GUSTAVE MASSON, B.A. . Extra fcap. 8vo. *stiff covers,* 1*s.* 6*d.* *cloth,* 2*s.*

Molière. *Les Fourberies de Scapin.*
Racine. *Athalie.*
} With Voltaire's Life of Molière. By GUSTAVE MASSON, B.A. Extra fcap. 8vo. 2*s.* 6*d.*

Molière. *Les Fourberies de Scapin.* With Voltaire's Life of Molière. By GUSTAVE MASSON, B.A. . . Extra fcap. 8vo. *stiff covers,* 1*s.* 6*d.*

Musset. *On ne badine pas avec l'Amour,* and *Fantasio.* With Introduction, Notes, etc., by WALTER HERRIES POLLOCK. Extra fcap. 8vo. 2*s.*

NOVELETTES:—

Xavier de Maistre. *Voyage autour de ma Chambre.*
Madame de Duras. *Ourika.*
Erckmann-Chatrian. *Le Vieux Tailleur.*
Alfred de Vigny. *La Veillée de Vincennes.*
Edmond About. *Les Jumeaux de l'Hôtel Corneille.*
Rodolphe Töpffer. *Mésaventures d'un Écolier.*
} By GUSTAVE MASSON, B.A., *3rd Edition* Ext. fcap. 8vo. 2*s.* 6*d.*

Voyage autour de ma Chambre, separately, limp, 1*s.* 6*d.*

Perrault. *Popular Tales.* Edited, with an Introduction on Fairy Tales, etc., by ANDREW LANG, M.A. . . . . . Extra fcap. 8vo. 5*s.* 6*d.*

Quinet. *Lettres à sa Mère.* Edited by G. SAINTSBURY, M.A. Extra fcap. 8vo. 2*s.*

Racine. *Esther.* Edited by G. SAINTSBURY, M.A. Extra fcap. 8vo. 2*s.*

Racine. *Andromaque.*
Corneille. *Le Menteur.*
} With Louis Racine's Life of his Father. By GUSTAVE MASSON, B.A. Extra fcap. 8vo. 2*s.* 6*d.*

Regnard. . . . . *Le Joueur.*
Brueys and Palaprat. *Le Grondeur.*
} By GUSTAVE MASSON, B.A. Extra fcap. 8vo. 2*s.* 6*d.*

Sainte-Beuve. *Selections from the Causeries du Lundi.* Edited by G. SAINTSBURY, M.A. . . . . Extra fcap. 8vo. 2*s.*

Sévigné. *Selections from the Correspondence of* **Madame de Sévigné** and her chief Contemporaries. Intended more especially for Girls' Schools. By GUSTAVE MASSON, B.A. . . . . Extra fcap. 8vo. 3*s.*

Voltaire. *Mérope.* Edited by G. SAINTSBURY, M.A. Extra fcap. 8vo. 2*s.*

Dante. *Selections from the 'Inferno.'* With Introduction and Notes, by H. B. COTTERILL, B.A. . . . . . . Extra fcap. 8vo. 4*s.* 6*d.*

Tasso. *La Gerusalemme Liberata.* Cantos i, ii. With Introduction and Notes, by the same Editor. . . . . . Extra fcap. 8vo. 2*s.* 6*d.*

GERMAN, GOTHIC, ICELANDIC, &c.

Buchheim. *Modern German Reader.* A Graduated Collection of Extracts in Prose and Poetry from Modern German writers. Edited by C. A. BUCHHEIM, Phil. Doc.

Part I. With English Notes, a Grammatical Appendix, and a complete Vocabulary. *Fourth Edition.* . . . Extra fcap. 8vo. 2*s.* 6*d.*

Part II. With English Notes and an Index. Extra fcap. 8vo. 2*s.* 6*d.*

Part III. In preparation.

Lange. *The Germans at Home*; a Practical Introduction to German Conversation, with an Appendix containing the Essentials of German Grammar. By HERMANN LANGE. *Third Edition.* . . . . . . 8vo. 2*s.* 6*d.*

Lange. *The German Manual*; a German Grammar, a Reading Book, and a Handbook of German Conversation. By the same Author. 8vo. 7*s.* 6*d.*

Lange. *A Grammar of the German Language*, being a reprint of the Grammar contained in *The German Manual.* By the same Author. 8vo. 3*s.* 6*d.*

Lange. *German Composition*; a Theoretical and Practical Guide to the Art of Translating English Prose into German. By the same Author. *Second Edition* . . . . 8vo. 4*s.* 6*d.*

[*A Key in Preparation.*]

Lange. *German Spelling*: A Synopsis of the Changes which it has undergone through the Government Regulations of 1880 . *Paper cover,* 6*d.*

Becker's Friedrich der Grosse. With an Historical Sketch of the Rise of Prussia and of the Times of Frederick the Great. With Map. Edited by C. A. BUCHHEIM, Phil. Doc. . . . . Extra fcap. 8vo. 3*s.* 6*d.*

Goethe. *Egmont.* With a Life of Goethe, etc. Edited by C. A. BUCHHEIM, Phil. Doc. *Third Edition.* . . . . Extra fcap. 8vo. 3*s.*

Goethe. *Iphigenie auf Tauris.* A Drama. With a Critical Introduction and Notes. Edited by C. A. BUCHHEIM, Phil. Doc. *Second Edition.* Extra fcap. 8vo. 3*s.*

Heine's *Harzreise.* With a Life of Heine, etc. Edited by C. A. BUCHHEIM, Phil. Doc. Extra fcap. 8vo. *stiff covers,* 1*s.* 6*d.* *cloth,* 2*s.* 6*d.*

Heine's *Prosa*, being Selections from his Prose Works. Edited with English Notes, etc., by C. A. BUCHHEIM, Phil. Doc. Extra fcap. 8vo. 4*s*. 6*d*.

Lessing. *Laokoon.* With Introduction, Notes, etc. By A. HAMANN, Phil. Doc., M.A. . . . . Extra fcap. 8vo. 4*s*. 6*d*.

Lessing. *Minna von Barnhelm.* A Comedy. With a Life of Lessing, Critical Analysis, Complete Commentary, etc. Edited by C. A. BUCHHEIM, Phil. Doc. *Fifth Edition.* . . . Extra fcap. 8vo. 3*s*. 6*d*.

Lessing. *Nathan der Weise.* With English Notes, etc. Edited by C. A. BUCHHEIM, Phil. Doc. *Second Edition.* . Extra fcap. 8vo. 4*s*. 6*d*.

Niebuhr's *Griechische Heroen-Geschichten.* Tales of Greek Heroes. Edited with English Notes and a Vocabulary, by EMMA S. BUCHHEIM. Extra fcap. 8vo. *cloth*, 2*s*.

Schiller's *Historische Skizzen:—Egmonts Leben und Tod*, and *Belagerung von Antwerpen.* Edited by C. A. BUCHHEIM, Phil. Doc. *Third Edition, Revised and Enlarged, with a Map.* . Extra fcap. 8vo. 2*s*. 6*d*.

Schiller. *Wilhelm Tell.* With a Life of Schiller; an Historical and Critical Introduction, Arguments, a Complete Commentary, and Map. Edited by C. A. BUCHHEIM, Phil. Doc. *Sixth Edition.* . Extra fcap. 8vo. 3*s*. 6*d*.

Schiller. *Wilhelm Tell.* Edited by C. A. BUCHHEIM, Phil. Doc. *School Edition.* With Map. . . . . . . Extra fcap. 8vo. 2*s*.

Schiller. *Wilhelm Tell.* Translated into English Verse by E. MASSIE, M.A. . . . . Extra fcap. 8vo. 5*s*.

Schiller. *Die Jungfrau von Orleans.* Edited by C. A. BUCHHEIM, Phil. Doc. [*In preparation.*]

Scherer. *A History of German Literature.* By W. SCHERER. Translated from the Third German Edition by Mrs. F. CONYBEARE. Edited by F. MAX MÜLLER. 2 vols. . . . . 8vo. 21*s*.

Max Müller. *The German Classics from the Fourth to the Nineteenth Century.* With Biographical Notices, Translations into Modern German, and Notes, by F. MAX MÜLLER, M.A. A New edition, revised, enlarged, and adapted to WILHELM SCHERER'S *History of German Literature*, by F. LICHTENSTEIN. 2 vols. . . . . Crown 8vo. 21*s*.

Wright. *An Old High German Primer.* With Grammar, Notes, and Glossary. By JOSEPH WRIGHT, Ph.D. . . Extra fcap. 8vo. 3*s*. 6*d*.

Wright. *A Middle High German Primer.* With Grammar, Notes, and Glossary. By JOSEPH WRIGHT, Ph. D. . . Extra fcap. 8vo. 3*s*. 6*d*.

Skeat. *The Gospel of St. Mark in Gothic.* Edited by W. W. SKEAT, Litt. D. . . . . Extra fcap. 8vo. 4*s*.

Sweet. An Icelandic Primer, with Grammar, Notes, and Glossary. By HENRY SWEET, M.A. . . . . Extra fcap. 8vo. 3*s*. 6*d*.

Vigfusson and Powell. *An Icelandic Prose Reader*, with Notes, Grammar, and Glossary. By GUDBRAND VIGFUSSON, M.A., and F. YORK POWELL, M.A. . . . . Extra fcap. 8vo. 10*s*. 6*d*.

MATHEMATICS AND PHYSICAL SCIENCE.

Aldis. *A Text Book of Algebra (with Answers to the Examples).* By W. STEADMAN ALDIS, M.A. . . . . Crown 8vo. 7s. 6d.

Hamilton and Ball. *Book-keeping.* By Sir R. G. C. HAMILTON, K.C.B., and JOHN BALL (of the firm of Quilter, Ball, & Co.). *New and Enlarged Edition* . . . . Extra fcap. 8vo. 2s.

*** *Ruled Exercise Books adapted to the above.* (Fcap. folio, 2s.)

Hensley. *Figures made Easy: a first Arithmetic Book.* By LEWIS HENSLEY, M.A. . . . . Crown 8vo. 6d.

Hensley. *Answers to the Examples in Figures made Easy,* together with 2000 additional Examples formed from the Tables in the same, with Answers. By the same Author. . . . . Crown 8vo. 1s.

Hensley. *The Scholar's Arithmetic.* By the same Author. Crown 8vo. 2s. 6d.

Hensley. *Answers to the Examples in the Scholar's Arithmetic.* By the same Author. . . . . Crown 8vo. 1s. 6d.

Hensley. *The Scholar's Algebra.* An Introductory work on Algebra. By the same Author. . . . . Crown 8vo. 2s. 6d.

Baynes. *Lessons on Thermodynamics.* By R. E. BAYNES, M.A., Lee's Reader in Physics. . . . . Crown 8vo. 7s. 6d.

Donkin. *Acoustics.* By W. F. DONKIN, M.A., F.R.S. *Second Edition.* Crown 8vo. 7s. 6d.

Euclid Revised. Containing the essentials of the Elements of Plane Geometry as given by Euclid in his First Six Books. Edited by R. C. J. NIXON, M.A. . . . . Crown 8vo.

May likewise be had in parts as follows:—

Book I, 1s. Books I, II, 1s. 6d. Books I–IV, 3s. Books V–IV, 3s.

Euclid. *Geometry in Space.* Containing parts of Euclid's Eleventh and Twelfth Books. By the same Editor. . . . . Crown 8vo. 3s. 6d.

Harcourt and Madan. *Exercises in Practical Chemistry.* Vol. I. *Elementary Exercises.* By A. G. VERNON HARCOURT, M.A.: and H. G. MADAN, M.A. *Fourth Edition.* Revised by H. G. Madan, M.A. Crown 8vo. 10s. 6d.

Madan. *Tables of Qualitative Analysis.* Arranged by H. G. MADAN, M.A. . . . . Large 4to. 4s. 6d.

Maxwell. *An Elementary Treatise on Electricity.* By J. CLERK MAXWELL, M.A., F.R.S. Edited by W. GARNETT, M.A. Demy 8vo. 7s. 6d.

Stewart. *A Treatise on Heat,* with numerous Woodcuts and Diagrams. By BALFOUR STEWART, LL.D., F.R.S., Professor of Natural Philosophy in Owens College, Manchester. *Fifth Edition.* . Extra fcap. 8vo. 7s. 6d.

Williamson. *Chemistry for Students.* By A. W. WILLIAMSON, Phil. Doc., F.R.S., Professor of Chemistry, University College London. *A new Edition with Solutions.* . . . . Extra fcap. 8vo. 8*s*. 6*d*.

Combination Chemical Labels. In two Parts, gummed ready for use. Part I, Basic Radicles and Names of Elements. Part II, Acid Radicles. Price 3*s*. 6*d*.

HISTORY, POLITICAL ECONOMY, GEOGRAPHY, &c.

Danson. The Wealth of Households. By J. T. DANSON. Cr. 8vo. 5*s*.

Freeman. *A Short History of the Norman Conquest of England.* By E. A. FREEMAN, M.A. *Second Edition.* . Extra fcap. 8vo. 2*s*. 6*d*.

George. *Genealogical Tables illustrative of Modern History.* By H. B. GEORGE, M.A. *Third Edition, Revised and Enlarged.* Small 4to. 12*s*.

Hughes (Alfred). *Geography for Schools.* Part I, *Practical Geography.* With Diagrams. . . . . Extra fcap. 8vo. 2*s*. 6*d*.

Kitchin. *A History of France.* With Numerous Maps, Plans, and Tables. By G. W. KITCHIN, D.D., Dean of Winchester. *Second Edition.* Vol. I. To 1453. Vol. II. 1453–1624. Vol. III. 1624–1793. each 10*s*. 6*d*.

Lucas. *Introduction to a Historical Geography of the British Colonies.* By C. P. LUCAS, B.A. . . . . . Crown 8vo., with 8 maps, 4*s*. 6*d*.

Rawlinson. *A Manual of Ancient History.* By G. RAWLINSON, M.A., Camden Professor of Ancient History. *Second Edition.* Demy 8vo. 14*s*.

Rogers. *A Manual of Political Economy,* for the use of Schools. By J. E. THOROLD ROGERS, M.A. *Third Edition.* Extra fcap. 8vo. 4*s*. 6*d*.

Stubbs. *The Constitutional History of England, in its Origin and Development.* By WILLIAM STUBBS, D.D., Lord Bishop of Chester. Three vols. . . . . Crown 8vo. each 12*s*.

Stubbs. *Select Charters and other Illustrations of English Constitutional History,* from the Earliest Times to the Reign of Edward I. Arranged and edited by W. STUBBS, D.D. *Fourth Edition.* Crown 8vo. 8*s*. 6*d*.

Stubbs. *Magna Carta*: a careful reprint. . . . 4to. *stitched*, 1*s*.

ART.

Hullah. *The Cultivation of the Speaking Voice.* By JOHN HULLAH. Extra fcap. 8vo. 2*s*. 6*d*.

Maclaren. *A System of Physical Education: Theoretical and Practical.* With 346 Illustrations drawn by A. MACDONALD, of the Oxford School of Art. By ARCHIBALD MACLAREN, the Gymnasium, Oxford. *Second Edition.* Extra fcap. 8vo. 7*s*. 6*d*.

Troutbeck and Dale. *A Music Primer for Schools.* By J. TROUTBECK, D.D., formerly Music Master in Westminster School, and R. F. DALE, M.A., B. Mus., late Assistant Master in Westminster School. Crown 8vo. 1s. 6d.

Tyrwhitt. *A Handbook of Pictorial Art.* By R. St. J. TYRWHITT, M.A. With coloured Illustrations, Photographs, and a chapter on Perspective, by A. MACDONALD. *Second Edition.* . . . . 8vo. *half morocco,* 1 s.

Upcott. *An Introduction to Greek Sculpture.* By L. E. UPCOTT, M.A. . . . . Crown 8vo. 4s. 6d.

Student's Handbook to the University and Colleges of Oxford. *Ninth Edition.* . . . . Crown 8vo. 2s. 6d.

Helps to the Study of the Bible, taken from the *Oxford Bible for Teachers,* comprising Summaries of the several Books, with copious Explanatory Notes and Tables illustrative of Scripture History and the Characteristics of Bible Lands; with a complete Index of Subjects, a Concordance, a Dictionary of Proper Names, and a series of Maps. . . . . Crown 8vo. 3s. 6d.

*** A READING ROOM *has been opened at the* CLARENDON PRESS WAREHOUSE, AMEN CORNER, *where visitors will find every facility for examining old and new works issued from the Press, and for consulting all official publications.*

☞ *All communications relating to Books included in this List, and offers of new Books and new Editions, should be addressed to*

THE SECRETARY TO THE DELEGATES,
CLARENDON PRESS,
OXFORD.

London: HENRY FROWDE,
OXFORD UNIVERSITY PRESS WAREHOUSE, AMEN CORNER.
Edinburgh: 6 QUEEN STREET.
Oxford: CLARENDON PRESS DEPOSITORY,
116 HIGH STREET.

23

www.ingramcontent.com/pod-product-compliance
Lightning Source LLC
Chambersburg PA
CBHW020752020726
47495CB00008B/2388
* 9 7 8 3 3 3 7 3 4 2 8 3 8 *